W9-BPO-567

# TALES FROM TETHEDRIL

Books published by The Ballantine Publishing Group
are available at quantity discounts on bulk purchases
for premium, educational, fund-raising, and special
sales use. For details, please call 1-800-733-3000.

# TALES FROM TETHEDRIL

## Edited by Scott Siegel

### Building on a story by R. A. Salvatore

A Del Rey® Book
THE BALLANTINE PUBLISHING GROUP • NEW YORK

Sale of this book without a front cover may be unauthorized. If this book is coverless, it may have been reported to the publisher as "unsold or destroyed" and neither the author nor the publisher may have received payment for it.

A Del Rey® Book
Published by The Ballantine Publishing Group
Introduction and compilation copyright © 1998 by Siegel & Siegel Ltd.

"Gods' Law" copyright © 1998 by R. A. Salvatore
"Ice Magic" copyright © 1998 by Douglas Niles
"Family Tree" copyright © 1998 by Dan Parkinson
"The Lazy Man" copyright © 1998 by Nick O' Donohoe
"The Sword of Dreams" copyright © 1998 by Ed Greenwood
"The Ultimate Weapon" copyright © 1998 by Christie Golden
"Blood of the Lamb" copyright © 1998 by Mary H. Herbert
"The Greatest Gift" copyright © 1998 by Mary Kirchoff
"The Sleeping Sauran" copyright © 1998 by Elaine Cunningham

All rights reserved under International and Pan-American Copyright Conventions. Published in the United States by The Ballantine Publishing Group, a division of Random House, Inc., New York, and simultaneously in Canada by Random House of Canada Limited, Toronto.

"Tales from Tethedril" is a creation of Siegel & Siegel Ltd.

http://www.randomhouse.com

Library of Congress Catalog Card Number: 98-92824

ISBN 0-345-39444-5

Manufactured in the United States of America

First Edition: August 1998

10  9  8  7  6  5  4  3  2  1

# Contents

# Introduction

*T*his is the genesis of Tethedril, a world created and fully imagined by today's most gifted fantasy authors. *Tales From Tethedril* weaves together stories of high drama, clever comedy, and searing action to bring the history of its fabled inhabitants to vivid life. Through words, ideas, actions, and characters, you will come to feel a kinship with the peoples of this world and a sense of belonging to its places.

It was my great pleasure to commission this project, an enterprise that afforded me the opportunity to invite an extraordinary cast of writers to collaborate on the founding of an indelible world. With style and imagination, they did just that. Consider the authors whose work you will find between the covers of this book . . .

Six-time *New York Times* bestselling author R. A. Salvatore, who has taken the fantasy world by storm with more than four million books in print. It was his original short story that became the basis of this volume.

Mary Kirchoff, who is among the fantasy world's most gifted writers, and who would be among its most famous had she not been so busy guiding other authors to fame and fortune as one of the genre's most influential editors.

Douglas Niles, the masterful writer who penned *The*

*Moonshae Trilogy*, which launched the hugely successful *Forgotten Realms*.

Dan Parkinson, who is, without doubt, the most original voice in fantasy and science fiction today and the author of the ingenious new series *The Gates of Time*.

The legendary Ed Greenwood, who has an imagination so fertile that even his ideas have ideas.

Elaine Cunningham, who is fast becoming one of the hottest, as well as one of the most respected, new authors in the genre.

Mary H. Herbert, one of fantasy's most elegant writers.

Nick O'Donohoe, a storyteller without peer.

Christie Golden, who writes like a dream.

Each one of these authors has written extensively in the fantasy genre; many of them have a shelf or more of published novels to their credit. This book offers you the chance to get to know them—if you don't already.

Mostly, though, this book offers you the chance to enter a freshly created world that is, at once, exotically original yet fundamentally familiar. You will not find the entire history of Tethedril here. In each of the stories— they are set in different times during the evolution of this remarkable place—there is a piece of the larger tapestry.

Should these tales ignite a fire of interest in you to discover still more of Tethedril's secrets, then more will surely follow. In the meantime, though these stories may exist in a book, they are intended to live in your heart . . .

SCOTT SIEGEL
New York City

# Gods' Law

## R. A. Salvatore

*R*asha Arc, the Godtalker, watched the battle raging at the bluff with fists clenched in utter frustration. He was a young man, strong of arm, and he could wield his clobber, a heavy club fashioned out of the trunk of the eldercactus, complete with short, hooked spikes, as well as any man in the tribe.

To watch his kinfolk fighting now, and dying, while he had to remain far back of the battle with the children was nearly more than Rasha Arc could take. If the saurans had come north to wage war just two years before, Rasha would have been in the front line of defense, throwing his javelins, then taking up his clobber to meet the charge. But that was when Tawni Arc had been Godtalker of the One Tribe. Tawni Arc was dead now, and Rasha had heard the calling, had seen the vision of Altos the One God in the Sacred Pool. He was the Godtalker now; he could not be put in jeopardy in open combat.

And so he watched as the stubborn saurans, lizardlike bipedals with mottled skin, patched black and yellow green, charged the bluff yet again, hissing their rage, flicking forked tongues leading the way. They were smaller than the men on average, slender and short, most not reaching twelve handbreadths while the men usually touched the fifteen-hand mark, but what they lacked in bulk they made up in strength and agility. Their lighter weapons, spears mostly, and whipcords, reflected their quicker attack routines. The saurans were indeed cunning adversaries, for those spears, fashioned of soft jungle trees, often splintered inside their victims, cutting multiple holes with a single thrust.

Rasha Arc winced as he noticed one sauran stab hard for the groin of Terka, a friend. Terka fell back, out of range, rolling down the back side of the grassy bluff, and Noltin, the man standing next to him, slid over a step and bashed down with all his strength and weight, his clobber caving in the head of the sauran. Rasha Arc nodded; they had chosen their ground well for this campsite. They were bordered on the east by the Silver River, swift and deep, and on the north by Godtalker Mountain, wherein lay the Sacred Pool. The saurans would not dare to cross that holy place, where Rasha Arc's magic was at its strongest. Bluffs lined the areas south and west of the camp, effective for defense, and so the humans held strong now, beating back the vicious saurans.

A cry from one of the children behind him turned Rasha Arc about to see a handful of the lizard creatures climbing out of the Silver, with others swimming in behind them. No strangers to battle, the nearly one hundred women of the One Tribe took up their weapons and forged ahead, racing to the riverbanks.

"Cursed," muttered Rasha Arc with a deep and profound sigh. The women were fine warriors, but were too valuable to be lost on the ends of sauran spears. The One Tribe was not populous, numbering no more than three hundred in this, the fifth generation of Man since the Day of Reasoning, and while one man could sire many children, the women were much more limited and often died during childbirth.

To lose even one now would be unacceptable.

Rasha Arc had hungered for battle, and now came his chance. He lifted his clobber, one of the heaviest in all the tribe, and charged ahead, reaching his free hand into a pouch of herbs tied about his waist. He led his way to the closest pair of saurans with a thrown handful of those herbs, which spun like glittering flakes through the warm air.

The slitted, reptilian eyes of the sauran pair began to sting immediately, their vision doubling. One looked back to the river—a true mistake, for every sparkle on the water magnified a thousand times, blinding the creature.

Rasha Arc came in ferociously, feigning a high, overhead chop and falling to his knees at the last moment, swiping across. He caught one of the saurans on the side of the leg, collapsing the beast, the clobber's thorns tearing through the overlapping, scaly hide and through the ligaments beneath it. Hardly slowing, Rasha Arc slid his feet back under him and lunged ahead, butting the other, blinded sauran square in the chest, knocking it back toward the water.

The creature's feet moved quickly, keeping its balance, and it came right back at the Godtalker, a straightforward thrust that Rasha Arc easily anticipated and dodged. He started to counter, but was beaten to the strike by Tilsa, daughter of Tawni, as she raced by, putting her slender ripperstick against the sauran's throat. The hooked thorns of the ripperstick bit hard and efficiently tore out the creature's larynx as Tilsa continued past.

Rasha Arc merely altered the angle of his ensuing blow, smashing the skull of the first fallen sauran as it lay

squirming in agony on the ground. Then on to the riverbank, where the women had formed a deep and strong
line, chasing those saurans who had made solid ground
back into the water and holding their line there, hacking
and pounding any lizard that tried to climb out. Already
most of the saurans had turned about, swimming for the
opposite shore. Only one woman had gone down, and she
didn't appear to be injured very seriously.

But before Rasha Arc could proclaim this area a complete victory, could call out the praises of Altos, he noticed
a pair of saurans holding steady in the river, almost to the
other bank, nearly a hundred feet away. The closest lizard
lifted its arms high above its head, holding some sort of
hollow tubing. The one behind it said a few words, and
the front sauran shifted the tube appropriately.

The Godtalker's sensibilities screamed at him to get
out of harm's way. He cried out to those about him to run,
or to get low to the ground.

But too late. The sauran at the back of the ten-foot pole
put its snout to the hollow end and blew hard, and one of
the women near to Rasha Arc jolted in surprise and cried
out, stung in the shoulder.

Retaliation came fast and hard, for two of these women
had made bowing poles, the newest weapon of the One
Tribe. They fitted notched short spears to the gut line tied
from end to end and pulled back their bowstrings, taking
careful aim.

Neither hit the mark; the shot was at the range limits of
the crude bows, but the near misses chased the saurans off.

"They have made a weapon to match our bowing
sticks," Tilsa remarked to Rasha Arc as the Godtalker
examined the woman who had been hit by the dart.

Rasha Arc wasn't surprised. Every time the One Tribe

fashioned a new weapon, the saurans responded with a similar weapon. When the humans had perfected the rippersticks, the lighter and quicker sharp-edged clubs, the saurans had responded with whipcords, a devilish weapon pointed like a spear on one end, and with a five-foot-long whipping thong, its tip barbed with claws, on the other end.

The Godtalker couldn't understand this newest weapon, though. The aim had been solid, the range at least that of a bowing stick, and yet the missile, a cat's claw, feathered on the back, did not seem so deadly. The woman, Neana, stood calm, more confused than hurt, though she admitted that the tiny wound in her shoulder did sting.

Most of the women, Neana included, dismissed the dart, and Rasha Arc did as well, though he held more trepidation than the others. His fears were confirmed a moment later, when the group, confident that the Silver River had been cleared of saurans, began to move back toward the center of the encampment. Their hopes brightened as they noted that the fighting at the bluff, too, had ended, the saurans running off across the grassy plain.

Then those hopes quickly turned to horror.

"I cannot feel my legs," Neana admitted, and she staggered a couple of awkward steps. A moment later, before Rasha Arc could even get to her, the woman doubled over in pain, clutching her stomach and gasping for breath.

It went on for more than an hour, with Rasha Arc using all of his skills as a Godtalker. He prayed to Altos over the wound, burned fires near Neana and near the four men of the tribe who had also been stung by the wicked sauran darts. He used every herbal treatment that his visions at the Sacred Pool had shown to him.

But it wasn't enough. Two of the men died of the cramps, unable to draw breath, and the other two, and Neana, just when the terrible wracking pains seemed to be abating, fell victim to yet another aspect of this most evil poison. Rasha Arc noticed it on Neana first, when the blood began to trickle from the dart wound once more, running as easily as if it was water.

The Godtalker tried to stem the flow, but the liquid's consistency proved too light. When Neana tried to speak out, Rasha Arc found her mouth also full of waterlike blood, fluid that was simply leaking from her gums. She died next, in agony, the remaining two soon after.

Rasha Arc stood alone, staring to the south sometime later. The sauran attack had not been unexpected. Summer had passed, and the week of the comet Aussasaur was fast approaching, bringing its heat that so invigorated the reptilians. Still, the saurans usually didn't come so far to the north in such numbers in the autumn approach of Aussasaur, for the cold winter would follow closely, and if the sauran raiding party got caught this far north when the first chill winds began to blow, they would be too sluggish to escape the wrath of the vengeful humans.

But Rasha Arc knew why they had come, knew that they had wanted to test out their latest weapon. They would be back in the spring, with Aussasaur's next fiery approach, he knew, in greater numbers and with more of the blowguns and poison-tipped darts.

"It has happened before," Tilsa, daughter of Godtalker Tawni, said to him. Rasha Arc turned to regard her. "The poisons," Tilsa explained. "The saurans once tipped their spears with such venom, so told me my father."

"Now they will be even more effective," Rasha Arc replied. He knew the tale of the poisoned spears used by the saurans during the war in the third generation after the Day of Reason, and he understood the basis of the process that had allowed the reptilians to acquire such a deadly poison once more. "They have found a high shaman," he said.

Rasha Arc looked again to the south, past the bluffs, past the rolling, grassy plain, past the sandy desert where grew the huge green eldercactus. His eyes could not go that far, of course, but his thoughts did, beyond the mountains called Arraroot, to the thick jungles and the great river that was home to the saurans.

Rasha Arc knew what he must do.

Kassis moved slowly through the tangle of the deeper jungle, respectful of the many dangers. The sauran high shaman knew well the great cats that prowled amid the wide-leafed ferns, and the giant constrictors that could squeeze the breath and life out of him before he had the opportunity even to cry out. Kassis' tribe lived on the river delta, at the edge of the jungle, and few of the saurans ever ventured into the deeper jungle.

Now the high shaman felt perfectly insignificant. Kassis had achieved the highest rank of his people, above even the chieftain on those matters he chose to make his own. But in here, beneath the towering blanket of twisted boughs and tangled vines, plodding through ferns taller than he, scrambling over roots as thick across as a sauran was tall, the high shaman was truly humbled. In here, Kassis recognized the power of Aussasaurian and knew that he was a blessed creature indeed to be given even the slightest taste of that godly might.

He came upon a short clearing, a patch of ferns that had been swept aside when one of the giant trees had tumbled, and there Kassis found his next catch. The nine-foot copper-colored serpent saw the sauran as well, and the taiperserpent, never shy, rushed forward, fangs dripping deadly venom.

Deadly, but not to Kassis. The sauran marveled at the grace of the snake, the sheer beauty of this creature, which saurans considered the embodiment of Aussasaurian. He studied the closing serpent's distinctive head, musing that its shape, that of the box that the humans used to bury their dead, was ever so appropriate. He marveled at its final approach, at the way the head held in place while the slithering body caught up to it, even came a bit ahead of it at one bend, and then, the blinding strike, too fast for Kassis to follow.

He felt the two cuts in his shin, though, and before he could even reach down to the wound, he felt two more.

The taiperserpent coiled for its third strike, and Kassis moved right for it, keeping his face, his only vulnerable spot, defensively back behind an upraised arm. The taiperserpent hit that arm hard, digging in, and Kassis was quick to grab with his other hand, catching the snake right behind its coffin-shaped head.

The high shaman held it up, marveling at its slender beauty. He kissed the serpent once atop the head, then stuffed it into a sack with the other four taiperserpents he had snared on this expedition.

Then he said his prayer. Aussasaurian had been good to him this day, and all of this journey. He was hoping to snare ten of the taiperserpents before returning to his tribe. He would milk the venom from them and then let them go—his edicts strictly forbade him from removing the serpents from their deep jungle home. Thus, Kassis had to remain in the deep jungle long enough to milk enough venom for the full-scale sauran attack on the human tribe to the north. The last battle had proven the effectiveness of the blowguns; now all that the saurans needed to ensure complete victory was enough poison to decimate the humans' front line of defense.

Kassis allowed himself a break while he tended the minor wounds. Minor wounds! Any of those bites would have surely killed another sauran, or a human. But to Kassis, the first high shaman in two generations, and only the third in the history of his people, the bites were not significant. The distinction between the rank of high shaman and shaman was the invulnerability to taiperserpent venom. All sauran shamans would be fed minor doses of the venom—when it could be gotten, and usually at the expense of at least one sauran life—over the first few years of their training, to build a resistance. The ceremony of high shaman would follow, with each of the respective candidates going into the deeper jungle and accepting a single full bite of the taiperserpent. Those who came out of the jungle, showing the trademark fang wounds, would be granted the title of high shaman. Four others had died during the week that Kassis had won his rank. Perhaps a great spotted jungle cat had gotten them, or a constrictor, or perhaps the true bite of the taiperserpent had been more than they could withstand. Whatever the reason, none of the others had returned, and Kassis alone had moved on to the highest rank of his tribe. Kassis alone now spoke with the pure voice of Aussasaurian; Kassis alone could venture into the deeper jungle in search of taiperserpent venom.

And how great his reputation would be when the saurans struck hard at the humans! It was something that Kassis wanted above all else. He was old, the oldest in his tribe, had seen more than fifty passes of Aussasaur, and he would not likely live much longer. This would be his triumph, his place of sauran immortality.

That fantasy led the high shaman back to the reality of his present situation. The week of the comet was fast approaching; already he could feel Aussasaur's mounting heat. He had five of the snakes, but at least twice that would be needed to collect enough of the venom to truly score victory.

The high shaman could not rest. He moved on through the thick tangle, but found no more snakes that day.

Rasha Arc had never been so miserable in all of his life. The tangle of the deep jungle assaulted his sensibilities as surely as the countless insects assaulted his flesh. He carried a hundred bites, some of them wickedly sore and swollen.

And the night was coming. Rasha Arc hated the jungle night worst of all, the complete darkness of the place, and the sounds! The jungle screamed louder at night than during the day, full of howls and roars and hissing—the hissing was the worst of all.

But he had to be there, the Godtalker reminded himself for the hundredth time that day. The Sacred Pool had shown him the way, and he was certain that the sauran high shaman was nearby.

Rasha Arc had also been snake hunting that day, though without the high shaman's immunities. He had to go about it much more carefully. He had used a forked stick to make the catches, and fortunately, he hadn't needed to get any closer than that to the wriggling serpent to enact the magic over it.

Rasha Arc climbed a tree and nestled in its lowest

bough. He would find little sleep, he knew, but he thought of Neana and the other victims of the sauran poison and considered his discomfort a minor sacrifice.

The day was hotter, Kassis noted, with a mixture of eager anticipation and worry. The week of the comet grew near, thus his time of glory fast approached. But his deadline for getting the venom and getting out of the jungle also approached, for the sauran forces would have to leave on the first day of the comet, at the latest, to cross the three hundred miles to the humans before Aussasaur's pass was completed. Those seven days of the visible comet were the best for fighting; during that short span, the saurans found their pinnacle of activity, were closest to their god.

So Kassis worked all the harder that day. He spotted a copper-colored snake up in a tree—a rarity, but not unheard of for the taiperserpents. Putting his bag over his shoulder, the old high shaman began his slow and steady climb, hand over hand, trying not to startle the snake. This was a small one, he noted, and while the younger taiperserpents had been known to be even more aggressive than the great nine-footers, they were also more unpredictable. Kassis could not afford to frighten this one off.

He inched closer to the snake, barely visible as it wrapped itself about a branch. It spotted him as he started to reach for it, and lashed out. Kassis' hand burned from the bite, but he hardly noticed the pain as he made his catch, securing the serpent about the head and gently unwrapping it from the branch.

Only when he had gotten back to the ground and was preparing to bag the snake did he take stock of its head.

Unlike the coffin-shaped head of the taiperserpent, this snake's was shaped more like a spade, more like the head of a fern-hanging viper. Kassis considered the creature carefully. Fern hangers were green, not copper colored. In fact, the taiperserpent was the only copper-colored snake in the deep jungle. Kassis knew this; he was a high shaman, studied in the word of Aussasaurian. How could he not recognize one of the god's own likenesses?

Before the old sauran's very eyes, the squirming snake's rich copper coloring began to fade away, replaced by a telltale green sheen.

Kassis gasped hard for breath. The viper almost slipped from his grasp, for the fingers of his hand had numbed. Purely on instinct, the old sauran grabbed the tail of the viper with his other hand and snapped the creature like a whip, shattering its vertebrae. Horrified by his own action, he dropped the viper to the ground.

"I have sinned, oh, Aussasaurian!" he lamented, eyeing his deadly work. In that moment of terror, Kassis had committed the worst crime possible, had killed a likeness of his god.

He fell to his knees, weeping. He reached for his sack, meaning to stick his head inside of it so that Aussasaurian's children could punish him.

The sack was taken from him, dropped to the ground. Kassis spun about to see a human—a human!—whacking at the sack with a heavy cudgel. The high shaman tried to rise, but the viper venom coursed through him now, stealing the strength from his limbs. Even worse, the human paused long enough to smack the old sauran, dropping him to the ground. Kassis doubled up in pain, and all the world grew dark.

When he awoke, and he was surely surprised that he

did open his eyes again, he was propped against the trunk of the tree, stripped of his loincloth and his weapons. The human, a young and strong specimen, stood over him.

Kassis' gaze went to the ground, though, to the dead fern hanger, to his ultimate sin.

Then he noted that the human was speaking, praying, to Altos the Cursed. Kassis looked up, meant to speak the name of Aussasaurian, but stopped as the man stopped chanting. Rasha Arc raised his clobber high and moved forward for the killing blow.

"How?" Kassis hissed at him, and the man hesitated.

Kassis looked to the fern hanger. "It was brown," he explained.

Rasha Arc lowered his club. "A minor magic," he replied. "A gift from Altos."

"You are shaman?"

"I am the Godtalker," Rasha Arc corrected indignantly. "I am the seer of the Sacred Pool. Altos led me here, to you, High Shaman."

"You know of me?" the old sauran gasped, hardly finding breath for the words. The pain burned terribly, the numbness in his limbs complete, and in truth, Kassis was surprised that he hadn't succumbed to the venom by this time.

"I know of your evil work," Rasha Arc replied. "I tended those you poisoned. I watched their horrible deaths—a fate that you will soon know, if there is justice!"

Kassis managed a hissing snort. "Justice," he echoed. "What would a human know of justice?" He looked directly at his adversary. "What would a human who kills saurans know of justice?"

"A human who fights back against evil saurans," Rasha Arc retorted.

"Evil?" scoffed the old sauran, and he coughed hard with the outburst, bits of watery blood spraying forth with the word. "Why so?" he asked after he composed himself. "Why are saurans more evil than humans?"

"You kill humans!" Rasha Arc cried.

"You kill saurans!" retorted the high shaman.

"We follow Altos," said Rasha Arc, as though that should justify everything.

"The Heatstealer," hissed Kassis. "Altos who stole the heat from the bodies of Aussasaurian's children in the days of creation. Altos who was jealous of the true god, and so wounded the work of Aussasaurian."

The tip of Rasha Arc's club drooped to the ground. He had never heard the tale of the days of creation, when Altos and Aussasaurian, the two gods charged to populate Tethedril, had done their work, told in that manner. "Aussasaurian brought the fiery comet," he countered, "that withers crops."

"To save her children!" snapped the old sauran. "Only the week of the comet gives us the energy to battle those who hold precious heat in their bodies. Only the comet gives to saurans the means to survive the cold winter, when humans move, but saurans must stand at rest."

"Aussas was human," argued Rasha Arc, looking for some advantage in this battle of logic that he seemed to be losing. From this one's point of view, it seemed that the humans weren't the only ones with a grievance here; the whole notion of good and evil seemed to melt together into the grayness of varied perspectives. "At first," Rasha Arc quickly added to quell Kassis' derisive chuckles.

"She took the more beautiful form," the high shaman replied, for even in sauran legend, Aussasaurian had begun the creation of Tethedril as Aussas, the sister of Altos, who did indeed wear the likeness of the humans. "Aussas changed herself and her children after the Great Deception," Kassis preached, "when Altos sent his lessers into the goddess' workshop to steal the heat from the bodies of her children. Evil Altos," the high shaman sneered. "He expected his sister to submit to him then, to recognize that his children and not hers would populate Tethedril, but Aussas, the true god of Tethedril, foiled his plans. She altered the sauran bodies, overlapping our skin into scaly folds, making us greater that we might survive the dangers of the warmer deep jungle. Then she, in seeing the beauty of her creation, took sauran form, and created Aussasaur the comet."

The sermon ended abruptly, in yet another fit of bloody coughing. During that fit, Kassis caught a movement to the side, in the sack. The clubbing hadn't killed all of the taiperserpents, it seemed.

Rasha Arc rocked back on his heels. He knew the tale of Altos and Aussas as well as any human alive, but he had never heard it put quite in that way. In his doctrine, both the races had been created without inner heat, but Altos, being the greater of the sibling gods, had found the way to improve his children. This had angered Aussas, and thus she had created the comet to heat the world, that her children would thrive and the children of Altos would die. But in that, too, Altos had defeated her, pushing her comet away for all but the two short passes each year.

The Godtalker looked upon the high shaman now with as much pity as hatred. If this sauran truly believed the legend it had told, then was the creature, in fact, any more evil than a human? Could Rasha Arc sincerely blame some creature for following the word of its god?

"By what name are you called?" the Godtalker asked.

The sauran looked up from its slumping posture, reptilian eyes scrutinizing the man, seeming suspicious. "Do you need my name to work more of your evil magic?" the high shaman asked bluntly. "To take my form, perhaps, that you might go to my people and lead them to disaster?"

"I am called Rasha Arc," the man said, stooping near to the sauran.

Kassis scoffed. "What does that mean to me, given so soon before I die?"

Rasha Arc let it go. He couldn't really blame the poisoned creature for its suspicions or its caution. "Our god legends are similar," he remarked. "Both of our peoples know of Altos and Aussas."

"Aussasaurian," Kassis promptly corrected.

"Aussasaurian," Rasha Arc agreed. "Heat bringers, both, in their own way."

Kassis managed to prop himself up on one skinny elbow. He couldn't believe that he was still alive; he could even feel a bit of tingling in one foot, as the numbness abated. Perhaps the venom of the fern-hanging viper wasn't so different from that of the taiperserpent. Perhaps his immunity would see him through the poison.

Rasha Arc noted the movement. He thought it reflective of discomfort and felt an unexpected pang of guilt. "You know why I had to come out here," he said.

Kassis didn't blink.

"I had to stop you." Rasha Arc went on. "The poison caused horrible deaths among my people. I knew that you would be out collecting more, and that I could not allow."

Kassis managed a strained nod. "We have to attack

before the winter," he rasped. "Have to hurt humans to keep them north before the time of cold when we are without defense."

Rasha Arc nodded. It made sense. "And I have to protect my people," he said.

"You performed well, Rasha Arc."

The human nodded, feeling an odd kinship to his counterpart. Both he and the high shaman were duty-bound enemies, each working for the good of their warring people. In just this short conversation, it amazed Rasha Arc how much he and this sauran were of the same mind, each performing as he must, for the safety of his people and in obedience to the edicts of his chosen god.

"We each have our duty," Kassis said, as though he had read Rasha Arc's mind.

The man smiled, even put a hand out to touch the sauran on the shoulder.

"Why must it be this way, Rasha Arc?" Kassis asked. "Why must we war?"

"The saurans—" Rasha Arc started to protest, but Kassis lifted a heavy hand, stopping the man short.

"Tell me not of the treachery of saurans," Kassis pleaded. "For I can match your every tale with one of the treachery of humans."

Rasha Arc lowered his gaze and snickered at the truth of it all. The two tribes had been at war since the Day of Reasoning, five generations of battle and murder. There were only about three hundred humans in all the land, and a like number of saurans, both populations kept pitifully low by fight after fight. In looking at the high shaman, in talking, actually conversing, with a sauran for the first time, Rasha Arc began to wonder why it had to be this way.

Kassis stirred again, shifted his leg. Rasha Arc looked at it in surprise.

The sauran hadn't wanted to reveal that the poison was abating, figuring that the human would merely cave in his head with that terrible clobber, but the game was up.

"Aussasaurian grants an immunity to some venoms to her high shamans," the sauran explained. "Over taiper-serpents, perhaps even over the bite of fern-hanging vipers. What other method will Rasha Arc use to kill me then?"

The question stung Rasha Arc to his very soul, to his merciful soul. "No method," he said, and he could hardly believe the words as they left his mouth. "Perhaps this talk which we have started will lead to greater ends."

"You would show me mercy?" the high shaman asked incredulously.

Rasha Arc squared his broad shoulders. "I care only for the benefit of my own people," he stated deter-minedly. He lost his bluster quickly, though, and admitted, "And perhaps I can learn to care for the benefit of the sauran people, as well."

"And I for the benefit of humans," said the high shaman.

Rasha Arc looked at him doubtfully.

"Though I do find you ugly!" the sauran added, coughing as he tried to chuckle.

Rasha Arc managed a slight smile.

"I am Kassis," the sauran said, and the tone of the rep-tilian's voice told Rasha Arc that he was not lying.

"My greetings to you, Kassis," the man said politely. He spent a long moment studying the pitiful creature. He remained suspicious, but he had taken all of Kassis' weapons and realized that he could defeat the old and weak sauran even if Kassis hadn't been poisoned. Rasha Arc offered an arm to the sauran.

Kassis struggled to his feet. He could feel the tingling of life in his clawed toes. The muscles in his legs were slow to answer his call, but his arms moved in coordinated fashion, and his grip on the human was strong.

"I may survive," the sauran admitted as Rasha Arc helped him through the first two steps. He slipped a step to the side, then doubled over in apparent agony.

"Fight it," Rasha Arc pleaded. The Godtalker's thoughts whirled now, following the potential course laid out by his discussion with the high shaman. He had never meant to talk to the creature, of course, except to taunt it in its last seconds of life. But now . . . now the possibilities loomed large. Perhaps the war would be ended; perhaps the misconceptions that had guided both the races through five generations could be untangled. Rasha Arc believed in Altos, and knew the legend well. That tale loomed as a grave warning against the sauran creatures, for in human lore, Aussas, mother of the sauran race, was the deceiver. Craving superiority over her brother, she had started the war of jealous sabotage, a war that Altos had won, but that his children had been charged with waging against the children of Aussas.

But Rasha Arc could not ignore the possibilities for peace. How much greater his people could become if the battling at last ended! How much . . .

The Godtalker was drawn from his contemplations when he noticed that Kassis, while doubling over, had reached for something. "What . . ." he started to ask, but stopped as the high shaman spun about quickly, reaching toward him.

Rasha Arc still did not fully comprehend the purpose of

the movement—was Kassis falling from consciousness?—
until the sack went over his head, until he felt the coils of
the dead taiperserpents looping down about his head and
shoulders, felt the slithering coil of one serpent that was not
quite dead.

The man fell back, and Kassis, without the support,
fell to the ground heavily. Rasha Arc fumbled desperately with the sack, got it off of his head, and pushed
aside four of the snakes. When he pulled off the fifth one,
though, the living one, he had to rip it right from his
neck, where its fangs had found a secure hold, pumping
in many times the amount of venom that had killed five
of his people. The taiperserpent hit the ground near to its
dead kin and tried to wriggle away. Its back had been
crushed, though, and it could do no more than flop pitifully, back and forth.

Stumbling with horror and with pain, Rasha Arc
retrieved his clobber and finished the wounded serpent
with a single heavy blow.

The laughter of Kassis turned him about. The high
shaman was still on the ground, propped on his elbows,
for his legs would not come to his call forcefully enough
for him to rise.

"Do you feel the bite of Aussasaurian?" the sauran
teased. "Do you feel her life blood mingling with your
own, stealing the heat from your body? Ever was mercy
the weakness of humans!"

Rasha Arc groaned loudly, more fearful of what would
happen to all his people, with him dead and the high
shaman still alive, than with the inevitable death that
loomed before him. He felt the burning venom coursing
through his veins, felt his muscles going slack, even his

chest, so that he had to concentrate and labor hard just to draw breath.

Rasha Arc fought hard to forget his own demise, to focus on the good of his people. He staggered forward a step, tried to lift his clobber.

Kassis laughed at him.

Rasha Arc saw double now. He tried to take another step, but tumbled facedown into the dirt.

Kassis laughed all the harder.

Rolling onto his side, Rasha Arc saw the sauran rise, then sway unsteadily. Kassis approached, and Rasha Arc instinctively reached for his clobber.

He found that he could not even lift the so-heavy weapon, and the sauran easily took it from him.

"I could show you mercy," the sauran said, standing, albeit unsteadily, over the prone man. "I could kill you quickly, with a single blow. Beg for that."

Rasha Arc rolled onto his back and stared blankly at the sauran.

"Beg for it," Kassis said again. "You will, soon enough!"

Rasha Arc shook his head.

Kassis laughed all the louder, but then stopped as he heard the not-so-distant roar of a jungle cat.

"Jaquar," the high shaman explained. "It smells you, human, not so hard a thing to do!"

Rasha Arc did not respond to the insult. He just lay on his back, fighting for breath, trying to find some way out—for himself and for his people.

"So I will not kill you," Kassis went on. "Linger in the pain of Aussasaurian's vengeance until the jaquar comes upon you. Let the cat play with its prey while I get far away."

Kassis took a step and nearly tumbled, his leg locking backward violently. He steadied himself quickly, though, and took another step.

Rasha Arc prayed with all his heart, called to Altos, begged his god to give him one moment of strength. One last moment.

Then he rolled onto his belly, put his numb legs under him, and lunged forward.

He didn't go far and couldn't even grasp with his reaching hand, but that whack across the ankle proved enough to topple the unsteady sauran to the ground. Ignoring the pain, forcing his knotted stomach to extend and not even bothering to force his breath, Rasha Arc scrambled forward, clawing at the sauran. He fell heavily across Kassis' legs and rolled higher. He hardly felt the blow as the sauran whacked him on the back with the clobber. And on he rolled, coming to rest limply atop the high shaman.

Kassis struggled fiercely, clawed at Rasha Arc's eyes until they were bloody pulps.

Rasha Arc didn't feel it, though. He was deep in prayer, far into meditation, basking in the thoughts of Altos. He could hardly breathe, but he somehow found the air to sing.

Kassis squirmed and clawed, but his weakened muscles would not easily shift him from under the large and heavy human. He punched Rasha Arc in the mouth repeatedly, trying to stop the song, knowing that it would bring the jaquar all the sooner.

Finally he got out and staggered to his feet. He spat a curse at Altos and brought the clobber heavily onto Rasha Arc's head, forever ending the Godtalker's song.

The high shaman glanced all about desperately. He

knew that the jaquar was close by, perhaps even watching him. But the cat would go for the easier prey, would feast on the large body of Rasha Arc for a long while, certainly long enough for Kassis to get away. He had to move slowly, he knew, steadily away, with no sudden jerks that might bring the jaquar springing upon him.

He slid one foot ahead of the other. There! He caught sight of the huge orange, spotted cat, several hundred handbreadths away, staring at him from between two trees.

Move slowly, the high shaman told himself. He understood the ways of the jaquar, and now that the cat was in sight, all that he had to do was hold its gaze with his own until he got to the thicker bush. Then he could move off, while the jaquar went to Rasha Arc.

He took another slow, sliding step, staring hard at the cat, and so intense was his gaze that he never noted the movement below him as, in his final act, in a movement inspired by his god, in complete defiance to the poisonous blood of Aussasaurian, Rasha Arc snapped his arm out and grabbed tight to the sauran's ankle.

Kassis went down heavily. He put his legs under him even as he hit, starting his dash to the underbrush.

But then he looked up, looked into the green eyes of the jaquar, looked at the white fangs of the growling cat.

Close enough to kiss.

# *Ice Magic*

## Douglas Niles

*T*allus sat on the high rock, watching the women work the nets in the frothing waters of the river. The spring catch was good, and there had been no sign of saurans—yet. Still, the warrior's keen eyes, of the same cold blue as the ice of the High Glacier, swept the far bank, where fronds of palm and thistle crowded close to the water. Wind momentarily rustled through that greenery, but as the breeze passed the leaves settled, motionless again.

The young man knew that the river provided a good barrier against a sudden attack from the south. The saurans wouldn't enter the chill waters, couldn't expose themselves to either the icy temperature or the powerful current. The real threat, if any existed, lay on this side of the deep flowage.

Uncomfortable and nervous, Tallus allowed his eyes to drift back to the fishers. The women of the Mountain Folk, under the watchful eyes of two warriors, worked diligently to harvest the spawning silvertrout. Dirondey was easy to distinguish among the powerfully built females who hauled at the nets. She was the youngest of the workers, and her hair of golden silk was gathered into a braid that dangled to her waist. Despite the sinew that rippled in her bare arms and legs, her waist was trim, and when she leaned back to brush a stray hair from her forehead the graceful lines of her figure made Tallus forget about everything else.

Everything, that is, but his ice. Even as he watched Dirondey, Tallus unconsciously carved the talisman of blue frost he had brought down from the High Glacier. During times such as this, when Aussasaurian approached with the scalding fires of spring, he tried to always have a piece of ice handy. In the hands of an icemaster such as Tallus, the frost of the High Glacier became a weapon of killing and confusion—a potent ally in the eternal war of humankind.

Working the frozen water as his eyes roved over the fishers and the surrounding wilds, Tallus felt the chilly power in his hands as a vague, comforting presence. Using the edge of his heavy flint knife, he carved several sharp shards from the block.

He looked to the nets again, seeing a dozen glimmering shapes wriggle and sparkle in the sun as more silvertrout were drawn to shore. Turning his attention to the mound of boulders on the far side of the fishing shallows, Tallus looked for some sign of Gartal. As if sensing his counterpart's gaze, that tall warrior rose to his feet, sending a casual wave toward Tallus before settling back into his guard post. One of the most competent and skillful warriors in the tribe, Gartal provided a solid anchor against surprise from downstream. If the saurans had somehow crossed that frigid barrier, he was the first line of defense.

Tallus dropped the thin chips of ice into his belt pouch, knowing that, near the coolness of his flesh, they would remain intact for a long time. Again he looked at the verdant jungle across the river, trying to suppress his sense of growing unease.

After all, he told himself, the water was high with spring runoff. The saurans, in the past, had occasionally crossed the river on dry boulders jutting above the low water level. These perches would be completely submerged for several more weeks, so the humans on this side of the icy barrier should be safe. Even so, the two warriors were posted strategically, ready for an unexpected attack.

His eyes drifted back to Dirondey, and Tallus allowed himself a moment of private reflection. Soon she would be his woman, sanctified by the rite of pledged mating common through the human tribes. Though she had stalled him for several years now, Tallus was fully determined that, under the sacred moon of midsummer, Dirondey would be sworn to him, would belong to him before the end of the warm season.

The first saurans exploded from Gartal's cluster of rocks, interrupting Tallus' musings with shocking suddenness, rushing at the women with silent speed. Sprinting on two feet, green and yellow blurs of deadly quickness, the reptilian attackers were in the midst of the fishers before any of the women screamed an alarm. Tallus felt a surge of irrational anger—*how* could Gartal have failed so completely? There was only one answer, and as he leapt to his feet a quick glance showed that his companion's watch post was empty. A thin river of crimson liquid flowed downhill from the concealed platform.

More fishers screamed, turning to slash at the snake-men with barbed spears. A sauran snapped the haft of one weapon with a bite of powerful jaws, then slashed a clawed forepaw, knocking the woman to the ground.

Others bounded through the group of humans with a singleness of purpose that brought terror to Tallus' heart.

A sauran went down, tripped by a net, then stabbed by Dirondey's spear. Two more of the snake-men leaped at the golden-haired woman, smashing her onto her back. Tallus ran down the slope toward the fishing grounds, deadly fear propelling him to reckless, bounding leaps over the broken ground.

With quick slashes of whiplike cords, the saurans bound Dirondey's wrists and ankles. More of the mottled warriors reached the melee, and four hefted her to their shoulders, taking off down the riverbank at a run.

Tallus sprinted frantically, his sauran-skin sandals bounding over the water-worn rocks. His bow was upright in his left hand, and he clenched the hollow reed shaft of an arrow in his right. Clamping the missile in his teeth, he reached into the belt pouch for a chip of ice, jamming it into the notch at the head of his arrow. From the vantage of a high rock he halted, drawing the weapon back in one smooth gesture.

He aimed for the one of the saurans carrying Dirondey, but already that group had scuttled around the rocks that had been Gartal's watch post. A few of the hissing, snapping creatures remained in sight, brandishing their knob-sticks, holding the infuriated fishers at bay. Tallus took a shot at one of these, and before the arrow struck, he was already flying down the hill again.

The ice-headed shaft hit the sauran in the shoulder, drawing a hissing croak of pain. The monster spun through a full circle, frantically grasping at the weapon—but before it could pull the missile free the snake-man had toppled backward, stiff and dead.

But the power of ice magic could not grant Tallus

wings, couldn't bestow the speed of the horned mountain rams that raced across the rocky highlands. He skidded on the rough ground, diving backward to avoid the whipcord of a sauran rear guard. Fanged jaws gaping, the creature leapt at the human's face, and Tallus dropped his bow in favor of the long-bladed knife of flint.

The sauran dropped to all fours, then pounced with lightning quickness. Claws bit into his shoulder as Tallus twisted away, then whirled back to make a desperate stab. The keen stone ripped into the sauran's belly, slashing soft skin, mangling twisted entrails. With a moan the beast dropped to the ground, thrashing, dying in pain. Stopping only long enough to sheathe his knife and snatch up his bow and arrows, the human raced onward.

The river foamed and spumed beside him, chill waters of icy gray mocking his power as Tallus sprinted along the winding trail. Rock outcrops loomed over his head, and an inner voice whispered caution—any number of places along here would make perfect ambush sites for the clever saurans.

But they had taken Dirondey! Every other fact faded into insignificance against the thought of the golden-haired prize in the hands of the tribe's vicious, jungle-dwelling enemies. Working chips of ice into several arrows, Tallus focused on the trail under his feet, ignoring potential threats on the heights above. He raced around another corner on a ledge where the river surged directly below, catching a glimpse of a green and yellow tail flicking around the next shoulder of the precipice. Tallus slid to a halt just before that blocking terrain, taking time to nock an arrow and draw his bow.

When he stepped into view he saw a slit-eyed sauran crouched a few paces away, ready to spring—but the

arrow flew first. With a strangled wail the brute went
down, squirming from a gut shot. Another sauran flew at
Tallus' face, but he unleashed his arrow a split second
before the wicked jaws would have closed onto his
shoulder. The missile plunged between fang-studded
jaws, driving the icy head deep into the sauran's throat.
The creature died silently, but the flying body slammed
into Tallus, sending him skidding from the sloping trail.
Crying out in fury and frustration, the man felt rocks
slam against his flanks as he tumbled downward.

The bow slipped from his flailing fingers, and then
water was all around, current surging and driving and
pounding. Another man, or any sauran, would have been
dangerously chilled by the immersion—for this was
water spilling from the High Glacier, barely a few hours'
thawed from the snowy heights that capped the world.
Yet the icemaster fought only the current, his already cool
body feeling no discomfort from the frigid temperature.

Stroking away from the largest rocks, Tallus swam for
the middle of the river, turning his feet downstream as
buffers against any hidden obstacles. He allowed the
current to sweep him along, catching an occasional,
blurry glimpse of the sauran war party working its way
along the rocky bank. Dirondey, still suspended between
four of the reptilian attackers, swayed and struggled
sickeningly on the high trail. Tallus suspected that she
would willingly cast herself to death on the rocks rather
than face the terrors of sauran captivity, knowing that
such captivity must inevitably end in an even more horrible fate.

Yet in his brief glimpses he saw that the reptilian captors had now secured the woman to a long, smooth pole.
The shaft had been pushed between Dirondey's bound

limbs, and more vines had been used to lash her torso. No less than six saurans carried the pole, and the captive could do nothing more than wriggle desperately.

The river spilled downward, entering the rock-walled chute of the Shadowgorge. It would be at least a mile before he'd be able to find a place to leave the river, and Tallus wondered how the saurans had crossed the watery barrier. He knew that if the creatures wandered too far down the left bank, they would run into the terrain of the Old Ones, the arrogant humans who still insisted upon calling themselves the One Tribe though they had known for generations about the Mountain Folk, Tallus' people.

But how had the saurans crossed the river?

His question was answered as the icemaster floated around a tight curve in the gorge. High overhead, spanning the lofty cliffs that bordered the river, stretched a long, spindly network of logs and heavy vines. This was where the saurans had crossed, and where they would no doubt return to the forested lowlands. Cursing the current that carried him with such speed, Tallus swam for the shore, riding close to the sheer cliff that rose steeply from the gorge.

Something brushed his legs and the man flinched, then realized that it was only a block of ice, broken free from the glacier and swept down with the strong, icy current. Seizing the opportunity, he wrapped his arms around the floating chunk, dragging it along as he floated beside the precipice.

For interminable minutes the bank of the river remained sheer, but finally the walls of the gorge tumbled away, opening into a vista of deceptively peaceful sky. Still clutching the block of glacial ice, Tallus kicked strongly, propelling himself into a shallow eddy, finally coming to rest on a sandy stretch of the river's right bank. Though rocky heights rose beyond, these were rough-hewn hillsides, not the steep cliffs that had bordered the gorge, and the icemaster knew that he would be able to climb away from the river. Still, the bridge of the saurans was nearly a mile upstream, and the creatures were undoubtedly already crossing with their prize, soon to disappear into the trackless jungle.

Tallus desperately wanted Dirondey back. For now, rage supplanted the aching desire that typically filled him when he thought of the woman, easily the most beautiful of the tribe's females. He had chosen her years ago, and now that she had reached maturity he would brook no further delays in acting upon his claim.

But how to reach her, rescue her? Now, at least, Tallus was on the same side of the river as that jungle. Though he had lost his bow, his stone knife remained in its deep sheath. And finally, there was this frozen block that had tumbled free and floated from the glacier. Squatting down to look at the chunk, Tallus was disappointed to see that this was frosty, opaque, surface ice. It would lack the potent magic of the deep blue glacial tunnels that were his favorite sources, would melt more quickly than the dense azure stuff that formed the core of the icemaster's powers. Yet it was far, far better than nothing.

The block was too heavy to carry, so Tallus set to work. Chipping deliberately with his flint blade, he started to etch a series of gashes, outlining the largest portion he could haul without seriously impeding his speed. Gouging deeper and deeper, trying to stifle his impatience, he gradually chiseled each gash to a depth of nearly a handbreadth.

When the outlines were regular and deep, he set down

his blade and placed his hands on the block. Slowly, gently, he began to exert pressure, pushing the cube he had etched away from the remaining mass. Eyes closed, lips moving silently, Tallus offered a deliberate prayer to Altos the Heatgiver, god of mankind.

The pieces of ice moved slightly under the inexorable pressure. Warmth flowed from the icemaster's fingers, focusing on the channel between the blocks, melting the cloudy ice, bringing small rivulets of water trickling from the gap. There was no sound, no sharp *crack* of release, but finally the two pieces fell apart, the smaller coming to rest in Tallus' hands.

Leaving the remainder on the riverbank, the man tucked the block, which was slightly larger than his head, into the crook of his left arm. Although the weight would hamper his movement, he knew that the ice also gave him his only chance of success. Clutching the knife in his other hand, Tallus started up the rocky slope, picking his path carefully between sharp, jutting boulders. Thorns ripped at his feet and leggings, but he kept his eyes turned upward, seeking sign of the hilltop—and, especially, of any lurking saurans.

He consciously tried to avoid thinking about Dirondey, from wondering about the savage rites that would claim her life in the heart of the steaming jungles. Yet these thoughts were too close to the surface, too piercing and real, for Tallus to have any chance of avoiding them. The fact that neither he nor any other human knew the real purpose for the taking of human captives only added to his dread.

It had only been in the last generation or two that the saurans had commenced the barbaric practice of capturing human women. For most of the long life spans since the One Tribe had been sundered, when the Mountain Folk had made their epic journey into the heights, the saurans had always attacked mercilessly, killing any human who fell into their claws, showing no interest in the taking of captives.

In those early conflicts, the tribe had fared well. Even before the discovery of the power latent within the towering glacial ice, Tallus' ancestors had found shelter from their ancient enemies in the snowbound heights. The saurans had displayed little stomach for climbing away from their steaming jungle domain. Building houses of stone, approachable only by steep trails on easily observed slopes, the Mountain Folk had found a home more secure than the realm of the One Tribe, which still inhabited the lands around Godtalker Mountain.

Tallus knew well the story of the Mountain Folk's history. The One Tribe had found itself with two men who desired to be Godtalker—and who possessed the skill to hold that exalted rank. It was the strife between these two that had splintered the tribe, sending the one named Diaqa Arc to the mountains. He had carried a skin of water filled from the Sacred Pool, and the stories said that with this he had tendered the glacier into the magical ice that had since served the tribe so well.

The only time of vulnerability known to the Mountain Folk were the times of year, such as now, before and during the arrival of Aussasaurian, the fiery comet that brought the saurans to their fever pitch of aggressive activity. At the same time, the humans were invariably short of food, since the winter's supplies had been depleted by the long, cold months when rivers were frozen, croplands buried beneath a frigid blanket of snow. One of the first food-gathering activities was always the fishing of the Glacier River—the silvertrout began their spawning with the warm weather, and skillful net wielders such as Dirondey could gather a tremendous amount of nourishing food in a single long day's labors.

Tallus remembered other captives, three or four of them taken in his lifetime. Always they had been female, and young—grievous losses to a tribe that strove desperately to increase its population. Previously the prisoners had been seized in the midst of harvesting in the foothills, always just before the coming of the comet in spring. One other thing each kidnapping had in common: None of the captives had ever been seen or heard from again.

"I *will* get her back," Tallus muttered softly, unaware that he had articulated the thought that burned in his mind. The memory of Dirondey's soft hair, her deliciously curved body, inflamed him—she was *his*, by the Heatgiver!

He thought wistfully of the quiet peacefulness of the mountain heights, where the only threats were plain and straightforward: avalanche, blizzard, or rarely, the predations of a starving ice bear. All these could be faced and, for the most part, mastered with human ingenuity and courage.

But the saurans were different. Every time the humans devised a tactic, the horrible creatures developed a counterapproach to negate humankind's ingenuity. Men had learned to fear the deadly blowguns with their killing darts, though fortunately the saurans rarely had enough poison to make a devastating attack. Still, the warriors of the tribes had developed shields of stiffened hides, and men often went to war in ungainly, but life-saving, costumes of dried bearskin, which had proved impervious to the stings of the sauran darts. Now the same leggings protected Tallus against the thorns and spines of the lush undergrowth.

He reached the crest of the hill and was greeted by a dense barrier of ferns, palms, hanging tendrils, ropelike vines, and the boles of numerous lofty, rough-barked trees. The icemaster halted, dumbfounded by the impenetrable nature of the verdant barrier. He knew that he would have little chance of discovering the captors' trail or the sauran gathering place if he merely plunged into the undergrowth and started hacking his way. Probably just the opposite, he realized—the noise of his passage would almost certainly draw the hateful snake-men right to him.

Instead, it made a lot more sense to follow the edge of the forest along the river, working his way back to the bridge. There he would find the place where the sauran war party had crossed the river, and that, at least, should put him on some sort of trail. Whether he would be able to follow the path, much less find the place they had taken Dirondey, was another matter. He banished such questions from his mind, concentrating on the best route along the jagged, stony hilltop.

Tallus scrambled along a steep crest of rock, knowing that he was mounting the lofty edge of the Shadowgorge. A perilous plunge yawned threateningly to his right, but the fronds and thorns of the jungle pressed so close to his left that he had no alternative except to follow the very brink of the precipice. With the block of ice nestled in the cool embrace of his arm and the knife carried at the ready in his free hand, the icemaster knew that his balance was not what it should be—but he had no choice. At the same time, the wounds caused by raking sauran claws and by his tumble down the opposite riverbank formed a dull throb in the background of his consciousness.

A fallen limb of darkwood dangled over the lip of the cliff, and Tallus crawled over the rough bark. On his sandals again, he trotted along flat rock where the greenery kindly halted several feet back from the edge. Coming around another bend in the constantly winding precipice, he abruptly found the view open before him.

In the distance, crowning the vista as it seemed to cap the world, rose the frost-limned ridge of Glacier Mountain. Spilling down both shoulders of the broad, flat-topped massif, creeping relentlessly through every chute and gully and ravine, fingers of ice sparkled whitely in the sun. They looked near enough to touch, and Tallus shook his head, convincing himself that the mountaintop was in fact far out of his reach.

Nearer, and of far more immediate importance, he saw the sauran bridge. Crouching behind a thick-leafed bush, Tallus looked around, scouring the cliff top and forest fringe for any sign of the snake-men. Wind tossed the lighter leaves and pushed scudding clouds through the sky. The gray waters of the river churned and roiled far below, but these were the only signs of movement that met the icemaster's careful inspection.

Still, he moved cautiously as he approached the near end of the span. The bridge of logs, tightly entwined with vines and tendrils, was clearly empty, but instinct told Tallus that a sauran—or a dozen of them, for that matter—could be concealed in the very fringe of the jungle. He stared at the bridge and nearby foliage for many heartbeats, finally convincing himself that the immediate surroundings were safe.

The crude structure was formed of three great trunks,

each lashed to the others with a tight weave of vines, some of the tendrils as thick as the icemaster's wrist. Heavy lines extended into the upper branches of a nearby tree, and Tallus saw with sudden clarity that this was how the creatures had lowered the bridge into place. First they had positioned the nearest, heaviest, timber. Then they had suspended the second, and finally the third, the lightest beam, had been pulled into place. The technique had allowed the saurans to cross a gap that was nearly twice as long as the tallest tree they had used in their bridge building.

The span was an ingenious construct, and yet another example of sauran cleverness. But, for now at least, Tallus decided that it was not a threat to his safety. No doubt all of the jungle warriors had already crossed back to this side of the river. The icemaster thought momentarily about cutting down the bridge: with his stone knife he could quickly saw through several key vines, and with those cut the entire bridge would collapse. Yet after a moment's reflection he decided that such effort would be a waste of time. Besides, if he escaped with Dirondey the bridge might even prove to be a useful avenue for their escape from the jungle. He could always cut it down later.

Tallus turned back to the verdant barrier that pressed so close to the rocky gorge. The path taken by the saurans was clearly visible, as the creatures had been forced to hack aside a mass of creeper vines in order to clear the way. Conscious of the ice slowly melting against his arm and side, the man nevertheless approached the jungle carefully, scrutinizing the gap in the greenery for any sign of ambush or trap.

Not content with a normal visual examination, Tallus

touched his fingertips to the block of ice, dabbing at the slickness caused by the warm air. When two fingers were wet, he raised them, touched them briefly to his closed eyelids.

Opening his eyes again, he looked at the gap with renewed clarity. His vision penetrated the initial fringe of leaf and trunk, though the image swiftly became blurred in a verdant tangle. A small furry mammal, frozen in place, stared at the man from a few paces into the jungle. Tiny brown eyes glittered on the edge of panic, though the creature was safe from observation by any normal vision. Enhanced by ice magic, Tallus saw it clearly—and the little rodent's presence reassured him far more than could a thorough visual inspection. After all, if any saurans were in the vicinity, the little creature would have sought shelter in a treetop lair or underground burrow.

As Tallus stepped forward the jungle rat scuttled away with just the softest flutter of rustling leaves. As his enhanced vision faded back to normal, the icemaster ducked under a trailing vine and, in a few more steps, found himself surrounded by greenery on all sides. Even a look backward showed just a bare glimpse of the sunlit rocks on the edge of the gorge, and two more steps carried him beyond view of even that image of daylight.

In fact, the atmosphere in the forest seemed like a whole different kind of air. The cooling breeze that swept downward from Glacier Mountain was nonexistent here, swallowed completely by the thick barrier of leafage. The temperature, too, climbed dramatically in just the space of a few steps, bringing an instant clammy sweat to the man's brow. The block under his arm steamed in the oppressive warmth, and Tallus clutched the chunk closer, seeking to shelter it with his cool body from the debilitating, melting heat.

Flies buzzed around his ears in droning, persistent circles. At first Tallus tried to brush the pesky bugs away, flailing with his long-bladed knife, flinching and swatting every time one of the insects landed on his arms or head. Despite the heat, he was grateful that the rest of his body was protected by his leather leggings and tunic—at least the supple material kept the flies from much of his skin.

A stabbing bite brought an involuntary gasp from the icemaster as one of the bugs chomped into his earlobe. Another sting burned at the nape of his neck, and one more nipped him through the thick hair that trailed in sweat-soaked strands over his temple. In disgust, Tallus abandoned his efforts to swipe the pests away, lowering his head to plod resolutely forward.

It was little consolation to learn that the bugs didn't seem quite so drawn to him when he wasn't flailing to keep them away. Even with the lesser attentions, he was bitten frequently, though the pain of the initial bites had exceeded the later insults significantly—almost as if he was getting used to having his flesh devoured, Tallus reflected grimly. He appreciated, more than ever before, the wisdom that had driven his ancestors to seek shelter in the high mountains.

A vine caught at his ankle, sending him stumbling along the narrow trail, and the icemaster cursed at the rustling, jarring sounds of his passage. He paused, catching his breath, listening for the sounds of alarm—but there was no noise that rose above the droning of those relentless flies. Moving more cautiously, he studied the ground before each step, taking the time to duck under the tendrils and limbs that would otherwise have smashed him in the face.

Clearly the saurans had carved this trail only recently, perhaps just before they built the bridge. Since the reptile-men averaged only about two-thirds the height of a man, they had naturally cleared only enough of the undergrowth to give themselves free passage. The ends of the slashed vines were clean, obviously cut by the sharp-edged blades of bone or shell occasionally borne by sauran warriors—weapons that made a different cut from the serrated stone-edged knives favored by humans. Fresh leaves already sprouted where the trail builders had hacked aside bushes and tree limbs, and Tallus shuddered under the very real apprehension that this jungle was a living, sentient being, actively seeking to reach out and block his passage.

Again he thought of Dirondey, pictured the brutal, thorny scraping that must have accompanied her passage through these tight confines. He forged relentlessly onward against the vines and creepers, sometimes hacking with the flint-bladed knife, otherwise ducking low to avoid a heavy limb or prickly branch. Always he pressed forward, following the trampled path of the sauran war party.

He lost track of time in the soupy air. The sun was a vague presence far above the canopy of leaves, unseen but certainly felt. The ground remained relatively level, though once the path dipped into the floor of a plant-entangled ravine. Here Tallus picked up the speed of his pursuit, trotting at full height since the overhanging canopy remained above the walls of the gully.

All too quickly, however, the trail climbed back to the forest floor, and the icemaster advanced in his half-crouching, scuttling gait. Despite his efforts to insulate it against the cloaking heat, the block of ice he carried continued to shrink at a frightening rate.

Abruptly the ragged trail connected to a real path. Tallus stepped forward onto the dirt thoroughfare before he even realized the significance of the find; by the time he shrank back into the jungle and cautiously looked to the right and left, he would certainly have been discovered by any sauran in the nearby vicinity. Fortunately, this stretch of trail seemed to be deserted, at least for now.

The hard-packed ground showed no sign of footprints, but Tallus knew beyond any doubt that this jungle pathway was used by saurans. The route to the bridge seemed to begin or end here—at least, there was no sign of a continuation in the tangle on the other side. Instead, the war party and their precious captive must have turned either to the left or to the right.

But which way? There were no footprints on the ground, and Tallus knew that he lacked the tracking skill that might have enabled a skilled hunter to find subtle clues as to the capturing party's direction.

Kneeling, the icemaster took his knife and carved a thick chip from the block of ice, a piece about the size of his little finger. Clutching the shard in his left hand, he closed his eyes and spoke a quiet prayer to Altos, feeling the Heatgiver bring warmth to his hand. Water trickled from his fingers, but he kept his eyes shut until the entire piece of ice had melted.

When he looked at the ground, he saw a line of wetness marring the dust, extending in a line toward the left.

Without hesitation the icemaster gathered up his shrinking block and started along the leftward path, unquestioningly following the results of his divination. The vines and limbs over this pathway formed a thick canopy high over the man's head—in fact, the lowest of these was barely within reach of his arm when he extended his knife hand upward.

There was still no breeze, but now at least the speed of his trotting advance caused a slight cooling effect, dank and humid air washing across his sweaty skin. He knew that it was dangerously warm in here as his body, like his ice, strove to stay cool. Still, Tallus remained grateful for the wide pathway and didn't bother to wonder why creatures as short as the saurans should maintain such a lofty trail.

Coming around a bend in the path, the icemaster saw a great beast crouched before him, barely a dozen paces away. The creature, nearly as large as a mature ice bear, growled as menacingly as one of the ursine predators of the heights.

Tallus froze, stunned by the realization that the trail was used by more than just the mottle-skinned enemies of his people. A pelt of golden fur, speckled with black spots in a curiously beautiful pattern, covered the lean yet massive body. The broad face wrinkled into a cruel grin, mouth gaping to display long fangs, including two tusklike teeth dangling from the upper jaw. The latter were as long as the icemaster's knife, wickedly curved and sharp. Golden eyes, slitted with dark pupils, blinked almost lazily, and the growl rumbling from that cavernous chest was almost a purr of anticipation.

He had heard of the great jungle cat, the jaquar, beasts reputedly ready to devour any creature unfortunate enough to meet their vicious talons and cruel jaws. Somehow, in the depths of his anger about his woman, Tallus had forgotten those tales of peril, had proceeded as if the only menace in this tangled forest was that represented by the saurans.

That mistake, he realized with a pang of bitterness, was likely to be his last.

Still, Tallus was not a man to surrender without a fight. Clutching the ice close to his flank, he stepped carefully backward, raising the stone blade that suddenly looked remarkably puny. The cat took a measured, careful step forward, then another, matching the man's retreat pace for pace.

Staring into those bright yellow eyes, Tallus saw the glittering slits return a glare of pure hunger. He threw down the block of ice, fearing this was a hopeless fight yet wanting both hands free. After all, ice magic was useless against the bears and cliff rams of his homeland. The chilling power seemed to be only effective against saurans, and the icemaster wasn't about to make a futile experiment against this crouching predator.

Edging backward around the bend, Tallus watched the big cat trot a few steps, keeping its prey in sight. The man wondered about hurling himself into the jungle greenery, trying to climb a tree or push through the creepers and vines, but he quickly discarded the thought—no doubt the cat would be far more at home in such an environment than would he.

Instead, the icemaster backed against the bole of a solid tree, clutching the hilt of his stone blade in both hands, awaiting attack. The jaguar crouched, tail lashing back and forth, unblinking eyes fastened on the man's face. Tallus heard the rumbling growls fade, sensed that the silence preceded a deadly leap.

The cat's piercing shriek froze the man in place. By

sheer will, Tallus kept his eyes open, wondering if the cry was an attempt to paralyze him with fear, to render him an easy victim for those cruel fangs. Surprisingly, the jaquar whirled to the side, snapping at its own flank in a blur of black-speckled pelt, then crouching low, gaping mouth turned toward the jungle, shrill cries mingling with deep, rumbling bellows of rage.

With a blink of surprise Tallus saw the spear. The wooden shaft of a dark, nearly black wood jutted from the cat's flank just behind the right shoulder. Vaguely the icemaster saw colorful feathers trailing from the haft, sensed that it must have been cast with powerful force, by . . .

By whom, or *what*? It was ludicrous to think that a sauran had attacked the cat, driving it into fenzied rage in the snake-man's attempt to save a human. Too, the spear shaft looked heavier, more polished than any sauran weapon in the icemaster's experience. In the space of an eye blink another spear flew from the woods, plunging downward from above, driving a jagged, stone-edged head into the cat's back directly between the shoulders.

Now the jaquar turned hate-filled eyes upward, rearing, rising high, swatting at branches overhead. Tallus saw his chance and sprang forward before he had time to think, to be afraid. The keen knife plunged into the cat's flank, piercing skin and muscle, driving between solid ribs. Gripping the hilt tightly, the icemaster tumbled away, pulling the weapon free and slashing it to meet the jaquar's swiping forepaw.

The padded foot met the blade sharply, and Tallus felt a hooked claw rip his wrist. He fell to the side, feeling the knife ripped out of his hand. Pitching into the tangled brush beside the trail, the icemaster kicked out with a sandaled foot, bashing the cat on the nose as it pounced toward him.

But now he was thoroughly trapped—and unarmed. Ignoring the throbbing pain in his wrist, Tallus scrambled to a sitting position, clutching for a stick, a stone, anything he could use as a weapon. His hand closed on pulpy fronds and lush ferns, nothing that would delay the cat for even an instant.

A dark figure flashed through the icemaster's vision, and again the jaquar uttered that shriek of fury and pain. Blinking in astonishment, Tallus saw that another fighter had entered the fray, dropping from an overhead limb.

The man was tall and lean, naked except for a narrow strip of jaquar fur twisted between his loins. He was armed with a short, heavy spear, identical to the two weapons already thrust into the great cat's body. Now the newcomer crouched beside the animal, plunging that third spear into the jaquar's haunches, then drawing it back.

Spinning to face the new attacker, the great feline stumbled awkwardly, sorely hurt. Roaring, the cat lashed its tail across the icemaster's legs, growling in the face of the nearly naked man of the forest.

The attacker brandished his spear with steadfast courage, but Tallus feared for him, knowing the deadly power of those talons and fangs. The fellow's dark features curled into a scowl of concentration as he held the spear over his head, pointed slightly downward as the cat gathered its muscles for a lethal spring.

Still lacking a weapon, Tallus could think of but a single tactic: He seized the feline's tail in both of his hands. Ignoring the steady throbbing in his wounded wrist, he held tightly as the animal leapt. The force of the pounce pulled the icemaster upward from his sitting position, but he didn't let go of the tail—and the drag of his weight brought the jaquar's pounce up short.

The cat fell to the ground in front of the strange human, and the man stabbed the stout spear downward, driving it into the neck directly beside the drooling fangs. With a last, strangled yowl, the jaquar shivered and stiffened, then grew still.

For a moment the only sounds in the forest pathway were the two men drawing deep, rasping breaths. Warily Tallus regarded his rescuer. He had never seen a man like this. Virtually unclothed, the fellow had skin of dusky bronze and was armed only with the stout spear with a head of jagged-edged flint. His hair was as long as a woman's, bound to the nape of his neck by a feathered band. The man's eyes were so dark they seemed almost black, and he held his handsome face high, regarding Tallus with a lofty, regal stare.

"I am Daithar," said the tall man, his voice curiously stiff and accented, but the words recognizable to the man from the mountains.

"And I am Tallus," the icemaster replied, staggering weakly to his feet. He retrieved his knife, wiping the blood on the jaquar's pelt before sliding the blade into its sheath.

"You saved my life," he declared frankly. "Why?"

"I have never seen a man like you. Not like the hunters of the One Tribe, who sometimes dare to enter the jungle. And not like the saurans, either."

"A curse of Altos on the saurans," Tallus declared vehemently.

"You seek your woman?" asked Daithar.

The question sent a surge of hope firing through the icemaster's breast, but he struggled to contain his elation.

"You have seen a female human?" he asked, as calmly as he could.

"In the hands of the saurans. They have taken her for the Great Fire."

"What fire is that?" growled Tallus.

"A magic blaze, ignited by the shaman. They light such a fire before the Great Comet comes. If they have the blood of a human woman to offer as sacrifice, the saurans believe that their power is increased when they embark on the raids of Aussasaurian."

"You have seen these fires?" demanded the icemaster skeptically.

Daithar shrugged, not taking visible offense. "I have heard tales from the elders of my tribe. I, myself, have been grown to manhood for but three comets, and the saurans have not brought a captive in that time."

*"Where?"* Tallus asked, feeling a sickening emptiness in his belly. All of his plans, his desires, his *need* for Dirondey were menaced by this vicious sauran rite. "Where is she?"

The jungle man looked at him for a moment, squinting shrewdly, before responding in that stilted accent. "She is very near to here. You were following the path to the village—before you almost became jaquar prey."

"Why . . . why did you save me?"

Daithar shrugged. "I am not sure that I know the answer to your question. You are human, of a strange tribe. And you are enemy of the sauran, who are my people's enemy as well."

"Your people? You have a tribe, here in the jungle?" The thought of humans dwelling under the very noses of the cold-blooded snake-men was a mind-boggling concept to Tallus.

"A small tribe," Daithar admitted. His shoulders stiffened, and he faced Tallus with a look of haughty pride, as if challenging the icemaster to ask him further questions.

But Tallus' thoughts had already veered back to Dirondey. "That woman—*my* woman—you saw . . . can you take me to where she is, to the sauran village?"

"I go where I please in the jungle. Now, it pleases me to take you to her. But not along the trail—by the time you took three hundred steps, the saurans would see you. And they would kill you before you knew you had been spotted."

Tallus looked at the tangled forest in dismay. "If not the trail, *how*?" he asked.

"Follow me." The dark man whirled and dove into the jungle, vanishing almost instantaneously.

Tallus overcame a momentary hesitation, then bent to retrieve his block of ice, which had shrunk considerably during the course of the fight. He ducked his head and followed in the direction taken by Daithar, surprised to slip almost soundlessly under a fringe of leaves. Watching his step, he avoided a gnarled root, then looked up to catch a glimpse of the jungle man scampering up the leaning bole of a heavy tree.

His sandals slipped on the rough bark, but Tallus was able to follow up the canted trunk. Gasping for breath, he caught up to Daithar as the other man finally paused. When he looked down, the icemaster realized that the ground was far below, lost to sight in the midst of thorny thickets and bristling fronds.

Up here they remained below the upper canopy of leaves, insulated from any glimpse of the sky. Nevertheless, a slight breeze wafted among the trunks, and Tallus was startled to see a gridlike network of heavy boughs extending horizontally among the massive trees.

"The tangle is all below," Daithar explained, seeing the icemaster's look of wonder. "Up here we, and the saurans, can move with ease."

Abruptly the jungle man scowled, his eyes coming to rest on the translucent block clutched in the crook of Tallus' left arm. "What manner of stone is that?"

"Not a stone, ice. Here, touch it."

The icemaster extended the block. Daithar reached out a cautious finger, then snapped it back as if it had been burned. The jungle man looked in wonder at the spot of wetness on his fingertip.

"It's just water." In the face of Daithar's rank skepticism, Tallus touched the block, then licked the meltage off of his fingertip.

"Why do you carry it here?"

"It might help us against the saurans." The thought of explaining his magic made Tallus unaccountably nervous; he sensed it was best to keep the extent of his power a secret. "How close to the sauran village are we?"

"I told you, not far. There will be sentries in the forest just a short distance from here."

"Wait a moment," Tallus leaned against the trunk of the tree, propping the block of ice between his knees. Chipping carefully, he broke away three chunks, each of which fit comfortably in his palm. The rest of the block he left intact, knowing that it gave them their best chance of combating the village of saurans.

He was about to work his enchantment when that sudden apprehension returned. Knowing that no human outside the Mountain Folk had ever seen the mysterious power of ice magic, he decided to be cautious; he would wait for a moment of privacy before enacting his magic.

Daithar watched skeptically, shaking his head. "I think I will trust to my spears—and wish you luck with your water stones."

Tallus nodded. "Show me the saurans," he said, slipping the ice into his pouch.

For long, silent minutes the two men worked their way along the high limbs. Tallus soon learned to balance on his sandals, moving almost as quietly as the jungle native. Seeing a momentary chance to be alone as Daithar moved around a heavy trunk, Tallus held back, squatting out of sight of the other man. The icemaster murmured a soft plea to the god of man, then brought a small bit of saliva onto his lips. Carefully, reverently, he kissed each of the three small pieces of ice, taking care to leave a little of the moisture from his mouth on each frozen chip.

His weapons now ready, Tallus moved quickly forward. He found Daithar crouching in visible tension. The jungle man gestured downward, toward a nearby tree trunk.

Leaning outward, Tallus saw nothing at first—but as he stared his eyes discerned a familiar pattern: the green and yellow that mottled the skin of the adult sauran. Two of them, he corrected himself, seeing the snake-men crouching in a crook of giant limbs. Their reptilian eyes were, for the moment, fastened on the ground below. Through a gap in the fronds, the icemaster caught a glimpse of brown dirt, knew that these were sentinels overlooking the trail.

Daithar shook his head, scowling in frustration and holding up two fingers. Tallus understood that his partner was dismayed to find a pair of guards here. Still, the jungle man slowly rose to a standing position on the thick bough, raising his spear to shoulder height.

The icemaster shook his head firmly, taking out two of his ice chips. Still skeptical, Daithar squatted low again, allowing Tallus to move into the most favorable vantage.

"Altos," the icemaster whispered. "Grant me the keen aim of your steady hand and eye."

Cocking back his fist, Tallus threw the first chip. The ice sailed true, striking one of the saurans in the shoulder before the creature had even detected the toss.

The second guard hissed in alarm, turning to look at his companion, who hadn't moved, hadn't blinked since being struck. Standing, raising a blowgun to his scaled lips, the remaining sentinel turned his slitted eyes upward—and immediately spotted Tallus, still perched on the limb.

But now the second chip was cast, and the ice struck the standing sauran directly in the chest. The snake-man froze immediately, blowgun almost touching his mouth, forked tongue flicking outward, stiff and cold.

"They are dead," Tallus explained. "They will remain thus for a short time, then collapse."

Daithar looked at the block of ice with new respect. "Your water stone bears potent magic," he allowed laconically.

Following a few more high-altitude traverses, the pair reached the fringe of a jungle clearing. Peering carefully out from the shadows of a mighty trunk, Tallus saw a collection of crude grass huts surrounding a central platform of loosely piled rocks. Even here, the leafy canopy was nearly intact, though a small circle of sunlight spilled through a gap in the center of the verdant dome.

If he hadn't seen the huts, the crude altar, and the multitude of saurans, the icemaster's nostrils would still have told him that they had reached the village. The reptilian stench of the creatures was overpowering, a slimy stink that reminded him of damp holes in the ground, of the festering waters of a swamp in late summer.

Atop the village platform, which had been smoothed with a floor of split beams, a tall post jutted into the air. Dirondey, slumped and motionless, was bound to that pole. Her golden hair lay in a tangle around her shoulders, and only the rhythmic rise and fall of her breasts told Tallus that she still breathed.

"She is *mine*!" the icemaster reminded himself, furious to see his woman thus used by the snake-men.

Saurans were everywhere in the village below, some squatting in a group around a large fire pit, others bearing bundles of twigs or heavy boughs toward the edge of the pit.

"Look. The shaman comes. Her time of dying is near," whispered Daithar.

Tallus saw an unusually large sauran emerge from the grandest hut, a structure standing near the village center. The snake-man bore a wicker cage in his hand, and within that container a coppery shape twisted and writhed about.

Though he had never seen a taiperserpent, Tallus had heard about the deadly, venomous snakes, source of the saurans' most virulent poison. Now his heart froze as cold as his block of ice while the shaman, bearing his deadly pet, stepped toward the raised platform where Dirondey slumped in listless apathy.

"You see your woman," Daithar whispered, his voice mere puffs of air. "But I do not understand how you might save her life."

"I have one chance," Tallus replied, in the same almost inaudible tone. Mindful of the one small ice ball still melting in his pouch, he raised the rest of the block that he had carried through the jungle. Even protected by the masking coolness of the icemaster's body, it had shrunk considerably; he could only hope that it was still big enough for his purposes.

"How can we get down from here?" he whispered.

Daithar gestured to a pair of stout vines that trailed from somewhere above. The tendrils dangled nearby, looping downward before curving to vanish onto a limb dangling over the village. "With these, very quickly," replied the jungle man.

"Then it's time for my magic," Tallus declared.

He took the block of ice and held it before his face. Again he murmured the prayer to Altos, though this time he did not kiss the ice. Instead, he drew in a deep breath, held the air in his lungs as he meditated on a silent intonation. At last he exhaled, very slowly and rhythmically. Breathing directly onto the ice, he watched as steam condensed around the block, coating the slick surface in an opaque cloud of shifting fog.

In a smooth gesture he stood and cast the heavy block toward the center of the village. The ball of melting ice tumbled through the air, then struck the ground near the feet of the sauran shaman.

Immediately the ice vanished in a spuming cloud of fog. White mist billowed upward, thick as a blanket, pouring from the block and churning into the air. Within two heartbeats the entire dais had disappeared within the murky concealment; by the time four more heartbeats had passed, the entire village area was masked within a cloud of unnaturally heavy fog.

"Let's go!" Tallus cried, reaching out to seize one of the vines.

His expression locked in disbelief, Daithar nevertheless took the second vine, pushing off from the trunk even before Tallus leapt. The two men swung through the air with dizzying speed, the ground coming up so fast that Tallus tripped and stumbled, sprawling headlong. Springing to his feet, he continued forward, certain he was on the right direction to Dirondey.

A form materialized in the fog, and he saw the shaman, reptilian jaws spread wide, hissing in fury. The sauran reached a hand to the latch on his wicker cage, but Tallus cast his last piece of ice. The chip struck the shaman in the face, freezing him with his fingertips just short of the cage door. The coppery serpent within writhed and hissed as Tallus passed, scrambling up the rocks onto the plank-lined platform.

He found Daithar there, already sawing through Dirondey's bonds with the tip of his spear.

"Tallus!" she gasped. "How—?"

"Talk later," Daithar interrupted, slashing the last bonds. "Now we must *run*!"

He took the woman's hand, brandishing his spear into the fog while Tallus drew his knife and followed on the other side. Together the trio of humans stumbled and groped through the mist, striking out at any flash of green or yellow that moved in the thick fog. Several times the stone weapons met sauran flesh, drawing shrieks of pain or alarm. So complete was the confusion caused by the misty cloud that the snake-men apparently couldn't discern the nature of the threat, much less find the humans making the desperate escape.

Then green jungle surrounded the trio, fronds of welcome shelter dangling overhead. Tendrils of mist rolled along the ground, wisping away from the village, but most of the magical fog remained trapped by the bower of vegetation that surrounded the sauran settlement.

Daithar led the way, bare feet pounding in a blur along the smooth dirt of the pathway. Dirondey followed, at first stumbling along, obviously stiff and cramped from her bonds. But soon she worked the knots out of her muscles and sprinted as fast as the jungle man.

Tallus held back, clutching his blade, wishing that he had more ice. Despite his nervous backward glances, he saw no sign of pursuing saurans. Perhaps the loss of their shaman had thrown them into disarray, or maybe the shock of the attack had been such a stunning development that they had all fled in different directions. In any event, there seemed to be no threat from the rear quarter.

"Here back to the bridge!" Daithar called, halting in the middle of the trail. Tallus would have run right past the place, had not the jungle man called his attention to the location. Now the icemaster saw the sliced vegetation, the choking confines of the temporary pathway he had followed from the river.

"You lead the way," suggested the other, hoisting a spear as he looked back down the trail. "I'll watch for saurans."

"Sure." Tallus took Dirondey's hand and together they started through the tight, choking passageway.

Firmly she pulled her hand from his. "I can run by myself," she explained curtly.

They moved as quickly as the confining vegetation allowed, soon pushing through the ravine that the icemaster remembered from his earlier trek. Then they were back on the jungle floor, ducking halfway over to avoid the hanging tendrils and hooking thorns.

"Where's . . . that man?" Dirondey said, after a long, desperate interval of flight.

Tallus looked back, realizing that Daithar had vanished, apparently choosing not to follow them.

"Maybe he thought we were safe. He might have gone back to his own village."

"He lives *here*, in the jungle?" Dirondey's face scowled in disbelief.

"That's what he told me. It's a good thing he disappeared though; I didn't want him to learn where we're going."

"Why? Without his help, we never would have escaped."

"*I* found you," Tallus replied, unwilling to take the time to argue. Still, it vexed him that Dirondey was not more appropriately delighted.

"I can't believe that you did," she admitted, holding her chin firm and high. "I was praying to Altos for a merciful death."

"I'm glad he ignored you," Tallus said, pausing, allowing a hint of a smile to crease his lips. "By all the ice on the glacier, I never thought to get you back. I only wish I could have killed more saurans."

"We're not back yet," Dirondey pointed out, pulling away as he moved to embrace her.

Once more they pressed through the tangled brush, until a glimmer of daylight showed the promise of open terrain before them.

"Here—the gorge, and the bridge!" Tallus exclaimed as they pushed through the last fronds. His plan was firm in his mind: They would cross on the span, and then he would saw through the supporting vines, tumbling the bridge into the river.

He halted in shock and chagrin on the narrow fringe of rock between the jungle and the gorge. A few loose tendrils of vine lay on the stones at his feet, but there was no sign of the wide span. Tallus snatched up one of the vines, saw that the edge showed the chopping marks of an irregular, sawing cut.

"It's been cut down!" he cried in sudden outrage. He had never known the saurans to carry serrated cutting tools, but that fact seemed secondary to the thwarting of their immediate escape.

"Up the river," Dirondey suggested. "In the shallows where we were fishing—we can cross there!"

Tallus agreed, and they started along the lip of the lofty gorge wall. Immediately he felt the oppressive heat, but it wasn't until they crossed a region of broken rocks, beyond the overhang of the jungle canopy, that they got a good look at the sky.

"Aussasaur has come," Dirondey observed, her voice remarkably calm.

Tallus, too, saw the great, blazing light, brightness rivaling the sun, shimmering waves of heat spilling over the face of the world. At the same time he heard a series of loud cracks from the direction of the mountains, and knew that the seasonal heat was, as always, breaking pieces from the High Glacier, melting the ice and sending great chunks plunging into the frothing waters of the river.

They had no choice but to continue their flight. Jogging and sprinting, sometimes crawling, the two humans pressed along the lip of the precipice. Gradually the cliff fell to lower heights, until finally they were following the very bank of the river—though the water was too rapid here to allow for safe swimming. Frequently great blocks of ice floated by, but none of these came close to shore, and Tallus didn't want to take the time to retrieve one and carve off a usable piece. Instead they kept running, now staggering over a shoreline of broken boulders.

"Up here—I think we can swim it," Tallus said, pointing to the water that was finally smooth and placid. "Then you will be safe." He looked directly at her, wanting her to understand the full import of what he was about to say.

"When we return to the mountain you will be wed to me immediately—I shall not wait until midsummer. The woman of the icemaster must be protected; you are too important for tasks such as fishing! From now on you shall remain in my house, protected from danger, tending only to my needs."

He paused, glaring sternly at her. "Those needs are great—and I have waited long enough."

She stared back at him, curiously unmoved by his declaration. Tallus wondered if imprisonment had numbed her senses.

"Follow me!" he commanded, leading her toward the gravelly shallows.

Churning waters swirled into eddies between the great rocks, and the two humans splashed through shallow pools, then scrambled up a steep-sloping boulder, a face longer than a man's height. Pulling himself to the flat top, Tallus stopped and looked around, then yanked Dirondey up to the crest of stone.

"You're hurting me—wait!" she objected, pulling away from him.

"You *will* come with me, now!" he declared, flushing

at her show of resistance. He faced her angrily, considered striking her in his impatience, but decided to show forbearance. They would have plenty of time for her to learn her role once they had attained the safety of the heights.

The blow from behind caught the icemaster utterly by surprise. A sharp pain shot through his shoulder, and he tumbled face first off the boulder. Shallow water broke his fall as he slammed onto the sandy bank and lay stunned for a moment. Drawing a breath of water on his first reflexive inhalation, he coughed and gasped, nearly drowning before he rolled over.

When his teary eyes cleared he saw Daithar and Dirondey standing atop the rock, looking down at him. Tallus' shoulder throbbed as he lurched to a sitting position.

Then he noticed the spear, tip still bloody, that lay on the bank nearby. One of Daithar's trademark weapons, it had fallen out of the shallow wound when Tallus fell. Looking at the serrated tip, Tallus remembered the roughly sawed vines that had felled the bridge. They had been cut with a tool no sauran had ever used.

Only then did Tallus realize that Daithar held another spear, this one upraised and ready for a plunging cast into the icemaster—or a sideways stab into Dirondey, who stood perfectly still on the rock beside the jungle man.

"Why do you attack me?" the icemaster demanded, feeling a glimmer of fear amid his growing outrage.

The jungle man ignored the question.

"You could turn away from the heights, and the cold, and the water that is hard as stone. Come with me, instead," Daithar declared, speaking to Dirondey as his eyes—and spear—remained focused on the icemaster.

"You would learn to relish the warmth of the forest, the clear pools of water, the breezes that wash the heights of the trees. Let this man of ice go back to his frozen water."

"She is *mine!*" Tallus declared, astounded by the jungle man's words.

"I am nobody's," Dirondey responded, looking at the icemaster with narrowed eyes. "This is a thing you will never understand."

"I claim you!" shouted Tallus.

Dirondey sighed, shaking her head. "In truth, I am tired of coldness, of ice walls and dark winters—and of a man who tells me always what I must do. It is an interesting thing, to have a decision that I myself can make. Perhaps I *shall* choose a life of warmth."

As he listened in astonishment to Dirondey's statement, something brushed against the icemaster's hand in the shallows, something cold and smooth. Tallus stared straight into Daithar's eyes, willing him to keep speaking. Noting that the jungle man had only the one spear in his hand, Tallus knew that Daithar must be careful. If he cast it down from the boulder, he would have no weapon with which to intimidate Dirondey. And surely, when relieved of that threat, the woman would make every effort to escape. She could not have been serious with her crazy words!

"How ... how big is your tribe? How long do you think you can survive in the jungle?" asked Tallus, gingerly feeling the smoothness of a small piece of ice beneath his palm. The shard had tumbled from the High Glacier with the melting heat; now Altos had seen that it came to his icemaster's hand. Tallus had a grip on the block, which was little bigger than the chips he had thrown at the trio of saurans.

Yet it was not the size, nor even the power, of the ice that mattered. Tallus watched the pair on the boulder above him, waiting for his chance.

The jungle man looked at Dirondey then, his face soft, his expression strangely curious and pensive. "Come with me and you shall have many choices, I promise you."

"Jump!" cried the icemaster as soon as Daithar's attention shifted. "Swim away!"

Dirondey didn't move as the icemaster sprang to his feet and raised the piece of ice in his hand. He challenged Daithar with a missile ready to throw upward simultaneous to the deadly cast of the spear.

The jungle man's face was stony as he looked down at his newly made enemy—and at the block of solid water in his hand. Tallus returned the stare, taking care to spread his fingers, allowing the pearly white of the ice to show.

"Shall we both live, jungle man? Or both die?" challenged the icemaster. "Though, perhaps, I won't die. Your first spear did not kill me, after all, and now I'm ready for you. Dirondey, flee into the river. He will not harm you, not with my ice to strike him."

"I would never harm her," Daithar said calmly. "But if you throw that stone, you claim that I will die?"

"As surely as the saurans who felt the sting of my ice," Tallus declared, drawing back his arm to full extension, ready to throw. "You have seen it strike, killing in an instant."

Daithar, his eyes narrowed shrewdly, studied the icemaster. The spear did not waver.

"You will not die," Dirondey declared suddenly. "Ice magic is only deadly to the saurans, because they lack the heat of a human heart—as, indeed, some men lack that heart."

"Come with me!" Tallus demanded.

"You are like your ice, cold and hard," she replied. "And you would have *me* become that ice as well, a tool that you would work and shape, using me only to enhance your own power. No, Icemaster ... I choose warmth."

"Then," declared Daithar, smiling tightly, "I decide that we all should live. We know that there are at least three tribes of humans in the world. Why fight among ourselves, when the saurans would kill us all?"

"I fight anyone who steals my possessions, as you have done with my woman!" Tallus retorted.

"He steals nothing!" Dirondey cried, at last giving vent to her rage. "I go freely!"

"And we go back to the forest. Take your life and return to the heights, Icemaster. And know this: If you follow me into the jungle, I will kill you." Daithar and Dirondey stepped backward, dropping down the boulder out of the icemaster's sight.

Tallus thought for a moment of pursuing, of meeting the dangers of Daithar's spear with his knife. Yet an inner voice of caution suggested that Dirondey was more than a mere prize—that if he fought her chosen partner, she would join in that battle.

And, against the two of them, Tallus would inevitably lose.

Defeat was bitter bile, a stinging surge rising in the icemaster's throat. Almost blinded by fury, he slashed out at the great boulder, scraping his knuckles against the hard stone. His wrist throbbed, and the bruises along the length of his left side suddenly seemed to sap the very strength from his body.

No, he would not pursue . . . would never go back into that jungle. There were other women, other prizes to be claimed among the Mountain Folk. He would let this one go. Indeed, he should be relieved to be rid of her.

Yet as he swam to the far bank of the river, pushing through the shallows, Tallus wondered why his heart felt as hard and heavy as the blocks of frozen water that gave him power . . . and ruled his life.

# *Family Tree*

## Dan Parkinson

*I*n the night the flowers closed, and the first stirrings of migration trembled the deep soil of Southrange. Though the starlit air was very still, forest leaves quivered here and there, only a few at first but then more and more until the entire woodland seemed alive with the trembling of foliage. Vegetation twitched alive, twigs scraping, leaves rustling against leaves. The rustling grew steadily, from faint tremors to a deep, pulsating whisper—a sighing, singing murmur of quiet harmonies more felt than heard. Myriad tiny pulses blended in intricate rhythm, and the rhythm built upon itself.

The chorus was punctuated now by the little popping sounds of succulent roots withdrawing from moist soil. Calls of night creatures echoed through the vaulted darkness. Great flocks of birds took flight, and the forest floor was alive with scurrying movement.

Even in their sleep, high in the intertwined canopies of the great forest, the people knew that the vernal trek had begun. The rustling penetrated their dreams, and they knew its meaning. The time of the firestar was at hand, and the forest was on the move.

One by one they awoke—men alert and crouching like shadows among the branches while women tended their children and gathered the little things that were important to them.

By first light—the tentative glow of a new dawn creeping through high foliage—they could see below them a slow tide of vegetation, flowing northward. Most of the forest creatures were gone by then, great masses of warm-blooded things of all sizes, wandering ahead of the moving plants, driven by the rising, writhing motion of the forest around them. But the people were not concerned about the creatures. When the forest settled again, in the northern reaches of the great valley, the forest creatures would return. They always did.

High in the branches of a huge, ancient tao tree, Leaf stretched himself and turned full about, wide eyes searching the intricate panorama of the forest in all directions. Through the soles of his feet he felt the tree's own waking resonance, the slight tremble of gnarled bark quickening to the pulse of new sap as the tree readied itself for its journey. It was a comforting resonance, as familiar to the man as his own heartbeat. Shaking back his long mane of flaxen hair, Leaf crouched on the great, high limb. His sensitive, furred tail stroked the limb while his eyes roved beyond, to lower levels where his people were moving about among the branches, readying themselves for travel.

There, directly beneath him, was Lia, strapping their infant son to her shoulder with a vine sling. As though feeling his eyes upon her she looked upward and smiled, that quick, dazzling smile that always made Leaf's heart flutter. There was pride in his woman's gaze, and a serene confidence as she gazed upward at the man who was leader and protector of the people—her husband.

Her smile told him that his presence made her feel

safe, and the knowledge of that made Leaf feel very strong. Lia was not afraid of the perils of their world. She had faith in him . . . just as all of the people did.

Lia knew—they all knew—that Leaf would not fail them. He was first among them, as he had been since reaching adulthood. He was their leader. Whatever came, Leaf would know what to do.

Again he sensed the tingling in the tree bark beneath his feet, and he squatted there to rest a hand on the rough surface. "Mighty Graybole," he muttered. "Better than any of us, you know the ways of the world."

The tree shifted slightly, reassuringly, and Leaf stood.

From his high perch he could see all of the nests and the branch paths, the entire wide grove that was home to his people. There were dozens of the huge tao trees here, a massive cluster that would assemble itself in this same pattern at the other end of the vernal trek. Monarchs of the great forest, the taos stood among their lesser cousins—the rank and file of trees that covered the valley floor from mountain range to mountain range—and towered above them.

And now among the taos—as among all the forest plants—the dance of the branches began. Interwoven limbs withdrew from one another, curling back gracefully, breaking the paths from tree to tree, making each tree a separate, unencumbered thing. And below—far below, in the shadowy depths where smaller plants flowed past, there was the deep, grinding sound of shifting earth—massive tons of soil being broken as great roots lifted from their deep, moist beds. Like dark twins of the branches above them, the huge roots lurched upward, freeing themselves. Secondary roots writhed alive and bunched their filaments into great, fistlike appendages that spread and writhed on the hove ground. Uprooted, the tao was a firm-footed giant, its stance as wide and sturdy as the spread of branches above.

High in the upper branches, Leaf's senses were tuned to a fine pitch. Now was the menace of the jungles the greatest, now when the trees were occupied with beginning their massive march, and all the animals of the forest were gone ahead. This was when—at times in the past—the creatures of the southern jungles had chosen to attack. Man-sized lizard things, they had come with their slashing tools and their serpent escorts, seeking the warm blood of the people of the trees . . . and the sweet sap of the trees themselves.

Each time they came, the people repelled their attacks. But always there were losses and great suffering. Yet even at such times there had been warning. The bromeliads of the swamps and orchids in the jungles spoke in their way to the salt grasses of the wastelands, and the grasses whispered their news to the brambles and the vines, who told the tangles bordering the great forest. In their own ways, the plants communicated.

But in the time of migration, with their roots withdrawn from the nurturing soil, the trees were deaf. Now the people must protect them. It was his responsibility as leader, Leaf knew, to sense and understand the murmurs of the plants, so that the people would not be taken by surprise.

Leaf listened now and heard the whispers, but there was nothing in them of creature movements in the jungles. On this day the jungles were only jungles. The lizard things and their minions were elsewhere, and for a time the forest was safe from them.

Relaxing slightly, Leaf clung as the branch he was on

swayed ponderously and the tree began to turn. A third of
a turn it made, then settled and shuddered as far branches
on the other side swayed northward. From below came
the deep, crunching sound of huge root-feet thudding
into moist soil.

From the shadows drifted the sweet scent of fresh
loam as mosses scurried to attach themselves to the
moving roots, baring the clean, dark soil beneath to the
open air.

The tao had taken its first ponderous step. Now it took
another, and another, and a steady, slow rhythm settled
upon it as other taos all around began their march, in
step with the patriarch tree. Far below, ferns and bushes
rustled frantically, skittering aside to make way for the
giant trees.

Leaf leaped to another branch, his furred tail waving
for balance as he soared across the void. Now he could
see the path behind. The ground there, far below, was a
vista of upheaval—tumbled piles of dark loam that had
been the root beds of the forest. Laggard brambles scurried past among the mounds, spindly shadows lurching
on stiff roots, and again there were the whispered reas-
surances of the thickets. No threat lay behind. The vernal
trek had begun, and there had been no sign of the jungle
dwellers.

Leaf sighed and perched easily on the moving branch,
enjoying the music of the march. Then with full daylight
filtering through the nodding boughs above, he strode to
the great trunk, slung his spear behind his shoulder, and
scrambled downward, heading for Lia's nest. All would
be secure there, he knew. Lia would be waiting for him,
and her eyes would shine with the excitement of the trek.

On other trees, within sight, other men scrambled

among the moving branches, seeing to their families, seeing to their nests, glancing ahead—northward—and awaiting word from Leaf before starting downward, toward the ground.

The men would walk most of the way, as always, scouting ahead of the trees. It would be a time of foraging for food, scanning the horizons, and watching for the occasional predator beast that might double back on the march to prey on stragglers.

Sometimes the women and children would come down, too, to walk on the ground. They would bathe in the streams they would cross, gather herbs, and fill the water pods. But always they—all of them—would stay with the trees. The forest was their habitat, and the taos were their homes.

"My people," Leaf thought fondly, gazing around at the tableau of great trees and nimble people making their northward journey.

The firestar would come, and its heat would make Southrange intolerable for many days. But the forest would not be there, then. The forest—and the people—would be well on their way toward Northrange by the time the firestar appeared, and on Northrange they would settle in comfort while the trees bedded their roots and cast their pollen. For half a year they would remain there, until the forest decided it was time to migrate southward again. Then they would uproot and return to Southrange.

And by the time they returned, the firestar would have come and gone again, and it would be time for the people to make their rest. The grown young would be choosing mates then, and the older children must be schooled. Tools and fabrics would be crafted, and the men would make throw-darts and hunt among the grassland herds for fresh meat.

And they would practice their skills with spear and woven shield.

Once, in the time of memory, the people had numbered many hundreds. But then the lizard creatures had come—and again and again. Now the people were few, and it saddened Leaf's heart to see how few they were. Still, there were the young among them, and each season brought a few more. In recent times their numbers had increased.

They had changed since the times before the jungle threat. The lizard creatures had made them change. The people had learned to fight back.

"The people," Leaf whispered to himself. "My people."

At their nest, Lia met him and watched proudly as he inspected the lashings she had made for their belongings. Their sheltered nest—a comfortable lodge of twined limbs, vines, and woven jute nestled in a fork of great branches—swayed happily with the motion of the tree, and all its contents were secure.

When he had done his ritual inspection, Leaf wrapped a strong arm around Lia's shoulders and hugged her, grinning at the bright-eyed infant she carried in its sling. The baby returned his gaze with wide, serious eyes—eyes like his own, as deep and blue as morning sky. "Little Bud," Leaf mused. "Our little Bud."

"And one day he will lead," Lia said.

At the first blush of spring, Chalik the Wend led his tribe down from icy mountains that they had spent many seasons crossing. Below them lay a vast valley, stretching lush and fertile into the distance. Coming down through the last foothills, Chalik paused to sniff the air. His nostrils twitched with approval, and strong teeth glinted through his thick, dark beard.

Ahead of them now lay a broad grassland, stretching off to the east. South of it was a huge, shadowy forest, but that was many miles off their path. Chalik's tribe had never been forest people, but the grassland—rippling across the miles like waves of yellow green in a warm wind—called to them like an old friend. The place from which they came, which many of them barely remembered now, was grassland.

But that was far away now, and long ago. Those grasslands of their fathers' time had once been home. Now they were home to others, and nothing remained there for the Wends but bitter memory.

Here, though, there was no sign of those others. No smoke arose; no cleared trails could be seen; there were no fields or herds. There was no hint of any human presence.

Spreading his young men in a scouting line, Chalik led his tribe down from the slopes and into the grasses.

There was game everywhere. Deer trails crisscrossed through the waving fronds, and there were the tracks of larger grazers among them. Great flocks of birds arose at their approach and soared aloft, filling the sky with beating wings.

As the scouts spread outward, they heard the grunts of buffalo along a slough, and hooves thundered away as the animals caught sight of the people.

The valley was rich with life, abundant and lush. Chalik knew that where there were grazers there also would be predators, and it was no surprise when they found

numerous tracks of bears, wolves, and great cats. But
carnivores held little fear for the tribe of Chalik the
Wend. The furs of such creatures provided fine robes and
garments for them, and their teeth and claws were used
as adornments.

Several miles into the valley, Chalik found a high
place and stood atop it to survey the terrain. The valley
was huge, extending from the high mountains behind
them to another, far-off mountain range barely visible in
the distance. To the south, several miles away, were the
dark fringes of that great forest that bordered the grasslands as far as the eye could see. To the north were rising
ranges of stony hills, shadowed by the storm clouds of
the season.

Here and there, at Chalik's direction, men drove spear
shafts into the soft earth, pounding them deep, then
brought them up to smell and taste the soil that clung to
them. Oddly, the rich loam was dark and pungent with
layered mulch, in the way woodland soils might be. It
tasted of ancient leaf mold, like forest loam. But this was
grassland, and the nearest forest was miles away.

Chalik was puzzled at that, as he was puzzled at the
abundance of deadwood scattered about beneath the new
grasses and the thousands of little pits and mounds that
were everywhere, as though great masses of soil had
been lifted and turned—and not so long ago.

It was a mystery. But then, the world was full of
mysteries.

Through that day and the next, the men roved outward,
exploring as they went. Their reports were glowing. A
dozen good streams had been found, carrying clear, fresh
water down from the mountains. Along the streams were

stands of cane and precious jute and whole fields of wild grain, all flourishing in this temperate climate.

And there was meat everywhere. The animals fairly swarmed in the high grasses, numerous beyond count. It was as if animals from many places had gathered here, to feed and fatten.

Never in the long years of travel—never even in old memory—had the tribe seen so lush a land. And no sign of humans anywhere. At the campfires in the evening, Chalik listened to his people. They were tired of wandering. They wished to make this place their own. Finally he climbed again to the high place and turned slowly, letting the land impress itself upon his senses.

Though it was night now, still the landscape was bathed in good light. The wandering star they called Brighteye—with its fiery glow and its long tail—had returned in recent days, and now it stood high above the distant crags to the southeast, its brilliance dimming the lesser stars. And with Brighteye's appearance came warm winds from the south, caressing Chalik's bearded cheeks.

"Is this the place we have sought?" he asked the wind. "Let there be a sign, if it is not."

The wind told him nothing. It was only the wind. But its warm caress was a welcome. Chalik turned again, fixing the terrain in his mind.

That forest to the south . . . somehow it seemed closer now than it had the day before. Yet it was only a forest, as the wind was only the wind.

Chalik the Wend raised his stone-tipped spear and held it high, calling to his people. "This place is our place!" he proclaimed. "This is where we belong!" Strong shoulders rippled as he brought the spear down, driving its point into the rich soil.

All around him, his people understood and began raising poles for their lodges. There would be council fires, and the men would talk and rest. Then, with the dawn, they would hunt.

From the upper branches of a lean-rooted conifer marching in the forward ranks of the great, moving forest, Leaf saw the fires. He trilled a warning to others of the people, farther back. Fire was the thing the trees feared most of all. Fire was the enemy of the forest.

One other time, on another trek, lightning had set the grasses ablaze across the valley as the trees approached. Flames danced and billowed along a fire line that extended for miles in any direction, and shifting storm winds drove it southward, toward the approaching forest. The grasses had moaned with dread, and thick clouds of smoke and ash drifted into the forest, for the succulent leaves to taste.

That migration had dissolved into a rout—trees, bushes, and vines scurrying aimlessly, crowding this way and that, entangling their roots and shattering their limbs as they tried to avoid the spreading fire. Fortunately, rain had extinguished most of the blaze, and the people had put out the rest. But that had been a bad season. Plants in the southern reaches of the migration had been stalled. Many scorched and died from the heat of the firestar. And the entire forest had been a month late in planting itself on Northrange, so that pollination was delayed, resulting in a late seeding of Southrange. And that year had seen the first season of the lizard creatures from the festering jungles to the south.

The people had suffered in that season, along with their trees, and they remembered—fire and lizards. The people had been almost defenseless then, just as the forest, once rooted and settled for a season, was helpless before fire.

Even on the march, the trees dreaded the taste of flame.

So now, when fires were spotted a few miles ahead as the forest approached its summer range, Leaf's strongest men raced to the fore, carrying water pods and damp bales of woven jute.

But these fires were not like those before. They did not seem to be spreading. There was no panic in the night whispers of the grasses, no wild-eyed, stampeding herds of animals, no heavy pall of smoke drifting across the fields. There were fires, but they seemed to be controlled fires.

The forest moved onward, unperturbed. Without eyes to see the landscape, the plants were unaware of danger unless they were told of it by the vibrations of other plants, or until they tasted the smoke in their foliage.

With wide eyes, Leaf peered into the starlit distance ahead. The fires were three distinct points of light, a few miles away. And there were shadows moving around them—upright creatures that came and went busily.

Creatures like people! But Leaf knew of no people other than his own people. He thought of the fierce lizard-like jungle dwellers to the south and wondered if these could be the same creatures. The thought brought a dread to him. The lizard-people were his mortal enemies . . . and yet, he had never heard of the creatures coming this far north, this far from their steaming lairs.

He could not count the shadows around the distant

fires, but there were a lot of them, maybe more than his people. Quickly his mind reviewed his people, seeing each face, hearing each name as he counted them. Thirty-two men, counting himself. Thirty-eight women, a dozen infants and small children, and seven old people—too old to hunt or to fight, but not too old to think. The old were the keepers of wisdom and were cherished by their families and all those around them.

"We must go and see what makes the fires," he told the men now. "We must protect the trees."

With two volunteers—the grizzled Twig and a younger man called Flower—Leaf headed north, traveling fast. The three carried jute shields, slings, and thorn-head spears. Behind them Lia cradled her infant son and watched with frightened eyes as her man disappeared into the tall grass beyond the forest. They were people of the trees, and those miles of open grassland—not yet occupied by the approaching forest—were daunting to all of them.

But Leaf was leader of the people, and he must do what was required.

The intruder was well within the camp before sharp-eyed Wendish guards spotted him, but when they did it took only a moment to capture him. Surrounded by torches and ready spears, he offered no resistance. Still, some of them were brutal. They seemed to want to hurt him. One especially—a burly man with a long scar across his face—seemed to take pleasure in hitting the stranger.

They took from him his woven shield, his spear, and

his sling, then they herded him into the center of the camp where Chalik awaited.

"He speaks man words, Chalik," Scar-face said. "But what kind of man has hair the color of straw?"

"And a tail," another pointed out. "What kind of man has a tail?"

The captive glanced around at them with large, curious eyes. Though surrounded by hostile strangers brandishing spears and clubs, he seemed unafraid. "What kind of man doesn't?" he asked. Then he fixed his gaze on the dark-bearded countenance of the one who stood before him. This, obviously, was their leader. "I am Leaf," he said. "Who are you?"

"Chalik," the leader rumbled. "I am Chalik. This place belongs to us."

Leaf tipped his head, trying to understand. "But this is Northrange," he said. "And here where we stand is the bed of Graybole. How can this place be yours?"

"Who is Graybole?" Chalik demanded.

"A tree," Leaf explained, speaking slowly as if to a child. "That is not truly his name, but we call him that. Only he knows his true name."

"A *tree*?" Chalik stared at him.

"A tao," Leaf said. "This is his root bed for the time of the flowering. Graybole needs this place. All of the trees need their places. You will have to go somewhere else."

"This creature is addled," Scar-face declared. "Let me kill him, Chalik."

Chalik raised his hand. "Wait," he said. Squinting at Leaf, he asked, "Are you ordering us to leave here because of a tree?"

"Not ordering," Leaf said. "Only telling you that you should leave."

"Do you think you will make us go away?"

"No. But Graybole will if you are in his way when he comes."

"Crazy," Wends muttered in the gathering crowd. "There are no trees here."

"There will be." Leaf shrugged.

"My people want to kill you," Chalik told Leaf, curiously. "What do you say to that?"

Again Leaf shrugged. "I don't see why they should."

"You aren't like us!" some of the crowd shouted.

"You're mad!" others snarled. "Madness must die!" Leaf looked around at them, counting them. There were hundreds, it seemed, and all as strange looking as their leader. Tailless and stocky, they seemed to have all been pressed from the same bark, and to Leaf's eyes that was not attractive bark. These people were noisy, hostile, and ill mannered. Still, they seemed to be human.

"Maybe you people are only seedlings," he suggested. "Maybe you will change with time. Maybe your ugliness will wear off."

"Kill him!" outraged voices cried, becoming a roar.

Chalik stifled a grin, started to hush them, then decided against it. The creature was amusing, but he could not stand by while his people were insulted. He was leader, and he must defend his people or lose them. Shaking his head, he turned away. "Kill him, then," he said.

The nearest of the guards—the scar-faced one— leveled his spear and lunged toward Leaf, tensed for the impact of his spearhead ripping through flesh. Instead, though, his target seemed to whirl away before him, and an instant later he was flat on his back. His head ached, and Leaf stood over him, holding his spear.

"I don't want to be your enemy!" Leaf shouted. "We are all humans here!"

But his cry was drowned by outraged shouts as a dozen more dark-bearded men rushed him, spear points glistening in the firelight.

In the shadows slings hummed, and stones shot from the nearby grasses. Two of the attackers went down, then two more, bright blood flowing, their skulls smashed by the whistling missiles.

Chalik roared a challenge, grabbed a spear, and hurled it at the stranger, but it was too late. The tailed man was away, flitting into shadows like a ghost. For an instant others like him were visible in the tall grass. Then they were gone.

With morning light, Chalik's hunters picked up the trail and reported. There had been only three of the strange men, despite the damage they had done.

Chalik heard the mourning of women, grieving over the four men who were dead, and he saw the wounds on three others who had been struck by stones. The tailed men must be found. They were the enemy, and they must be tracked to their lair and killed.

But there were other, more immediate concerns now.

The distant forest was no longer distant. Morning light showed it to be less than a mile away—close enough now to see its massive movement. Like a huge army extending as far as the eye could see, it was advancing up the valley. And all around, the tall grass swayed as brambles, vines, and bushes pushed through it, scurrying along on dancing roots.

\* \* \*

"Those are our enemies now," Leaf told the people gathered around him high in Graybole's swaying boughs. "I hoped they would just go away, but they want to fight instead."

"Then we have enemies at both ends of the trek," Lia said sadly. "But what will these do when the rooting begins? Will they invade our nests?"

"They have no tails," Leaf reminded her. "They would be clumsy in the boughs. They are ground people."

"I wouldn't want to be on the ground when the trees root," Twig said.

"Maybe they will see before it is too late," Lia hoped. "Maybe then they will just go away."

"They haven't gone away yet," Flower said, listening carefully to the marching rhythms of the forest. "They're coming. They're in the forest!"

Chalik's trackers leading, nearly fifty warriors pushed forward into a forest that marched to meet them. At first they encountered little thistles and other green thongs, skittering through the tall grass around them. Then there were larger plants, more and more of them—a tide of moving vegetation that flowed around them, going north, the way they had come.

It was worse than distracting, this stampede of things that should not move. It was terrifying, and a few of the warriors broke and ran. But the rest went on, following their leader. "The tailed ones came this way!" Chalik barked at them. "We can, too."

The flowing mass of plants became taller and thicker. A Wend spearman, dodging a bramble, was caught up in a huge thorn bush and carried away screaming. But still the men pressed forward, and suddenly they were through the thickets of the verge and in a nightmare world of waving shadows where great trees drummed the sod as they walked imperturbably northward. The soil underfoot shook with mighty, rolling impacts.

Everywhere were writhing, heaving roots, swinging forward like wide, many-footed pedestals as the trees they carried swayed crazily above them. A warrior tripped and went down, and a ponderous root descended on him, crushing him.

The men scrambled frantically, trying to keep their footing as they dodged the swinging, walking roots.

Then, in the lead, a scout pointed upward and shouted. "There!" he trilled. "There they are!"

Overhead, high above, riding the boughs of striding trees, were dozens of the tailed people. Some of Chalik's men heaved their throwing spears, which rippled through the patterns of light and shadow as they streaked among the strangers above. They were answered by a rain of sling stones and deadly thorn-head javelins from the branches.

A tree dweller tumbled from aloft, pierced through by a Wend spear. Three Wendish warriors fell, and two of them were crushed where they lay, by descending roots.

Chalik led a howling attack up giant, writhing roots to the great trunk of a moving tree, but the climb from there was thrown back by club-wielding tree men who clung and scampered up and down the rough bark as if it were flat ground.

For long minutes the Wends pressed their attack, but it was futile. "Withdraw!" Chalik shouted. "We will try another way! Withdraw and make torches!"

Above him Leaf heard the order and shivered. "Fire," he murmured. "They will use fire." As the Wends raced for open ground, desperate tree men followed them, carrying weapons, water pods, and woven mats.

In the advancing verge of the forest, now only a stone's throw from their own camp, Chalik and his men made fire and lit their torches. The winds had shifted. If they could ignite the grasses now, the flames would meet the forest head-on.

But even before they could spread to set their blazes, the tree men were on them. Whipping mats of wet jute beat back the fire, and streams from water pods doused the torchbearers. With fierce strength born of desperation, Leaf led his best men to the attack.

Slings hummed, stones whistled, and javelins flew. Then it was spear and club, man against man as they closed, and the high sun radiated on a scene of madness, where blood flowed and spattered on trampled grasses.

Though outnumbered, the sheer fury of Leaf's people pushed the Wends back step by step. Quicker and more nimble than the grassland people, the tree men seemed to be everywhere. Then came a rain of stones thrown by women creeping through the grasses.

For a time, the Wends were disorganized. But then Chalik's roaring commands brought a semblance of order to their ranks, and they held their ground, right in the middle of their own camp. And now there were reinforcements, as Wendish women and youngsters joined the fray.

Leaf fought furiously, but suddenly he found himself alone and surrounded. A wedge of Wends had cut him off from his forces, and he found himself face-to-face once more with the one who hated him, the one with the scarred face.

Dodging a spear thrust, Leaf countered with his barbed

club, and as Scar-face stumbled back the tree dweller
said, "I did not want to fight you, traveler. I came only to
warn you, the first time."

"To warn, or to ridicule?" Scar-face hissed, thrusting
again. "You are the enemy, tail dragger! All who are different are enemies!"

As Leaf blocked the thrust, Scar-face whirled and
thrust again. Leaf felt the agony of razor-sharp flint ripping into his side, tearing at his guts. He tore himself
away from the spear, tripped, and tumbled—and found
that he lacked the strength to get his feet under him.
Great gouts of blood flowed from his wound.

Scar-face the Wend stood over his victim, raising his
dripping spear. "You are dead, enemy," he breathed. He
started the spear downward, then shuddered as a javelin
sprouted in his chest, its thorn tip protruding crimson
from his back.

And Lia was there, crouching over Leaf, her eyes
flooding with tears. She still had her baby—their baby—
in its sling at her back.

Scar-face staggered, roared his rage, and turned his
spear. Swinging it like a long club, he brought it down
with bone-crushing force across Lia and her infant. They
pitched forward across Leaf, as still as death.

Still roaring, Scar-face raised the spear again, and a
shadow fell across him. His roar became a scream as a
huge, dark root descended upon him and writhing root
tentacles encompassed him. He fell beside his victims,
and the great root descended, covering them all.

He awoke slowly, as from a long, dreamless sleep, and
for a time he was in darkness. Gradually he became

aware of comforting sounds, little rhythms in the silence. His heart was beating, and he could hear it—his and two other hearts that beat within the shared warmth of small bodies pressed close to his own.

"Lia?" he whispered. He tried to move, and for a moment could not remember how. Then it returned to him, and his hands moved, exploring. "Lia," he whispered. "Little Bud."

As if responding to his motion, massiveness above him lifted slightly, and there was muted light as a screen of root tendrils parted.

Leaf sought the light, pulling Lia and Bud along with him. Where they had lain—three together—was a warm, dark nest between moist loam below and dark root above. Someone else had been there, too, but no longer. His searching eyes saw the skeletal remains of a human hand—a bony hand clenching a spear shaft.

Slowly he crawled from the hollow beneath the root and brought his family with him. In the light he studied Lia's sleeping face, and the infant's.

Their clothing was almost gone, like his own—just dark shreds of fabric clinging to them—but they seemed uninjured. They had simply slept.

Beyond the opening in the roots, others waited.

"Graybole has kept you for us," Twig said. "He told Flower that you were here."

Leaf stood and looked around him. The forest was in full flower, its foliage high and succulent with burgeoning life. Far above, among the high boughs, were the nests of the people—his people.

"Those others," he murmured. "Those strange people. Did they go away?"

"They went," Twig nodded. "But not far. They have moved into the hills north of here. Sometimes we see them, and I have even spoken with Chalik. But there has been no more fighting."

"We have all lost too many of our own," Flower added. "I think they are as tired of fighting as we are."

"Soon it will be time for us to move southward," Twig said. "The forest sings now of seeding. I have thought that maybe when we go, some of those others might follow along, to hunt the herds. Chalik thinks so, too."

"It would be a good thing," Flower said. "They could help us defend against the lizard creatures."

Leaf knelt beside his loved ones, gazing at them. They were awakening now, and Lia looked up at him with puzzled eyes. "I thought we had died," she whispered.

"Graybole kept us," he said.

"Graybole has need of you," Twig offered. "You are his family."

The infant Bud stirred, and Leaf lifted him. He brushed the clinging soil from the little face and pressed his own against it, washing it with his tears. Then he raised the boy high and looked at him more closely. There was something different about him, something Leaf had noticed only now.

Bud gazed down at his father with wide, wise eyes—eyes that had been the color of morning sky.

But those eyes were not blue now. They were as green as the high foliage of the tao tree.

# The Lazy Man

## Nick O'Donohoe

### I

**A** spine-fin fully the length and thickness of Karlor Dehn's leg, its namesake spines alone the length of fingers, rose toward the surface. It stared, walleyed and unblinking, at the struggling leaf-leaper floating impaled on a thorn. The fish rolled sideways, fixing one eye on the bug and opening its great mouth, the size of two fists together, as it drifted upward—

"Did you catch anything yet?" a voice brayed.

The spine-fin dove. Karlor sighed. "No, Lathas. Almost, though." He brushed tangled hair back from his eyes as he stared despondently at his bait. "How about you?"

Lathas shook his head, his curly hair waving. No matter how long it grew, it never hung down. "Only one, right away at sunrise. It's a rosebelly, a third the size of that one you—" He waved an arm at the Silver River, eyes widening "—could have caught if I hadn't shouted. Forgive?"

"Altos gives when he wants. Forgotten." Karlor loved Lathas, but ever since Lathas had first begun talking, ten years ago, he had a gift for talking at the wrong time.

Karlor pulled in his line resignedly. "Baltuth says the

tribe needs us to catch twelve, one each. He says most of them should be big. He says—"

Lathas wrinkled his nose. "Karlor, what's his other name? You're Karlor Dehn. I'm Lathas Bai. What's Baltuth?"

Karlor glanced involuntarily at the bluff above them. Silhouetted against the sky, leaning on a thin staff, was an angular man at least eighteen handbreadths high, well above most grownups and towering over the boys he tutored. Karlor half thought he could see the usual grim, almost angry smile. He shuddered. "Baltuth," he said flatly, "has always been Baltuth."

"But he wasn't always the Godtalker," Lathas said earnestly. "He spent time alone, and prayed, and ate little, and spent a night by the Sacred Pool." He watched Karlor expectantly.

"On Godtalker Mountain," Karlor said, and rubbed his legs automatically. "Which is incredibly large." Karlor looked around quickly himself before asking, "Did anyone miss me?" He glanced fearfully toward Baltuth.

"He asked, yes. I told him you were being lazy again, off sleeping. He'll thrash you, that's all."

"Thanks."

"It's better than being caught in a blasphemy." Lathas was beside himself with curiosity. "I wish I'd gone."

"You were afraid to go, and you wanted to know about it." Karlor wouldn't admit his own curiosity. "Now you'll know."

"Did you see the pool? Was it ringed with flowers, and was there the sound of chanting songs in the air? Did voices speak to you? Did they know your name?"

"Nobody spoke out loud at all, except for bird songs. The pool was ringed with plants—flowers and herbs mostly. I've never seen any like them down here." Karlor hesitated, realizing that he knew their names now.

"What was the pool itself like?"

"Round. Clear. It had—" He puckered his forehead. "When you look into the river and see the sky, and it's calm and you can see every detail? It's like that, even when the wind blows." He stared into Lathas' eyes. "But it's not the same sky."

"As over the river?"

"As over the pool. Not the same day, or the same place. Maybe it shows the sky that would have been, more clouds, or more birds." He waved his arm. "The more you look, the more you know it's different."

He leaned forward. "And what did you see, when you looked?"

"Not a lot," Karlor muttered. His friend prodded him, and he admitted finally, "I fell asleep."

Lathas stared in disbelief. "At the Sacred Pool? At midday? Karlor, you're not supposed to sleep by it until night."

"I was tired from climbing. It was shady. I slept. I was thirsty, too," he added unwillingly.

"And you drank from the pool." Lathas shook his head. "And here you are, same old Karlor. No change in you."

"Maybe it only works at night or on people like you and Baltuth."

Lathas sighed. "Some day I hope that I'm the Godtalker."

Karlor shoved his friend gently. "Get back to your own pool before the real Godtalker looks down."

As Lathas ran off, Karlor tossed his line back out. He reeled it in slowly, then with quick tugs, then skipped his bait across the surface. In his mind he could hear Baltuth's dry rasp. *Throw it and leave it; this is the fish's toy, not yours.*

He settled into the shade, keeping out of the midday sun. First Heat under Aussasaur was forty days away, but it was warm enough to be uncomfortable for humans. He was glad to be wearing a loincloth and no more.

But he couldn't sleep; he had to keep holding the line. "It's too much work," he said sleepily. There had to be a better way to catch fish . . .

Karlor got an unfocused, dreamy-eyed look. He sprang up and began searching the stand of trees below the bluff. He found two sticks and pounded one, forked end up, deep in the clay and mud of the riverbank. The other, more slender and springy, he laid in the fork, but frowned at it. The first tug from a fish and it would be gone. He had a spare line, but Baltuth would be angry if he lost the first line when something took the bait.

He ripped the drawstring from his loincloth and tied the stick. He had half the string left over. He rubbed a sharp rock against it until the line broke, then found two more sticks and tied them as he had the first. He tied his spare line on the second spring-stick.

He put his spare thorn on, baited it, and flung the line out. After a moment's thought he stuck the two pieces of loincloth, now separated, one on the back of each spring-stick. He stepped back to check his work, then ran to see Lathas.

Lathas was stunned. "You broke the loin string?"

"I didn't break it; I cut it."

"On purpose? Karlor, those are hard to make: It's a lot of weaving . . . What's wrong with your eyes? You have a far look, like you're staring somewhere else—"

"Give me your loincloth."

Lathas unhesitatingly handed it to him and watched with only faint apprehension as Karlor snapped the drawstring, created two crossed-stick fish catchers, and cast their bait out. "When either of the loin pieces flies up, run back and grab the line."

He had to explain it again, but he had barely finished when Lathas dashed downstream. "Where are you going?" he shouted.

"To teach Dalyssa and the others."

Karlor shrugged and walked back to his own lines, breaking into a run when he saw that one of the lines was up. He reeled in the struggling, full-grown spine-fin, gaffed it on a stick, and dug the stick into the river bottom. Then he strolled back to the shade and went to sleep.

In late afternoon the twelve boys and girls walked the trail up the bluff. As they came, the men and women of the One Tribe gasped and pointed.

Each child had two and in some cases three fish gaffed on sticks. Two boys had a carrying pole slung over their shoulders and were struggling with no fewer than five spine-fins, one of them Karlor's prize catch. All twelve boys and girls were naked.

Nudity was unimportant; the destruction of the clothes scandalous. Shortly Karlor found himself digging a toe in the dirt and daydreaming uneasily, waiting outside a Council meeting.

Baltuth emerged. "I return. O Karlor the Un-Sewer. Or can you sew, perhaps?" He scrutinized Karlor with mock hope. "Naturally not. Some are made to create clothes, others to destroy them. Did you think what you did was frugal? Prudent? Wise?"

"I thought it would catch fish," he said unhappily.

The tutor peered at him. "For whom? You told no one but Lathas, who shared with the other enterprising unmakers. What a shame it wasn't colder! Then you could have destroyed breeches and cloaks."

Karlor said nothing.

"Long ago, when the saurans stayed farther away from Silver River and life was simpler, the Godtalker could have set your punishment without answering to a Council. Now that is their task to assign."

Karlor relaxed.

"Fortunately, the Council has asked me, as your tutor, to give you a fit punishment," Baltuth all but purred. He picked up his staff where it lay beside the door and frowned at it. "What a pity this isn't more substantial."

He spoke as he swung the staff. "Clothes are not for destroying." *Whack*.

"When you save work for yourself, be sure you aren't making work for others." *Whack*.

"And never—" *Whack*.

"Never—" *Whack*.

"Never make it your goal to work less for the tribe than anyone else does." He lowered the staff. "The One Tribe cared for you all, and clothed you. Now it must clothe you twice."

Karlor, watching Baltuth stride away, muttered unhappily, "But I *like* fish."

■

A year and a half later, Karlor was running along the bank, checking a row of twenty fish lines. There were eight rosebellies and two spine-fins. He gaffed them and rebaited the hooks, enjoying the freedom and the certainty of peace. The saurans, sluggish and vulnerable, avoided the One Tribe in the cool season.

But the undergrowth rustled; Karlor hid quickly. A moment later, Baltuth strode by, his quick eyes glancing left and right on the opposite bank for saurans. Baltuth never took anything for a certainty.

Satisfied, he squatted on a sandbar: From his knapsack he took out thost meat, flatbread, and a pouch. He munched reflectively, opening the pouch with his free hand and rubbing a blue herb powder on his left foot, grunting as he stretched.

Karlor stood. "Why are you doing that? We're in no danger."

Baltuth glared at him; Karlor cringed. At such moments, Lathas would sigh loudly and say to Karlor, "I hope you're done getting in trouble by the time I'm Godtalker."

"I do it to practice a skill," Baltuth said finally. "Don't you practice the things I've taught you?"

"Practicing is too much work. Is it always that hard for you to touch your foot?" he added with interest.

"Only in cold weather, so far." he said with some annoyance. "You find that hard to understand?"

"Oh, no. You're old," Karlor added flatly as if it explained everything.

"And you're fourteen now, and I wonder if you will see fifteen."

Karlor didn't understand the sarcasm: He was drifting into the "far look." "Does *kmerkaas* work on river water?"

Baltuth looked at him in astonishment. "Does what work on the water?"

Karlor pointed to the blue powder. "*Kmerkaas.* Can

you draw power from the river by stepping on it, like you do to pull forces from the earth?"

"The powder would wash off."

"Not if you coated your foot with grease."

Baltuth stood carefully, holding his foot away from the earth. "Tell me why I would want to."

Karlor slapped his hand against the water. "If you let all that power loose in the water, it might be an even easier way to fish."

Baltuth's interest gave way to disgust. "Still finding lazy ways to do things."

"Just to get fish. I like fish." He looked wistfully at the river, then back at Baltuth, who was scowling. "How do you know what to do with *kmerkaas*?"

"I have slept by the Sacred Pool at night." Baltuth regarded him narrowly. "How do you know about *kmerkaas* at all?"

But he didn't wait for an answer, instead sifting a gray powder down on Karlor's shaggy head. Karlor blinked, then opened his eyes: For a terrible moment there was a blinding light not coming into his eyes, but *out* of them.

Baltuth's long, deft fingers cradled Karlor's cheeks as the index fingers held open his eyelids with unexpected gentleness.

The brightness faded, and Baltuth fell back. "By day." He stared at Karlor, shocked and deeply troubled. "You slept there by day."

Karlor backed away. "Will you tell the Council?" No answer. "What would happen to me if someone knew?"

Baltuth shook his head. "No one has ever prescribed a punishment."

"Will you tell them?"

There was a long silence before Baltuth said, "I am your tutor. I'm responsible for you."

At least he hadn't said he would.

Karlor turned to go, then spun back and said finally, "The Sacred Pool."

"Yes," Baltuth said tonelessly.

"If you learn lore and Altos' knowledge by night, what can you learn there by day?"

Baltuth looked down at his hands, still frozen as they had cradled Karlor's face. He said nothing at all. Karlor turned and walked into the woods.

When Karlor was out of sight, Baltuth rubbed fat from the thost meat on his foot, patting the herbs carefully in place. Using his staff, he hopped carefully down to the water's edge and held his foot against the surface. His whole body tensed at the surge of indrawn power; ripples pulsed from bank to bank as he lifted his foot.

When he slapped his foot down on the surface, the recoil knocked him backward his own length and more.

Karlor ran from the trees and, tactlessly, passed his prone tutor to stare at the river. "It worked! I thought it would." Bodies were rising in the water: spine-fin, rose-belly, hundreds of fish.

He felt a hand like stone gripping his shoulder as Baltuth pointed out all the other bodies: frog, lizard, even taiperserpent. The surface was dotted with bobbing, still bodies. "I killed everything so that you could catch and eat a few."

"Maybe they aren't all dead," Karlor whispered. "Maybe they'll live."

"No," Baltuth whispered. "I killed every living thing near me in the river."

Karlor looked away from the bodies, sickened. "Are you going to hit me?"

"Should I?" When Karlor didn't reply, he added, "The river flows; it will recover soon. This fault is mine; I did what you only dreamed." He poked at the water as a gathering of peepers drifted past and murmured, "I don't think I'll mention this to the Council just yet."

Karlor, shuffling back into the plant growth away from the river, muttered, "At least it would work against the saurans."

Less than twenty days later, it did. A sauran raiding party ambushed humans and drove them back across the river, then plunged into the waters in great numbers to cut off the retreat before they could call for others with rippersticks, clobbers, and the terrible bow spears. Baltuth hastily greased his foot, powdered it, and with one stamp destroyed the invaders. Eleven died, clutching their ear holes or their chests. The remainder, stunned and drifting with the current, were easily dispatched.

Baltuth was called before the Council and hailed for his heroism. If Karlor noticed members of the Council staring at him strangely thereafter, he paid little attention; he was always in trouble with someone.

### III

The grassers buzzed steadily under a listlessly waving stand of drum-stem. The sky was a deep, empty blue, cloudless and moistureless. Near the sun, a second bronze disk shone: Aussasaur was approaching again. Second Heat would choke all of Tethedril in less than thirty days.

Karlor greeted Lathas, Dalyssa, and the four others

with him carrying double buckets; behind them, younger children staggered under single buckets. He cleared his throat to speak, gave up, and pointed to the gardens. The wilted grain and vegetables said more than he could.

"How long must we water these plants?" a girl of ten asked querulously.

"Today," Karlor said tiredly, "and two days from now, and four days, and as long as we can keep them alive." He glanced at the silhouette of Baltuth, who had a thicker staff these days and leaned on it often. "It's too much work." He stared resentfully at the upright stones, nearly shoulder high, walling in the garden he needed to water. "Best we start."

"When I'm Godtalker, I'll find a way to make plants grow without water," Lathas said.

"When you're Godtalker," Karlor said tiredly, "*I'll* grow without water." He saw Lathas' face and felt suddenly guilty. "Or at least I'll be a hard worker. And you'll be the tutor for layabouts like me." He lifted his full buckets again and strode to the garden, wiry muscles bearing up under the load.

He resented the upright stones but understood the need for them: Small herds of fat-sided thost would graze through the gardens otherwise. Karlor wondered idly if they could ring a garden with dead eldercactus, but abandoned that thought immediately; he had seen the ugly gray beasts rub on cactus and break the plants in two.

He tossed his burden of water over the stones. The garden soil darkened, but moisture on the tassels and leaves disappeared almost immediately. Soon Silver River would be a trickle. The crops would fire, and everyone but the saurans would hide in the shade until

Aussasaur had passed. Even now, it was too warm and the air too dry to grow plants anywhere but near the river.

Karlor slumped, worn down by heat. He picked up a fallen piece of drum-stem, still amused and fascinated by how light it was. He turned the broken top end toward himself and peered into it cautiously, remembering the day he had rolled a log and nearly been bitten by a spotted madlegs for his curiosity.

But there were no spiders. He could see clear through the tree stem; the segments dividing each section had crumbled. On a whim, he put it to his mouth and blew it like a horn, enjoying the hollow sound. Hollow . . .

Karlor pushed the nearest live drum-stem, stepping carefully over the splintery stump as it fell. He shoved a sharp stick through the stump end of the tree until he could reach no farther. Then he poked in the other end, grunting when his stick slipped from his fingers and slid through the trunk.

To let the tree reach all the way to the garden he had to dig a small channel from the falls, ending it in a spill pool and lining the pool with clay so the water wouldn't simply seep into the rock. As he expected, the water poured through—a small, steady runnel inside the garden wall.

He lay down on the highest hummock in the garden, watching the drum-stem do his work. Finally he shut his eyes, barely listening to confirm that it was still working.

He woke, sputtering: The patter of falling water had become a splash. The hummock he slept on was nearly submerged. He blinked up at the midafternoon sun, then stared at the grass waving gently below the edge of the hummock—

He stared at the garden. Only the tips of the grain were above water; the walls had dammed it in.

Karlor leapt up, frantic. In some parts, the water was nearly to his waist. His stick floated near him: He grabbed it and dug frantically at the foot of a crack where two stones met. He shifted and turned the stick as he met resistance from other stones and finally pounded the end of the stick with a rock, ignoring the raw rub of the stick in his right hand and the grazing of his fingers on the rock in his left.

When he thought the end of the stick was beyond the wall, he pulled it free, sighted down on the crack in the stones, and plunged it deep in the earth.

As he pulled the stick free, water gurgled out immediately, and he relaxed. It wasn't until the water had arched to a height of eight handbreadths and the fountain was as thick as his arm that he realized his mistake; by then it was too late.

Baltuth arrived as the first stone fell, its support eroded by the churning water. A flood gushed out of the gap then, carrying mud and plantings with it. The water vanished quickly, leaving behind a black delta of topsoil that half buried the already wilting grain.

The other waterers peered from behind him in awe. Baltuth turned around. "Perhaps you'd like to learn from Karlor, again, and do as he did."

They shook their heads slowly, awestruck at the damage.

"Wisdom from the young. Finally." Baltuth turned back to face Karlor, and it seemed to the boy that Baltuth's staff was larger and stronger than it used to be. "And now I will go ask the Council's permission to devise a punishment for you." He left, striding rapidly and leaning only slightly on his staff.

*   *   *

The Council meeting was surprisingly long. Baltuth, emerging, nodded to the waiting Karlor. "Best we finish this now, while I have all my energy to devote to it."

Karlor would have been willing to postpone it until the older man was exhausted or short of time, but wisely refrained from saying so.

Baltuth added, "And now, tell me: If you could take back a part of your life, which not even the god Altos could—and believe me, He would, if only to bring mercy to others—what would you change now?"

"I'd pound a section of drum-stem under the wall," he said dully. "That would drain extra water in the soil. It would save the field when it rained, too."

"A fine idea." Baltuth beamed at him. "Doubtless the next time you destroy our food, you will do an even better job. Unless, of course, you intend to farm fish."

Karlor stared without seeing. "We could."

Baltuth, warming up his muscles by spinning his staff in his palms, paused. "How?"

"Catch them and pen them inside walls like the garden. Run river water through the pens, like I did today." He winced and finished hastily, "At least the fish would keep fresh until First or Second Heat."

Baltuth nodded slowly. "I see that. Possibly even beyond, if enough water flows through to keep them cool." He caught himself and smiled grimly. "Restrain yourself from flooding another field to find out." He swirled his staff. "And now, a short lesson."

Karlor tensed.

"When you are assigned to water the gardens, the object is not to carry the least number of buckets." *Whack.*

"The object is not to make your garden the wettest of all." *Whack.*

"The object—" *Whack.*

"Is to make sure—" *Whack.*

"That the garden—" *Whack.*

"Produces enough food that we will not starve during Second Heat."

Karlor, still braced for a final blow, looked up cautiously. Baltuth was completely ignoring him, staring sadly down at the delta of mud and the now-brown plants. "Karlor, if only you would think of others before doing these things, you might never get in trouble at all."

Karlor, rubbing his sore back, waited until Baltuth had limped off before muttering, "But then I might never do them at all."

# IV

By the start of the next year, all the river fields were irrigated, and the tribe could devote more crop space to growing flass for cloth. By year's end, there were two walled fish ponds with running water.

Over the next two years, Baltuth taught Karlor and the others a range of tasks for the One Tribe. Karlor, sometimes to his own regret, found more and more ways to save time and make less work.

He developed a foot-turned wheel for pottery and for a grinding stone. Once he perfected the ratio of large turning wheel to small, the speed was too much for the grinding stone, which broke free and ran through the tribe's encampment, chasing an old woman named Ryallnor the Full who, up until then, was justly proud of how large she had become.

He assembled an upright wheel that turned in the waters of the Silver River and ground two millstones against each other to make grain into powder for bread. Unfortunately, he thought of no way to stop the wheel. When the great rains after Heat-Break came and the river flooded, the wheel spun madly; its axle rubbed until it caught fire. Ryallnor the Full lost one-third of her remaining crop and, in a moment that Karlor cherished until his own thrashing, beat with her fists repeatedly upon Baltuth for "tutoring children with no god at all."

Tired of cultivating gardens, Karlor lashed together a platform of wood—thanks be to Altos that the tribe now stocked rope—and bound stones down into the soil, with weights to press down the frame and cultivate soil as he dragged the frame forward. It was a wonderful idea and would allow one man to plow a large garden with little effort.

Sadly, the two thost to which Karlor tied the frame had never felt anything around their necks. They panicked and galloped up the bluffs, tearing the harness through the home of the One Tribe, chasing the retreating form of Ryallnor the Full. Astonishingly Ryallnor, goaded beyond endurance, turned on them and, in tears, chased them back through the entire camp, thus avenging the dishonor that the laughter of others had made her feel but doubling the damage to the campsite.

So Karlor's life went, his dreams and their disasters growing larger every year, and it seemed to him, Baltuth's stick growing thicker and heavier as Baltuth grew grayer, angrier, and more dedicated.

He was seventeen when his dreams were interrupted again by battle with the saurans. He was with Lathas and

Dalyssa, chipping flints into shape for fist axes; he had hit his knuckles twice and was tired of Dalyssa laughing at him and Lathas admiring her for it. Lathas' friendship with her had changed noticeably of late: He spoke of her at all times, noticing when she made a meal, won a race, tied her hair back to work in clay. At first Karlor was jealous of Dalyssa. Later he shrugged and concluded that he wouldn't want to be the reason that his best friend sounded like a babbling idiot.

A warning sounded on a hollowed thost horn; Karlor looked up in confusion. Baltuth was holding the horn with one hand, gesturing with his staff with the other. The saurans had crossed the river, headed for the camp. The women assembled immediately as a battle group and charged down the narrow paths on the bluff in teams, two with rippersticks, one with a bow spear. The men followed behind, carrying clobbers for themselves and additional rippersticks, bows, and notched bow spears for the women.

Karlor and Lathas followed the team led by Dalyssa. Lathas, his eyes never leaving her, stumbled. Karlor caught him before he impaled himself or a companion. "Watch your feet."

"Sorry. Doesn't she look wonderful, a born leader?" he added fervently. "Isn't she a fit mate for a god?"

Karlor, watching the oncoming saurans, said absently, "She is pretty, except for that scar on her right leg." Lathas glared at him, and he caught himself. "She's a star come down. Our children's grandchildren will still sing about her beauty. To ensure that we have them, would you mind watching the war?"

"You sound like Baltuth," Lathas muttered.

"Don't talk that way while I'm holding a bow spear."

He threw an arm out for balance as he slowed: There was now a gap of only ten strides between them and the saurans. "Thank Altos it's too windy for their blowguns." The humans stopped within bow spear range, but just beyond the range of those terrible whipcords.

One of the saurans flipped his arm. The whipcord whipped upward across the gap, impossibly far; sunlight gleamed off something at the tip. The shining cord end buried itself in Dalyssa's shoulder.

Her eyes widened as she dropped to her knees from fear. The women to either side gasped in horror as Karlor leapt on her, gouging her shoulder with the point of a bow spear. Blood drained quickly and freely as the cord-end fell free.

He cradled her for a moment as she fell back on him. "Go and wash your shoulder," he said.

He spun her around and dropped her as the sauran roared, drawing the whipcord back for a second snapping attack.

Karlor held the bow spear up, letting the whipcord tip wrap around the stick until the silver piece hooked on its own cord. He stood, tugging hard; the sauran, startled, fell forward and dropped the whipcord. The women charged, shrieking furiously; the sauran never rose again.

After the brief attack was repelled, the shiny piece Karlor had hooked worried the tribe more than Dalyssa's near death. Baltuth washed it free of taiperserpent venom and turned it in his hand carefully. It was heavy enough to travel well in the wind and carry far. It was shaped like a claw, but from what animal?

Desperate for understanding, Karlor sidled up to Baltuth and asked, "What is this thing?"

"I have no idea. And nothing of nature can hide from me," Baltuth added defensively.

"Then it's a made thing." Karlor left thoughtfully; Baltuth watched him in silence.

He found Lathas washing Dalyssa's wound; he was not surprised. It was deep but clean and would scar without infecting. Baltuth had given her a poultice, which Lathas couldn't keep from adjusting.

"Karlor!" Lathas said earnestly and unsteadily. "My friend, you saved my life by saving—"

"What was the shiny piece?" Dalyssa interrupted more practically.

Karlor slumped beside them. "Nobody knows. Not even Baltuth." He looked up. "That's not true, is it?"

"But you just said—"

"The saurans know," Karlor interrupted, half to himself.

Dalyssa and Lathas looked at each other. Lathas spoke first, with the caution of long friendship. "You have the 'far look' again. What are you going to do?"

"I'm never sure what I'm going to do," Karlor replied with some truth. But he added, "If I asked the two of you to do something now—something dangerous, perhaps crazy, something the One Tribe might not like—would you do it?"

Even knowing Karlor, Lathas answered immediately. "I would give you my life."

Dalyssa answered more hesitantly. "I owe you that."

"Good," Karlor said. Dalyssa, expecting some disclaimer, looked disconcerted. Lathas, more perceptive, nodded tiredly. "Here's what I want . . ." Karlor went on.

The next dawn found Lathas waiting for Karlor by the ford, a series of stones by which a man could cross the river. It was unguarded; only a fool of either species would cross.

Karlor stumbled to the ford, panting. He had a bow spear, a lashed wood framework, a foul-smelling pouch, and three empty water skins.

Turning up his nose at the pouch, Lathas turned to the skins. "Do you really need these?"

"Badly." Karlor stooped, retrieving a handful of clay. He daubed it on his body in irregular streaks, then patted a mix of freshly chopped leaves on the clay. Some leaves were dark, some light, one or two flowered at the leaf edge. "Stick some grass onto me."

Lathas dutifully tucked and knotted swamp grass onto Karlor. When he was done, Karlor reached into the stinking pouch. "Smear this on me." It was a mixture of thost dung and long-dead fish.

Lathas looked unhappy but did as he was told. Karlor gagged, then braced himself and inhaled deeply through his nose. "Now it won't bother me again." He gestured to the skin bags beside him. "Fill these with spring water and come back."

Lathas left quickly, glad to be away from the smell.

When he dragged the frame back, the skins were already dewy with sweat where the humid air struck them. Karlor tugged on it. "Now go back up, and say you don't know where I've gone."

"But I—"

"No. You don't know. That's best." Karlor grinned. "Go, or do you want me to hug you?"

Lathas backed up hurriedly. Karlor, grunting, dragged the frame across the rocks and stood by the trees on the other side.

Lathas, watching, gasped. Karlor, a mass of green and

brown patches instead of a man shape, disappeared as he stepped into the trees.

Karlor tugged on the frame, struggling with it as quietly as possible. He knew enough of saurans to hate them, but he had also thought about them night and day; dragging the skins of spring water would be worth while.

He moved cautiously at first, then more confidently. As he moved away from the area where scouting parties moved silently, he guessed that the saurans would be noisier.

True enough; he heard two clacking, hissing voices arguing before he saw them. The older one wore a necklace that seemed to show rank. Karlor was too far away to hear, but he saw enough of the argument to sympathize, automatically, with the young one.

The elder finally gestured disgustedly and moved away into the trees. Karlor saw that he was on a trail; near the end of the trail was a break in the trees and—

He blinked. For some reason there was a pile of bare, chipped rock near the trail's end.

The young sauran made a gesture of his own, behind the back of the elder, and sniffed the air cautiously, swinging his head from side to side. At one point he shook his head in disgust but, satisfied he was alone, strode toward Karlor.

Karlor rose up suddenly and put his spear against the sauran's breastbone. "Shout and you die."

The sauran froze in place, nostrils flaring. He squinted at Karlor's patchy body and distorted outline, and he hissed, "How can this be? I hear you, but you are not here."

Karlor jabbed lightly with the spear. "Now do you know I'm here? Lie down."

The sauran did as he was told. Holding the spear one-handed, Karlor quickly pulled the rack of water skins across the sauran and stepped on the frame, pinning the reptile underneath it.

The sauran cried out. "The cold!"

"Yes. Cold conquers even your bravest. Not ours," Karlor added with pride. "Answer my questions."

"What about?" Already the sauran's speech sounded sluggish. If Karlor were right, his will would relax before he fell asleep.

"This." He dropped the whipcord tip into the sauran's front talons. The sauran cried out with naked fear. "Don't be afraid; the venom is washed from it. But what is it?" Karlor asked with his whole heart.

"Moon metal." The sauran's voice sounded dull and far away. "We call it that because it shines bright, darkens over time until we polish it so that its bright face returns. As the goddess Aussasaurian polishes Sister Moon for Her people, to help them remember warm daylight through the cold darkness." There was pride in the sauran's voice. "I found it first."

Karlor was envious. "How?"

The sauran hesitated. "We are careful what rocks we choose for chimneys. Some have water in their cracks, and explode when hot. Some of the black rocks burn— we don't know why. I was careless—"

Karlor wasn't sure what a chimney was, but he nodded. "And you chose the wrong stone. It comes from the rocks," he murmured to himself. It seemed as if he had known it before asking. "What happened then?"

"Part of it ran into the fire, as if it wept." The sauran's eyes cleared. "Like your people. We never weep."

"Tears aren't hard, though."

"No. It wasn't rock tears, but something in the rock. We were afraid, until we understood," he added frankly. "We thought a weeping rock was a sign of disaster. When the fire died, the tears hardened. We felt they were sharp. Are tears sharp?" he asked.

Karlor remembered the sting in his own eyes—at punishment, at deaths . . . "In a way."

"Yes. I thought so. We ground the rock tears on stones, and made them sharper," the sauran said proudly. "We rub stones against its edges until it can cut a drifting leaf in half."

"And you learned to control its shape in the heat," Karlor murmured. "And you learned how to cool it in that shape."

The sleepy sauran opened his eyes at that. "How did you know? It took us many tries to learn to do that."

"It would be less work than grinding. Go on."

"I went back where I found the rock, and found more. We dug under those rocks, and found still more, like a hardened stream of it, stretching into the ground."

"Then there is more?" Karlor said thoughtfully.

"Not where we can get it."

"Why is that?"

"We dug a pit," the sauran said. "Then we dug a cave in it, following the metal stream into the rock." He gestured in slow annoyance, his anger moving him against the cold of the skin bags. "Then we stopped."

"Why didn't you go into the ground for it?"

"The cold." The sauran's arms pulled in, a hopeless attempt to conserve body heat in a body that never could.

"Why didn't you build fires in the hole?"

The sauran regarded him with contempt. "Fire underground makes the Dark Sleep. I'm not surprised that your kind don't know that."

"So you have no way to get more moon metal by yourself," Karlor said thoughtfully.

"Your voice sounds strange, heat stealer." Even his hatred was dulled with the cold.

Karlor pulled the water skins off. "Warm yourself in the sun, then take me to your tribe." He added, enjoying the shock the sauran showed as he said it, "So I can help you mine your metal."

It took Karlor less time to reach the saurans than he expected; the river valley was narrow, and they were disturbingly close. A plain strewn with dark rock outcroppings, stretching in long lines, ran parallel to the river. Beyond it were the mountains. The saurans had a camp in the rocks.

The camp circled a large, nearly circular pit in the ground, with a pile of chipped rock at one end rising out of it, and a fire in the pit center. The pit floor was littered with stone adzes, similar to the One Tribe's fist axes but visibly damaged even from here. At the far side of the pit, a hole extended into the ground.

He walked in with his captive, trying to look unafraid. It was less hard than he expected; he was obsessed with examining the hole.

A sauran rose and came before the others. "I am Gassiga," he said, hissing slightly as they all seemed to. "Tell me why you have taken Saggasz."

Without answering, Karlor let the other sauran go. Saggasz strode forward and spread his arms in hope and wonder. "He says he will help us with the mine."

"Not 'will,'" he broke in. "'Can.' I will need promises."

"Why will you do this?"

Ignoring Gassiga, Karlor strode down the stone steps to the pit floor. As Saggasz followed him, he added, "Can you give me light? The tunnel is shadowy." He frowned at it. "The rocks fall in, don't they?"

Saggasz, descending with an unlit torch, stopped. "How did you—"

He gestured impatiently at the fresh scars in the entrance ceiling, at the stray rock on the floor. "You would have cleared that. Aren't you afraid you'll be buried alive?"

"The True People fear nothing," he began, but sagged quickly under Karlor's backward glance. "Yes. To die there, in the cold and dark . . . a shameful, ugly death."

He nodded. "Do you build wood frames? Do you have wood buildings, with roofs?"

Saggasz lit the torch. "We have fought since creation, but we know so little of each other," he mused. "Yes. We worship Aussasaurian under pavilions." He came to the entrance, his mouth gaping slightly. "I see what you say: Make a roof under the rock, a roof inside a hole. I would not have thought—"

"No," Karlor agreed. He took the burning torch, glancing impatiently at the saurans ringing the pit. "How deep is the tunnel?"

"Two hundred, three hundred paces. Do not stay long; the torch smoke causes the Dark Sleep."

Karlor strode in, marveling at the fresh scars in the rock. The One Tribe did not dig deep or scar rock: They took their flints from a soft, chalky bluff near the river.

The tunnel angled downward quickly, and the floor was rough. As it turned, his torch was the only light.

Karlor went ahead, his curiosity outweighing any fear at the strangeness of being underground.

At the far end of the tunnel lay more digging adzes, and a wall. The torchlight was answered by a gleam in a streak nearly two fingers wide, crossing the wall diagonally.

Karlor shivered, wishing he had a cloak. Water dripped from the walls, partly coming from the air and partly from underground. Clearly, the saurans could barely move here. Holding an adze awkwardly in his five-fingered hand, he scooped loose a palm full of moon metal.

He stepped back outside, carefully looking unbothered by the chill. "You call me a heat stealer. What if I give back some heat, spending it in that hole of yours?" He held up the metal in his hand.

They regarded him in silence. Finally their chief said, "You alone can do little."

"I'll bring two others, a man and a woman." He felt faintly guilty about promising their help. "Possibly even someone else," he added as a thought struck him. "We can start tomorrow. But we take some of the metal."

After a long moment the sauran nodded. "The goddess Aussasaurian said, 'Be fair in all dealings.'" He clicked his jaw open and shut several times. "I can't believe that She meant dealings with you, but . . ." He gestured at the abandoned hole. "I never believed the god would offer us this."

Karlor sprinted out of the pit, showing off his energy. "No hole in the ground makes the One Tribe weak." Before he left the saurans, he gave a long, mocking bow.

The chief showed all his teeth on both sides. "Be here early. You have much to do."

To Karlor, this suddenly sounded uncomfortably like too much work. He dashed back to the tribe, carrying his sample of the moon metal and working over in his mind what he could say to Baltuth.

After a brief, bullying discussion with Lathas and Dalyssa, he felt up to confronting Baltuth. He gave Baltuth the metal and explained what he wanted, and the Godtalker looked at him in horror and disbelief before he gained understanding. Even then he made no answer.

Finally Karlor said impatiently, "Baltuth, will you do it?"

"For the saurans?"

"No. For the metal. Without it, they'll kill us all some day."

"Karlor, it was only one small weapon."

"It was only the first," he answered quietly. "I can think of more, and so will they."

"What you want . . ." Baltuth's face twisted with anxiety. "You have finally done it, Karlor: You have asked something so strange that only the god Altos can answer. I will listen to him. Then tonight I will go to the Council—"

"No," Karlor said tensely. "I'll speak. I know how to say it. And I don't want you telling your version and volunteering to punish me," he added with dislike. "That's over."

Baltuth stared at him a long time before answering. "I will speak after you, but you should speak for yourself. And I can't volunteer to punish you anymore." He limped away but paused and said over his shoulder, "When next you are punished, Karlor Dehn, it will be as a man."

* * *

Karlor abandoned his planned speech when he saw the Council. They listened emotionlessly, their backs against a low circular wall, lit by a fire in the center of the circle. They were familiar people made strange and powerful: Dalyssa's father had spots like the jaquar and wore wooden claws. Ryallnor the Full was painted as a thost and somehow looked powerful and wild instead of foolish. Karlor's own father's brother was crosshatched with green scales, fangs painted at the corners of his mouth. Lathas' mother was blue, yellow dots of stars shining on her.

He tried to explain why the moon metal was important. "We have nothing like it, have seen nothing like it." He explained what it could do. "If a whipcord travels farther with its weight, how far will a bow spear carry?" He argued that Baltuth's using his Godtalker's gift wouldn't help the saurans. "They could never learn to do it; Altos would not teach them."

In an impassioned undertone Karlor gave his final, most telling argument. "If Baltuth shows his power, the saurans will be afraid of us."

He tried not to think of what was in his heart as he looked on the silent Council: *These painted men and women touch the earth and sky, and all I can touch is a few tools and some dreams.*

Baltuth tugged at his arm. "Go now," he said quietly. He smiled his usual tight, grim smile. "I am still allowed to talk, since I am the Godtalker." He stepped forward with slow dignity as Karlor left.

But when Baltuth left the Council he was striding along quickly, almost furiously, though his face showed no emotion. "Take me to your reptilian friends," he snapped. "It seems I'm to show them my talents, that they may learn from me as well."

Karlor ran to get Lathas and Dalyssa. He was glad of the errand; he needed to grin at having outspoken the mighty Godtalker in Council.

## V

By agreement, Dalyssa and Lathas went with Karlor at dawn. Baltuth, alone and unguided, followed at midday.

The walk was obviously hard for him; he was perspiring when he arrived, leaning on his staff more than Karlor had seen before. Baltuth, his face showing constant disgust, watched over the work crew in the pit.

The humans had carried a large pile of rock to the side of the pit and a small one of metal to the fire at the center. For reasons Baltuth could not understand, one of the saurans squeezed a skin of air repeatedly, letting it blow over the fire. The coals glowed white-red, and a clay bowl with a long clay handle lay in the coals.

On the pit rim, the sauran Gassiga said heavily. "This is the one who kills with the powers of earth and water."

Karlor grinned slightly at "of water" but carefully looked solemn before the sauran turned back to him. "He has no tools," the reptile said, "no extra workers, and his legs are thin and weak. Can he truly help us?"

"Speak to me," Baltuth said sharply.

The sauran spun around, agile in the midday warmth. "To you, then. If you are the only one with your power, will killing you save my people?"

Karlor paled, realizing for the first time the danger he had put Baltuth in.

"If you could kill me," Baltuth agreed, smiling grimly,

"it might save a few. Another Godtalker would rise in my place, more deadly still, avenging your insult to the god. Assuming you could kill me," he added with polite sarcasm. "Would you care to try?"

After a moment's tense silence he waved a hand in dismissal. "Good. In the meantime, I have changed my mind; speak to Karlor, not to me." He turned his back on the sauran and descended into the pit.

At the tunnel mouth, Baltuth removed the herbs from his pouch, then a small clay bottle with a wood stopper. These days, he fortified *kmerkaas* with oil; it compensated for the trembling of his leg as he tried to apply the powder.

Nothing about him trembled as he stood. He looked around at the saurans, whipcords in hand at the top of the pit, and he smiled. "Please don't feel ashamed if you're afraid," he said, showing no fear himself. "It happens even to the children of men, and as for your kind . . ."

He ignored the muttering and concentrated on his foot, lowered into the soil of the mine entrance. A few moments later the saurans gathered around sucked in air sharply; the rock beneath their feet hummed softly, then loudly. Baltuth raised his foot, pausing a little longer than was necessary on his staff. He focused his mind on the rear of the tunnel. He took a deep breath and stamped his foot.

A flash of light pulsed from the tunnel, brighter than daylight for the blink of an eye. A low rumbling came from underground, and dust puffed out in a swirling cloud. The elder saurans murmured in distress: the younger cried aloud. Karlor leapt forward and stared into the gloom. "Double your crews on the buckets tomorrow," he said to Gassiga.

Gassiga narrowed his eyes and hissed, but nodded obedience. Baltuth, weak as he was, looked astonished.

Karlor added to Baltuth. "And you—" He caught himself, glancing at the saurans. "Great Godtalker, can you arrange for us to have another worker for the mine?"

"If one is needed, it may happen," Baltuth said impassively. "Are you sure one is needed?"

Karlor dashed in as far as he dared, holding his breath, and emerged quickly, covered in debris. "The roof held. The tunnel is deeper, in the direction we wanted." Baltuth, appalled, stared at him on that *we*, but Lathas and Dalyssa leapt forward, digging tools in hand. Karlor caught their arms. "Not yet. Wait until the dust falls."

Lathas coughed and nodded, then turned and bowed to Baltuth. "Thank you, Godtalker."

Karlor, distracted for a moment from the business of mining, grinned crookedly and groveled at Baltuth's feet. "Down!" he whispered to the other humans. Lathas and Dalyssa, confused, knelt beside Karlor as he cried, "Thank you, great Godtalker, for using so little of your power. More might have destroyed us."

Baltuth understood then. He stretched an arm over Karlor, careful not to let it tremble. "Do not ask often. If you anger me, you may have more moon metal than you wish." Bracing his legs, he raised his staff and pointed at the risen half-moon. The crowd of saurans murmured, suddenly frightened.

"Please no, great Godtalker!" Karlor shouted with what seemed like real terror. "Please, leave us our moon, I beg you." He gestured to the saurans. "They beg you also."

Several of the younger saurans bent at the knees, but hisses from their elders kept them upright. "It shall stay in heaven—for now," Baltuth said curtly. Using his staff as little as possible, he strode directly through the reptile tribe; they pulled back, clearly afraid. Baltuth smiled in grim satisfaction and strode away, ignoring the pain in his leg. Before he left, though, he stared back at Karlor arguing with the sauran smelters, and, for just a moment, he looked worried.

Although his presence was not required, he came with the additional worker the following day. He stayed for the morning, watching as the humans carried out the ore they chipped free.

From above the pit, Saggasz looked at the piled moon metal dazedly. "This is much more than we need for weapons."

Karlor opened his mouth to suggest other uses, but changed his mind quickly. "Then give it to us."

"Give? To you!" He laughed sharply, and several others echoed him. "Why would we do that?"

"For our cloth." Karlor gestured at his cloak; he had noticed the saurans, who of course could not use a cloak, admiring the fabric when he hung it near the pit. "We have more than we can use."

The saurans looked at one another. Finally one said, struggling with the unfamiliar idea, "You give us cloth and we give you moon-metal weapons?"

"Yes. No!" He said it quickly, sharply. "You give us only the moon metal; we give you the cloth and not the garments. We will show you how to sew, and you will show me . . . us—" For a heartbeat he showed the "far look." "—how to shape tools of moon metal."

"Tools? Of moon metal?"

Karlor bit his lip. He should have said *weapons*. "If

that's all the metal you have. There may be other, better rivers in the rock," he added, almost casually. "Moon metal can't be the only ore in the world."

Saggasz looked lost. Baltuth, near him, gave him a look that almost spoke of kinship.

A day later, a bearer came with the first shipment of woven flass. Baltuth came before him, looking angry. The saurans fell back automatically: His power had left an impression.

Karlor, half invisible with dust, met them. "Put the cloth over there." The saurans stepped forward toward it. He raised his palm. "Lay the moon metal beside it first." They snapped their jaws but did as he said.

The bearer left, staggering under the metal. Baltuth, following him as the nervous saurans parted still more, smiled grimly but looked over his shoulder at Karlor, his worry now open and naked.

Karlor wondered about that briefly, then forgot it as he shouted orders to Dalyssa, Lathas, and the saurans. They all scrambled under his direction.

## VI

Almost all of a growing season went by. Children, forgetting to be wary, played at the river without setting a guard; sentries for the One Tribe grew relaxed. Bundles of flass cloth, taken to the ford, were exchanged for baskets of ore from the saurans.

Baltuth made the trip to the mine twice more to break the rock wall with his powers. On the way back from the second trip, he stumbled without tripping over anything, and his left arm and cheek were frozen for two days. Thereafter his limp was even more pronounced.

Lathas mentioned it to Karlor at work—also, that Lathas and Dalyssa had become lovers. Karlor, preoccupied with the mine and learning the new skills of metal work, barely noticed any of this.

Then one day he descended the bluff to cross at the ford and found two sticks crossed before it. Hanging from them were a sauran whipcord and a bloody robe.

He ran up the hill, only to find Lathas laying out clobbers and rippersticks. "I found her this morning," Lathas said flatly, ignoring the tears in his own eyes. "Ryallnor Wai, called the Full. There was an accidental meeting of saurans and humans in the valley. Words were said, stones thrown. She was too old to run. She was my mother's sister," he burst out. "She nursed me."

Karlor held him a moment and walked away, dazed. There would be no more mine, no more metal or new knowledge. His eyes stung, suddenly, thinking of how his machines and changes had plagued poor Ryallnor; he remembered saying, somewhere, that tears were sharp.

A second party, this one of hunters, met a group of saurans by accident; the humans killed several saurans before retreating. The long quiet that had begun with working the mine was over.

On the One Tribe's bank, thost horns blared and drums made from hide and drum-stem banged constantly. The saurans patrolled the other bank, not in scouting parties but in large teams with any number of metal-tipped whipcords and even moon-metal daggers. The Council called for new weapons of the new metal.

In a makeshift workshop below the bluff, Karlor worked like a sand demon, smelting the supply of traded moon metal, pouring it into molds of baked clay and sand, quenching it in river water that fizzed and steamed. He constantly sketched new designs in the sand: spears with crosspieces, a curved sickle on a jointed handle, a toothed blade like some nightmare version of a ripperstick.

Dalyssa, pregnant and unable to prepare for battle, carved drum-stem and wrapped the handles; Lathas, a cloth over his mouth to avoid being burned by the sparks, sharpened the blades on a grinder wheel. Smoke hung over the sands below the One Tribe's village, and Karlor watched constantly for the saurans to come across the river.

But in the end it was men who came for him from the bluff above: stone-faced men acting for the Council. They tied his wrists with thongs to a tree trunk and took Dalyssa and Lathas with them. Karlor waited, wondering why they had left him as a sacrifice to the sauran attack.

Baltuth struggled down the entire bluff, and Karlor watched him indifferently. When Baltuth arrived, Karlor said, "So what took more talk—disposing of me, or planning how I would die in the war?"

Baltuth sat tiredly on a rock. "There will be no war."

Karlor stared at him.

"The saurans sent a messenger. He spoke high and nasty words, and called us the outcasts of Aussasaurian and miserable heat thieves, but let us know that they won't fight us."

He looked Karlor in the eye. "They want the cloth, you see. They need the mine labor. They won't fight us anymore until the next two Heat Seasons are done. Your co-miner Saggasz was stoned to death, for entering an agreement that prevented their choosing war."

After a scant moment of pity, Karlor's heart leapt. "Then we take war to them when we choose—"

His voice died as Baltuth said heavily, "Their envoy came just before the Council sent me to say we did not wish to fight until the mining was done. We want the metals—we need them now, for the needles and fishhooks you made. I don't see how we survived without them." He shook his head, sighing. "Karlor, what have you done? Altos and Aussasaurian gave us this hatred, burned it into us as surely as the comet, and as surely as love of war gave us teeth and nails. Did you know this might happen when you began mining?"

For the first time since the death of Ryallnor, Karlor was near tears. "I knew they had something new, and I knew what they would do with it, given time. I knew that we needed it if we were to survive. I wanted it more than anything." He reddened. "They think I betrayed the tribe?"

"Not *they*—be specific. I taught you better than that." He sagged again. "Some of the Council do, yes. They say you act against the god Altos and against the nature of the One Tribe. There is a penalty. It is seldom imposed."

"What is it?"

Baltuth said only, "You would be crushed slowly between two stones and . . . other things. They are horrible and sacred. I will tell you if it is necessary."

"It isn't necessary!" Karlor tried to slam one hand into another, failing when he remembered that he was tied. "You should know what I've done for the tribe. One day soon we'll mine our own metals. Other needles, hooks, knives, harvesting tools . . ." Even Karlor's rapid mind failed him. "Weapons." He was stopped, assailed by a stray thought. "Baltuth?"

"What?" The old man was startled. Baltuth hadn't

heard that tone from him since Karlor was young and craved learning.

"If we cooled a fire-melted spear of moon metal in the Sacred Pool, what could it do? Would it have any powers in war?"

Baltuth stared helplessly and burst out, "Don't ask me such things!" He fled, and Karlor realized bitterly that, just before the trial and the sentencing, he had frightened the man who had always returned from Council to punish him.

Karlor leaned against the cool rock of the bluff, waiting for death. Finally he heard a shout above and stretched as far out as the thong would allow.

Baltuth stumbled across the cliff face, every limb trembling. He walked doubled over, leaning on the shattered remains of his staff.

Lathas, shouting again, all but fumbled down the bluff toward Karlor.

"What happened?" Karlor shouted.

"He broke his staff." Lathas panted as he arrived. "Cracked it against the wall."

"You watched?" The enormity of it struck him. "You stole into the Council?"

"You're my friend," he said simply.

For once, Karlor was unsure what to say. "Are we to make war?"

"We can't." Lathas' face was a mix of disgust and wonder. "We need the metals too badly; they want the cloth. We've both agreed to let the war wait until two Heats from now, when the crops are in and the mines are closed."

"Am I to be crushed between two stones?"

"Not exactly." Lathas undid the ties around his arms. "You are to be reassigned, three tasks a season, until you have done every task we do."

Karlor stood with his forearms together, confused. At last he dropped them. "How is this a punishment?"

"It isn't. It's your new task. You're to look at how we all work, and find ways to make all our work easier. And you've been chosen the new Godtalker," he added as an afterthought, "if when you sleep by the Sacred Pool at night your vision is true."

He felt as if he had been staring into the sun. "But I thought I was a traitor. The Council—"

"Was convinced that everything you did with the saurans was for our best interest. Even postponing war will give time for a new generation to be born and our numbers to double."

Karlor rubbed his arms. "It would also give time for the saurans to double theirs."

"No. We will both begin fighting again after the mining is done; that's before they mate and nest."

"So it is." Karlor hadn't thought of that. "And who said that to the Council?"

Lathas grinned. "Who always defends you?"

"You, but you're not on the Council."

"Who always takes your life seriously, argues with you to do something with it, wants you to stop being lazy?"

"Baltuth?" He shook his head violently. "You're wrong. He hates me; he always has. I've never done a single thing he liked—"

"When you were to be beaten by ten men for ruining all our loincloths, he argued that you'd given us more fish for less effort. When you flooded the fields and were to be tied down in a field through the sun of Second Heat, he said you'd given us a longer growing season and that we should be feeding you by hand, instead of punishing you. And he always asked to punish you himself, and kept you from worse hurt."

Karlor blinked. "And this time?"

"He said that in the future the new metals alone would save lives, that you had made sure that if the saurans got metals, we did, too. He pointed out how hard you had worked for each of your new gifts."

"How hard I worked?" He tried without success to picture Baltuth saying these things of him. Reflexively he ducked. "He's always said I was the laziest worker in the tribe."

"He also said your gifts would only be really clear to the children coming now," Lathas, distracted, said happily, "including Dalyssa's and mine."

Karlor, completely lost, shook his head. "Did he say anything else?"

"The last thing he said was how your work in the mines made life easy for others, not for yourself. That it was the mark that you were an adult. He said that you would be chosen the new Godtalker when he was gone, because the Sacred Pool had already chosen you for day's knowledge instead of night's. And I'd like that," he added frankly. "You'd be asking Altos and not me to help do crazy tasks or to keep you out of trouble." He climbed back up without showing the slightest jealousy that Karlor had achieved by accident what Lathas had spent his life seeking.

"But it's too much work," Karlor said feebly. He rubbed his wrists and stared at the bluff above him, the fire-charred bank beside him, at the expanse of quiet river where, for the first time in his life, there was no threat. He tried to imagine what he should do from here, what people would expect of him.

In the end, the wood he had been tied to made his decision for him. He broke off a large limb, not too dry, and examined the three-pronged fork at the end with interest. He stuck the prong into the sand, leaning this way and that, feeling for it. Dreamy-eyed and full of the "far look," he pulled a moon-metal knife from his work pile and squatted on the sand to peel the bark.

Patiently and with great care he began carving a new, sturdy walking stick for Baltuth.

# The Sword
# of Dreams

## Ed Greenwood

*T*hey were supposed to be picking all the largest, ripest flyberries they could find, but it was very hot, and old Bhiilu was growing very deaf.

While he kept patient watch over the downgully the warriors of the Fleetfoot Tribe had stalked through earlier to drive out all snakes, gruntears, and other perils, Duara led all six of the berry-picking girls past him, out into the freedom of the wider forest. Bent double to keep hidden under the large, splayed plana leaves that grew in a thick bed beside Bhiilu's spear butt, giggling and hissing with suppressed mirth, they crept by the old warrior and went in search of more interesting things—but as was so often the way in the deep green forest of Araunra, more interesting things soon found them.

Duara knew all about boars and manyclaws and tree vipers and deathfangs, because the women of the tribe talked more about them to younglings than the most boastful warriors ever did—all about their rending fangs and cruel claws and deadly speed. And their watchfulness.

Unless you wanted to die, you could never not listen or smell or keep watch in Araunra, the women warned, because in the great forest something was *always* watching you.

It could be only a little bird or tree-creeper or the swift, timid fleetfoot whose name the tribe bore because fleet-feet gave the tribe most of their meals. Or it might be a deathfangs, the great prowling cat that could tear a warrior open with one slash of its gleaming fangs—or devour a child whole. The first rule of the Fleetfoot was: Be watchful—or die.

Duara Fallingstar had heard such warnings so often that her night fears had faded. When younger she'd often awakened trembling in fear, drenched with sweat and biting her lips to hold back screams—roused from horrid dreams of fleeing endlessly through unfamiliar stretches of the forest, falling often and in growing pain, until something she could never see that bounded along always just behind her grew tired of her panting screams, and pounced.

So when a long, hairy, taloned arm reached out from behind an olbol tree and snatched Irthagh from the damp moss right next to her, Duara thought she was in a waking dream for a moment, and that one of the men of the tribe was fooling with the always-irritating Irthagh for another moment—and then she heard the horrible damp crunching sound from behind the tree and knew that this was very real. It was a good time to scream.

They all screamed—Ruthra and Ermeth, Mlara and Shal—and sprang up, fleeing almost before they thought about it, even before the hulking, hairy mass of the manyclaws slunk out from behind the tree with bright fresh blood dribbling from its jaws! In all directions they ran, each girl taking her own path through Araunra on swift, hardened bare feet. Running was the best way to deal with many dwellers in the forest; the people did not call themselves the Fleetfoot for nothing.

Duara looked back fearfully as she bounded over a fallen tree, and so it was her eyes that the yellow gaze of the hungry manyclaws stared into . . . and she—lithe, brown-tanned little thing that she was, more unruly long hair and bony limbs than good meat—that it decided to hunt. With ponderous but ever-quickening speed it loped after her, swinging its many hairy arms to hasten itself along and uttering a low, growly, hungry grunt.

Duara screamed only once more, and then saved her breath for running—running as hard and as fast as she knew how, crashing along through ferns and spikebushes, plunging over limbs and moss-girt rocks and stumps, her ragged breath loud in her ears as the patient grunting of the manyclaws grew slowly closer behind her.

She could hear distant shouts from behind her now as the Fleetfoot warriors, alerted by the screams, came running from their vigils by burrow holes and rock clefts and other places where furry food might lair. Araunra came alive with crashings and birdcalls and excited whirrings of wings as the always-curious feathered ones swooped and darted around the excitement.

Duara Fallingstar ran as she'd never run before, gasping for breath, hoping the manyclaws would give up the chase or meet with one of the warriors and turn for battle. But as she grew weary and the fear rose slowly within her, that angry grunting was always close behind her. The manyclaws had chosen its prey—and when a manyclaws set itself after a meal, the Fleetfoot women said, its quarry was doomed.

Weeping in fear, Duara stumbled on, turning into a part of the forest her people always avoided—a place where the trees were thin, and much of the ground was tumbled rocks.

"Too good a lair for deathfangs," she remembered old Bhiilu growling, when she'd once asked him why they avoided the spot. And then Ermeth, along with the moss she was sitting on, had slipped slowly but helplessly off a rock taller than them all and fallen on her head with an indignant squeal. Bhiilu had made the grunt that served him for laughter, and told Duara, "That's another good reason, little spring of everflowing questions. Now get you all gone from this shunned place."

If she ran on, no Fleetfoot warrior would come looking for her. Duara looked back—and stumbled on loose stones, crashing to the earth. The manyclaws was close behind her now, its yellow eyes glittering in triumph. She rolled desperately to her feet and ran on, hoping to find some rock higher than a manyclaws could climb. If she did not enter the shunned place, bones were all any Fleetfoot warrior would ever find of Duara Fallingstar.

Sweat blinded her, and her fingers and feet were soon torn raw on sharp edges of stone as she climbed over a rocky ridge, across a fern-choked basin, and up a rock wall beyond. Behind her the ferns hissed as the manyclaws charged through them, its long-taloned arms sweeping the air in eager reachings for her.

Duara sobbed and climbed on, down the precipitous far side of the ridge, across a place of tumbled bare rocks where sunning serpents slithered hastily out of her path, and on up a much higher wall of rock beyond. This was higher than she'd ever climbed in any tree before, and her heart lurched in fear as a rock she was scrabbling over broke away from the stone all around and fell, numbing her knee as it went.

More stone crumbled away as she frantically threw herself to the right, clawing for a grip—any grip—on the beginnings of a ledge. Below her, the grunts of the many-claws were interrupted by a snarl of anger and the thudding of small stones on flesh. Altos grant that it couldn't climb all the way up . . .

And then she'd reached a place where she could stand, a sloping rocky shelf atop the ridge that was choked with bird dung and small bones—and as she whirled about to look back, one hairy taloned arm came into view just below her!

The manyclaws was wheezing now, and she could hear the rattle of dislodged stones as it slipped . . . and slipped again. Duara looked wildly about. On its far side the ridge fell away into thick green leaves—in a cliff she could not climb down quickly unless she wanted to fall into unseen depths beyond—but just above the manyclaws a spear of rock rose up like a tooth, anchoring a tumbled mess of sticks and withered grasses that must once have been the nest of a darkwings or an eater-of-the-dead.

Duara swallowed, fighting for breath, as the many-claws slipped again just below her. The jutting rock looked loose, held only by mud and other stones; if she could shift it so that it fell onto the manyclaws . . .

She threw herself against the rock and reeled back, moaning at the pain. It stood as firm as . . . well, as rock. Duara pushed at it, felt around its base, and tried to claw away some of the smaller stones. One came free. She snatched it up, peered around the rock tooth into the furious face of the manyclaws—and threw it, as hard as she could, into those blazing eyes.

It thumped home solidly, and she heard the manyclaws roar in pain and fury as the stone bounced off and whirled away through the air to crash down into the trees.

And then one hairy arm came up around the tooth of

rock, raking the air in search of her. Duara shrank away, swallowing. The questing claw could tear her open with one swipe. She heard again the crunching from behind the tree, shuddered, and looked along the ridge in search of somewhere—anywhere—to run.

And then two other claws curled around the rock tooth, and the hairy bulk of the manyclaws rose around one side of it—

And the stone beneath Duara groaned. Sun-baked mud broke away beneath her feet and she fell backward, staggering helplessly for balance. She had one glimpse of the rock tooth falling away with a roar, the manyclaws clinging to it and flailing vainly at the air—and then there was no more rock under her feet, and she was falling, too!

Down, down the unknown far side of the ridge a sickeningly long way, head over heels. With a despairing moan, Duara plunged toward the green foliage and the rocks that must lie waiting beneath.

She smashed into leaves and the woody vines that bore them so hard that the breath was snatched out of her and she was flung back up into the air for a dizzying moment before crashing down again, leaf edges and twigs jutting into her and slashing her bare limbs as she fell dazedly through them into darkness.

Her ribs and arms and one thigh burned as if flames were licking at them, and her head rang; something seemed to be circling slowly in front of her eyes, like a leaf blown around and around endlessly by eddying winds.

The sunlight was flickering around Duara, as if the fire in the sky itself was dancing. Her mouth felt dry and dusty, and the only feelings she had that were not more pain were the soft caresses of breezes all over her body.

All over her body?! The thought snapped Duara fully awake; she blinked in the leafy dimness and stared down, shifting her arms and legs slightly—and found that she was caught in a tangle of vines, hanging in midair above plants and rocks she could barely see in the gloom. Above her, leaves shut out the sunlight, and all around—

Turning, Duara found herself staring into the lidless, unblinking eyes of a serpent larger than she was—and almost close enough to touch. Its broad, flat head hung motionless amid the vines, only its tongue questing out from between its lips, darting at her again and again. It lifted that great head, just a little—and in spite of herself, Duara screamed.

In a trice the serpent turned away, slid sinuously along the vine it had been coiled loosely around, and slithered away into the concealing roof of leaves above. The Fleet-foot she-youngling who should have been picking fly-berries swallowed a sob and moved hastily in the other direction—too hastily.

One bruised, bloody hand slipped on a vine. Duara slid sideways through more leaves and plunged down.

She fell only a little way this time, to where three vines crossed each other, but the force of meeting them left her aching and yet numb. Hissing in pain, Duara struggled on, trying to climb downward without falling again.

She almost managed it, catching grimly at vines whenever she felt herself slipping again. The vines were more like trees this low down, thick and knotted and gray with age. A few jarring landings later, Duara found rocks under her feet again, rocks cloaked with the same sickly, yellow green scaly stuff that grew in caves and other places the sun rarely reached. Looking quickly overhead for the snake, she saw nothing but leaves and vines, so at last she dared to take a good look around—and gasped.

She stood in a long, narrow, shadowy place, amid tumbled stones. It was hard to see far in the gloom under the thick canopy of leaves that hung everywhere overhead, but it seemed that the stones in the center of the downgully had been gathered into three piles—piles like the Fleetfoot warriors made to cover honored dead.

For a moment Duara stiffened in fresh fear but then relaxed again, almost wearily. These piles had been made long ago; the skeletons of long-dead plants sprouted here and there beneath creepers that were themselves gray with age and sprawled in lazy longevity across stones that had been piled thus longer than Duara had drawn breaths.

Were these tombs the Fleetfoot wanted forgotten? Or something else? Duara stood still and silent for a long time, watching and listening for any sign of the serpent, the manyclaws on the unseen ridge overhead, or anything stirring around the three cairns.

Birds called and whirred, and she saw a harmless groundworm curl and glide across the ground a fair stretch away, beyond the nearest cairn; but nothing larger moved or made noise. At last, warily, Duara stepped slowly forward, watching the ground underfoot and the vines overhead as she walked to the left, around the cairns, until she could see what lay beyond.

In the narrowing end of this leaf-roofed downgully stood more rocks—and something more exciting. One side of the second cairn was gone, torn down into scattered rubble long ago. Its dark interior gaped open. Duara's mouth went suddenly very dry.

Swallowing, she peered and sniffed, then bent to pick up a rock that seemed the right size for throwing, knowing as she hefted it that it was a pitiful defense against whatever had broken the cairn open. The unknown tomb breaker had been large enough to split and gnaw bones that were larger than Duara.

The Fleetfoot she-youngling shivered in sudden fear and swallowed, her throat still raw and dry. A good lair for deathfangs, Bhiilu had said, and it seemed he'd been right.

She looked quickly all around, though there was no trace of the heavy, musky deathfangs scent she'd been taken to smell as soon as she was old enough to stand. Dust was on the old bones, and the dullness of age. The dung piles were dry and sagging dust, too. Nothing living had laired here for a season at least.

Emboldened, Duara glided forward, tense and alert, awaiting an attack that might come from anywhere. One pace. Another, and still the waiting silence held. Sudden hope rose within her that nothing would come . . . and then excitement, too: Something was gleaming in the dark heart of the shattered cairn in front of her. It was something strange, light where there should be no light.

The iron taste of fear rose again beneath her excitement, but Duara moved steadily forward, drawn despite herself by the glimmer in the darkness. The eerie light shone on something yellowed, smooth, and sticklike: more bones.

Duara looked all around once more, half expecting to see her death watching her triumphantly as it gathered itself to pounce, but she was alone in the shadowy downgully. Gathering herself with sudden determination, she strode forward.

The glimmering light was coming from one bone, broad and flat and beyond the others, lying by the hand of a skeleton taller than any Fleetfoot elder, even great Olboar. The bones oddly hadn't been disturbed by the tomb breaker. Wisps and crumbling fragments of what must have been robes or war armor clung to the skeleton here and there, clear in the dim, slowly pulsing light that was coming from a battlefang that lay by his hand—a carved bone sword as long as Duara stood tall.

For a long time the best berry picker of the Fleetfoot stared at it, entranced: She'd never seen anything so beautiful before, not even the bright-woven sash worn by Essa Firstwoman. Smooth and yet intricately detailed warriors struggled against stags, saurans, and manyclaws along the ivory-hued smoothness. Lost in wonder, not thinking of what danger she might awaken, her hand stretched forth to touch its ancient smoothness.

It *was* smooth, and warm, almost inviting . . .

And then her mind was suddenly ablaze with a sunlit scene: tall men and women, wearing armor of hide that was curved and fluted strangely, battling others who looked more like her own people, small nut-brown naked folk—but they were led by a sauran! It's snarling, scaled head was gray with age and as large as two men's heads, and it hurled short, barbed hand darts, not the long spears of the Fleetfoot. And behind them all was a mountain that spat smoke into the sky! One of the tall men used a club to smash aside one of the sauran's darts, and in his other hand was the bone sword, leaping into its parted jaws . . .

Duara winced. She was dreaming while awake, the bone sword smooth in her hands, and yet tingling.

Suddenly shivering with fear, Duara tried to let go of the blade, but somehow could not. Shaking her head to banish the vision of bloody battle, she found it suddenly whirling and wavering into a moonlit night where short, burly folk held high wooden bowls of fire as they danced in a ring around a giant of a man who wore the head of a stag over his own as some sort of mask. In his other hand was the bone sword, and he raised it suddenly and grandly to the stars, so that it caught the firelight.

Duara watched, unable to look away, as the sword was brought savagely down again, plunging into something she could not see, in the heart of the ring, and sparks sprayed as the dance sped into a frenzy.

Suddenly a stone turned under her foot, and she sat down hard on sharp stones, jolted back to the shaded tomb. Blinking, Duara stared around—and then down at the sword in her hands. Images began to swirl again before her, but she grunted and turned her head away, forcing herself to rise.

The sword rose a little in her hand, as if it was alive and lifting itself to get a look around. Duara swallowed and then quickly bent to the stones and set it down, shaking her hand to be sure it did not cling.

Backing away from the blade, she found herself drenched with sweat. She stood trembling in the gloom, looking down at the silently glowing sword, for a long time. Its glimmering light seemed to beckon.

In sudden haste Duara turned away, looking to one side of the shadowed place, where rocks with red streaks on their flanks lay tumbled. She could remember them, aye. Digging and tugging with feverish speed, she pulled aside enough of the smaller stones to hide the blade. When she laid it carefully to rest, the visions came again, swirling up as if to blind her to what she was doing and tug her forever into the dreams. But she threw herself backward into a roll, using her free hand to slap at the one that held the blade, and was free again. Drawing a ragged breath, she fought down fresh fear and swiftly but gently covered the bone sword over with earth and stones until it was hidden and yet it did not look as if anything had been buried there. She left a curving trail of stones, like a tail, trailing away from where the unseen hilt of the sword lay.

Standing back to fix the spot in her mind, Duara wondered who had fashioned the sword, and what it might do. Who were the folk fighting with the sauran? And the stag people? And how long ago had the fight and the fire dance been?

Suddenly, for no reason she knew, Duara found herself on the edge of tears again. She tossed her head, sighed, and turned away from the tomb and the sword to begin her climb back out of the gully.

She was almost at the top when she heard the drone of the calling horn summoning the Fleetfoot back to the fire from the far places of the forest. Whispering a prayer to Altos for keeping her alive, Duara seemed to hear a quiet answer: She should say nothing about the tombs and the bone sword.

*As Altos wills,* she thought, wondering if she'd ever see the bone sword again, or if she'd forget all about it in the seasons to come. Frowning, something of the wonder that had touched her still dark in her eyes, Duara Fallingstar came over the top of the ridge to be greeted by shouts of wonder from the warriors who were cutting up the dead manyclaws.

That night, she had the first of the dreams.

\* \* \*

"Why do this, Revered Elder?" Duara asked calmly, almost ten seasons later.

There was a murmur from the assembled Fleetfoot; no one ever dared speak against Stoneskull before all the people.

Yet the young, dark eyed, beautiful Duara had won her own standing in the tribe. Unwed, strong, and fast, she hunted with the warriors yet was not too proud to work at the cooking fires. She might have been no more than a proud wild-will, overdue to be humbled and broken by an elder, were it not for her ideas. They were wild ideas that worked: a "breakneck" pit for the hunters to chase the fleetfoot into, to bring thrice the meat with no risk of the point hunter being run down and trampled; rings of sharp stones around sleeping furs to keep serpents away; tree limbs cut and then propped up in boughs to dry out, for use in fires later. They were ideas too useful to dismiss or ridicule, ideas that only elders should have.

Duara dared tell no one she saw those ideas in her dreams—dreams that came every night down the long years and began and ended with the floating glimmer of the bone sword. It, or whoever had put it there, seemed to have chosen Duara, showing her things that had been much help to the Fleetfoot, things done by other tribes in places she did not know. In these visions, there were only two things she ever saw more then once: a high mountain valley that seemed lush and green and inviting, and a marker stone that stood by itself in the forest—oddly enough, in the very spot where she stood now, though there was no sign of it in the Fleetfoot clearing.

Perhaps its task was done. When she'd first seen it, she'd been drawn to it, but the dreams always ended before she reached it. It had been several seasons before the blaze of the bone sword had been tardy enough to allow her dream self to get close to the stone—close enough to see the open mouth carved in it.

It terrified her, that mouth, and yet fascinated her. Why was it there? Would it bite her, or speak? Was it just a carving, or did it have some meaning she must discover?

Three winters had passed before she'd managed— twisting and snarling in determination—to get close enough to touch the stone. A sound had begun to come from it before the vision of the sword whirled her away to wakefulness. Sweating and squirming on her sleeping furs, Duara had blinked awake furious but exultant. It had started to speak, to say something to her!

And so her dream visions had continued, night after night. Sometimes she reached the stone before waking, and sometimes she never saw it at all, or glimpsed it like a reproving finger in the dim distance before the bone sword came to herald her awakening. Another two winters passed before she'd learned its entire message, heard word by painstaking word: *Seek the safe place.*

Since then she'd not seen the stone again in her dreams, only the beautiful mountain valley. Perhaps it was the safe place. Last night, she'd seen the gully with the tombs again, and then, somewhere beyond it, the valley. Her dreams seemed to be telling her to seek out the valley, and that it lay to the far, sunrise side of the tombs.

All these years, she'd never told anyone about the bone sword. The Fleetfoot thought her wits touched by the dark spirits of the woods, she knew, but they said nothing against her when her ideas brought so much to the tribe. Yet the elders seldom smiled at her.

One was scowling at her now. The bald giant Stoneskull

was tallest and heaviest of the warriors, the only Fleetfoot man who'd ever met the charge of a gruntears, wrestled the hairy boar to a standstill, and then broken its back and flung it down by the hearth fire. That had happened long ago, but the older warriors of the tribe all swore they'd seen it done, and they told the tale often.

Stoneskull had risen to be chief among the elders of the tribe and along that trail had also become a harsh, cold-eyed man unaccustomed to having his words or ways challenged. And though this Duara might be the brightest of them all—and the most beautiful, so that he often growled at the mere sight of her—she was still a woman, and an uncloaked she at that, who'd not yet taken any suitor's cloak as her own. That would change soon, Stoneskull vowed.

After he'd broken her jaw and made her treat elders with the proper respect.

His voice was thin and cold as he answered her. "When any elder of this tribe bids you do something, she, there is no *why*. You do it, when and how bidden."

Silence fell as the Fleetfoot watched, awaiting Duara's reply. Many eyes were bright in anticipation of her humiliation, yet just as many darted dark glances at Stoneskull or—among the young men who were not yet warriors—looked at Duara with proud hunger. What a prize she: one who dared cross words with the revered elder!

"I'll cut longbark poles with good will," Duara told him calmly, "but I think the purpose for which we gather them unwise."

"Un*wise*?" Stoneskull roared. "For all the cold seasons I've seen, the Fleetfoot have gone to war with the Scaled Ones! Who are you to call all of us elders—and

all who came before us—unwise? Your tongue is far too
long, she! Hide it away, lest I put you to catching wing-
stings with it like a croaking one!"

He strode forward, raising massive fists. "Well?" he
bellowed, determined to have her submit to him aloud
and on her knees. All must see that Stoneskull ruled here,
or he'd have a hand's-worth or more of challenges from
old rivals to deal with before they reached the Hot
Forests. He towered over her. *"Well?"*

"Your roaring does not make a thing any the more
wise, or the less. I would put this to all the tribe," Duara
said calmly, looking up into his face.

Stoneskull raised a threatening hand, but a spear
stretched out to bar its descent.

Old Bhiilu stood hunched with age and trembling with
the shakes that took him often, now, but his voice was
strong as he faced the furious revered elder. "In my day
shes did not speak out against elders," he said calmly,
"but it is the right of every Fleetfoot to put any matter
before all the tribe. I have here heard her claim that
right."

"Stay out of this, old man," Stoneskull snarled.
"Your—"

"My hearing is as good as yours," Bhiilu told him
firmly. "And in my day, no elder was ever told to stay out
of *anything*. Nor did elders presume to strike shes of the
tribe—shes they are sworn to defend—except in judgment, *after* all had been decided."

The rebuke brought a chill to the silent clearing, but as
Stoneskull glared around at the watching faces, he saw
that the Fleetfoot were in agreement with the doddering
old one. And why not? He'd said out the laws clear and

correct, Altos take him! Abruptly the revered elder stepped back and waved a dismissive hand.

"Speak then, uncloaked she. Tell us of the unwisdom of our fathers and their fathers," he said heavily, "and we will judge. We will all judge."

They all knew Stoneskull had ordered longbark saplings to be cut to make war spears—spears that grew stonehard in a fire. Spears would be needed in this season's journey south into the Hot Forests where the Scaled Ones dwelt.

The Fleetfoot always spent the coldest months away from the chilling snows of their forest home in the Staglands, raiding the saurans. "The Scaled Ones are always ready and waiting," Duara told the silent circle of her people. "No matter how brave and strong our warriors, some fall every year, and the Scaled Ones strike back—and more of us die. Would it not be better to leave the Scaled Ones alone?"

Stoneskull's lips twisted. "They are our foes! Leave them to grow stronger, so that they can come here to hunt us down? I cast your own question back at you: Why?"

"The Scaled Ones never go where it's cold. We are safe here," Duara replied. "Our raids cost many Fleetfoot lives and win us only a few hasty chances to hunt tuskboars. And even then, we often meet with poisonous vipers and the thousandcoils instead!"

"Cowardly she!" Stoneskull snarled. "How are the men of the tribe to prove themselves warriors, if not in battle? Would you have us become hiders in the forest, like tree-creepers? I—"

"The she has put this matter before the tribe," Bhiilu said calmly, "not you. Let her speak a bit." He turned to Duara, amid murmurings from the assembled folk, and said, "If we do not go to the Hot Forests to fight Scaled Ones, what is your thought for how the Fleetfoot should spend the cold time?"

Duara hesitated and then ducked her head, took a deep breath, and said her dream aloud. "I would have us hunt for a safe place," she said, in a voice that was firmer than she'd feared it would be.

"And what is that?" Bhiilu asked calmly.

"A place with caves we can live in, and rock walls around it so that we can defend it," Duara said, her voice gathering strength as the familiar vision of the safe place grew vivid in her mind. "A valley with warm springs in it to drink from, where we can grow berries and nut trees and broadleaves to eat, instead of spending so much time searching for them. When we go out, we'd go to hunt fleetfoot by driving them into breakneck pits. If the Nundar or other enemy tribes came we could roll rocks down on them and climb away to the highest rock ledges where they dared not follow."

"And have you seen any such place of wonders?" Stoneskull scoffed.

"In my dreams," Duara said softly. "Often, in my dreams."

Some of the warriors snorted and snickered, and Stoneskull's voice was heavy with sarcasm as he asked slowly, "And just what else, O clever uncloaked she, have you seen in your dreams?"

Duara raised her eyes to meet his and said crisply, "Fewer Fleetfoot graves. More happy families, and more elders unhurt and hale, walking into longer years."

"We'd all like such things," Stoneskull said coldly, "but wishing things to pass does not change the trees and sky around us." He snatched a spear from a nearby warrior and waved it high over his head, turning for all the Fleetfoot to see. "*This* is the only thing that changes the fortunes of the Fleetfoot. Dreams—bah! Get back to the fires, she, and leave the leading of the tribe to those of us with wits enough to face life as it is!"

Duara looked calmly around the circle and saw thoughtful frowns on many faces. "Is this the judgment of all the Fleetfoot?" she asked, looking to several of the elders who stood together.

Slowly, almost reluctantly, one of them—Hustur—stepped forward under Stoneskull's hot glare and said to her, "Young she, it is. You speak well, and I would not have you suffer for what you have said here." He turned pointedly to look at Stoneskull—who stiffened and turned dark with fresh fury—and then looked back to Duara and added, "Yet we cannot live in dreams. Find this safe place to show us, if you would put this to the people again." He smiled and added mildly, "While we talk, the longbarks remain uncut."

Under his gaze, then, as he looked slowly around the circle, the Fleetfoot people began to move, the murmur of dozens of conversations beginning as they scattered to their tasks. Stoneskull stood glaring at Duara, but she turned away from his gaze and went to find her sharpstone, Shal and Aereth falling into step beside her.

Ildra, Shavvara, and Neleathe joined them before they left the clearing.

Hot eyes watched them go. "Ah, to have that one . . ." Talarth said in hoarse admiration, staring after the raven-haired Duara Fallingstar as the prettiest uncloaked shes left the clearing together.

"And be lashed with her tongue at sunrise, sunset, and

all the dark hours between? Not my chosen fate," Wuvaer said wryly. "What say you, Thorn?"

The darkest, quietest of the able young men who'd not yet been named warriors stared across the clearing for the last possible glimpse of Duara. "With those eyes and hands," he said softly, "she could scream all manner of crazed plans to the moon, and I'd spread my cloak for her happily."

"When you grow older, O lost-in-love," a reproving voice put in from behind them, "screams to the moon will start to grate on your patience just a trifle. Trust me in this."

The younglings swung around, flushed in embarrassment, and shifted away under the amused gaze of Malag, Thorn's father and one of the best-liked elders.

Another elder, Orgeth, stood at Malag's side. "What think you of the she's dream?" he asked them quietly.

The young men shifted uncomfortably. It was Wuvaer who answered for them all. "I hope this place she dreams of lies somewhere, and some tribe Altos favors finds it. But I doubt I'll ever live to see it." He lifted a hand to indicate the trees above and around them. "This is our home, and in winter, we go south to hunt Scaled Ones. That is what the Fleetfoot do."

The two elders nodded approvingly as they watched the younglings hasten away. They'd have been less content had they been able to hear Aereth, Ildra, and Shal wistfully plying Duara with questions about the safe place as many longbark saplings were cut and stacked.

That night, as the warriors expertly turned the pointed sapling tips in the flames of the dying cook fires, Stoneskull stalked through the gathering nightdark in a slow circle around the tribe, glowering at Duara as he passed. When he took his accustomed spot on the hillock at the center of the fires, the calling horn barked once, to call for silence, and the gathered Fleetfoot listened.

"When the sun rises again," the revered elder said shortly, "everyone is to prepare for the trip to the Hot Forests. The night after this is the last dark time that our fires will blaze here until the snows have come and gone again."

Stoneskull turned to face Duara squarely. It was too dark for their eyes to meet, but everyone there knew whom he was looking at. "Anyone who does not walk to the Hot Forests with the elders, and obey their orders, is no true Fleetfoot and may walk with the tribe no more." And with those grim words, the bald giant strode down from the speaking mound, into the darkness.

A silence colder than any night chill followed his words, and it was a long time before any chatter arose again.

Duara's dream that night was long and vivid. She was carrying the bone sword, going east from the cairn a long way through rolling forests unfamiliar to her, to where a tall peak rose like a standing man from the trees. A river splashed down from its heights and roared out from the tree-girt cliffs to a plain far below. The sword lifted in her hand until it pointed up to where that swift-flowing torrent first spilled into view—and flashed so brightly that she cried out and covered her eyes. Somewhere up that river she would find the safe place.

There was another flash, and pain with it this time— pain in her ribs. Duara shuddered, trying to curl up on her side as she blinked awake.

Another ungentle kick propelled her half out of her sleeping furs, fully awake and gasping for breath.

Eyes swimming, she twisted around to see her tormentor—and met the ugly eyes of Stoneskull. "You talk like a warrior," the revered elder said coldly, without further greeting. "It is time you worked like a warrior. This suntime, on our journey to the Hot Forests, you scout. Go with Malag; he will tell you what to do."

Behind the revered elder's shoulder, Malag nodded gravely to Duara in greeting. Lying bare skinned before both men, the most beautiful uncloaked she of the Fleet-foot eyed them both calmly and then rolled smoothly to her feet and said to Stoneskull, "I will not. I will find my safe place, and be happy there, while you send the Fleet-foot into death on the spear points of the Scaled Ones."

"Death?" Stoneskull roared at her, his voice loud enough to wake echoes in the trees around—and every Fleetfoot who yet slept. "We go to victory!"

"The victory Darth found?" Duara countered, naming a smiling warrior who'd been slain horribly by the saurans two fireskies ago. "Or the glory of Omran's passing? Or Perethain's?"

Flint eyed, she went on naming dead Fleetfoot warriors until the revered elder's paling face twisted in battle rage. His great war club swept up to strike her down—but Aereth and Ildra were suddenly beside Duara, shouting angrily, and another war club thrust forward from one side.

Stoneskull's club halted aloft, and he turned his head with slow menace to look along the weapon that blocked his clear strike—into the eyes of Orgeth the elder.

"Cast her out if you must, Revered Elder," Orgeth said sharply, "but she is the daughter of my sister who is gone to Altos All-Watcher. Strike her not!"

Stoneskull looked at him in silence for a long time, his

face slowly darkening, but Orgeth's club remained where it was.

At last the bald giant let out his breath in a long, slow sigh and let his club fall back to his side. Stepping around the end of the club, he strode past Duara, turning to say softly, "You are no Fleetfoot. Begone."

Duara raised her hand to him in a warrior's salute. The revered elder stiffened at the insult. She smiled into his blazing eyes, nodded to him as one equal to another, and said, "I am my own tribe now. The Fallingstar Tribe would look upon the Fleetfoot as friends." Raven-dark hair swirled in the revered elder's face as she calmly turned her back on him to bow to Orgeth in thanks. Then she walked away into the forest, toward the sunrise, without looking back.

After a long moment, all five of the other uncloaked shes who were her friends made their own bows to Orgeth and followed her into the trees. Stoneskull took one startled, furious stride after them—and found himself staring into the faces of Orgeth and Malag, standing shoulder to shoulder to bar his way. With a growl of dismissal, the revered elder turned on his heel and strode back to the main fires, ignoring the silent stares of his people.

He went straight across to the other side of the camp, where by tradition the young warriors-to-be slept, well apart from the uncloaked shes. There he caught the shoulder of the dark-haired one he'd often seen staring so hungrily after Duara and strode on into the deep woods, hauling the startled youngling apart from all others.

"I need your service, Thorn," the revered elder said, pointing toward the sunrise. "The Fallingstar she and five of her friends have just now left the Fleetfoot."

Thorn stared at him, eyes widening in wonder, and started to speak. Stoneskull shook him, not gently, and snapped, "Follow them, and stay unseen. See where they go, and what they find, that all the Fleetfoot may make use of it later. Let Duara go where she may and find the death that waits for her—but bring the others back if you can. Herself she may slay, but the Fleetfoot shall *not* lose five uncloaked shes over her wild dreams. One she of your choice shall be yours with my gifting, if you do this, and you shall be counted a warrior among us."

Thorn stared at him, face brightening in incredulous joy, and Stoneskull spun him around to face the sunrise and hurled him forward with a terse, "Go!"

Thorn looked down to his belt to be sure his fire-hardened stabbing fang rode there, looked back at the revered elder with a bright nod of agreement, and trotted eagerly away through the trees.

A twig snapped nearby, and Stoneskull turned toward the sound with a roar, unslinging his club with deadly speed. Another club parted some leaves not far away, and Orgeth stepped out to face him. The elder had obviously heard his words to the youngling.

The revered elder stared challengingly at Orgeth, who nodded slowly in approval.


Duara walked swiftly, cloaked in her thoughts, trying not to cry at having to leave everyone dear to her without even a farewell. It was a long time before she slowed to catch her breath—and heard the hastening footfalls behind her. Many of them.

She turned, dropping into a crouch. Was Stoneskull sending warriors to silence her? She had only her sharpstone . . .

Leaves danced, and then through them Duara caught sight of Shal and, behind her, Aereth and her other friends, and sighed with relief. There was a sudden tightness in her throat.

"It was good of you to give me a proper farewell," she told them, opening her arms to embrace Aereth and Shal together.

"Farewell? We're coming with you," Aereth said firmly, and at her shoulder Ildra nodded. Duara looked to Shal, and to Shavvara and Neleathe coming up to join the swiftly enlarging embrace, and saw the same eager resolve.

"All of you?" she asked, close to tears. There were nods and smiles.

In the midst of a flurry of reassuring patting and stroking hands, Duara shook her head. "Don't follow me!" she protested. "Stoneskull is cruel, but his arm is long and can't help but shield you better than I can. My road could lead to swift death."

"I believe in your dreams," Aereth said softly. "You will find this safe place, and the other things you have told us of, somehow. And I want to be there when you do."

"Even if you are cast out of the Fleetfoot? Never to have a man but as his captured slave? A Nundar man, or a Stagwind warrior who will eat you when he grows tired of you?"

Neleathe's face turned pale, and she stared at Duara in horror, lip trembling. Then she burst into tears, waved protesting hands at them in mute apology and farewell as she turned, and then fled blindly back through Araunra.

"The price will be high," Duara added softly, lifting a hand to indicate the fading rustlings that marked Neleathe's fearful flight. "Are you sure you want to walk with me?"

There were somber nods, and it was Duara's turn to weep, leaning into the embraces of her friends. Their shared tears and laughter came to an abrupt halt when a thin, shaky voice growled, "Is this some new way to lure beasts to the table?"

The women whirled around, reaching for sharp-stones—and stopped in surprise.

Old Bhiilu could move more softly than anyone would have suspected, it seemed. He stood blinking around at them all with his best war spear in his hand, his fingers busy at the lashings that bound a second shaft to it. As the women watched uncertainly, he got the second spear free.

"Old Wise One," Duara said gently, giving him the title he'd been known by when he'd taught them all which berries to pick and which to leave alone, long ago, "you may not have heard, but Stoneskull cast me out, and—"

"You all rushed off into the sunrise without a man for your new tribe," the grizzled elder grunted. "So my duty was clear."

After a startled moment of silence, the women shouted with laughter. Bhiilu gave them a dry smile and posed with one hand on his hip, moving his pelvis provocatively for a moment.

And then he tossed his own best war spear to Duara, and the laughter died away.

"I name you warrior, and chief of the Fallingstar tribe," he said calmly, "and I'll hunt for you, if you'll have me." The women stared at him in awe.

Duara swallowed, looked down at the spear in her hands, and then stepped forward, put her arms around him, and burst into tears.

\* \* \*

"How far is this safe place?" Shal asked wearily. "Do you know?"

"A long way yet," Duara said calmly as they fought their way through brush, eyeing the lowering light high on the trunks and leaves of the few trees that stood above the tangled thornbushes. "We'd best take to the trees—up there, where the land rises—and sleep for the night."

"I'll stand guard," Bhiilu grunted, and held up his spear. A plump longears dangled on the end of it.

Shal gasped. "I never saw you take that," she said, almost accusingly.

The elder shrugged. "Quick throw," he replied. "I'll need help gathering dry wood if we're to eat before full dark, though."

"You'll have it," Aereth promised him as they went up into the trees.

Night came down swiftly, and Bhiilu stood still and silent, looking like one more tree among all the others. He watched downslope from his tribeswomen so that someone falling out of her tree in slumber wouldn't land on him and be hurt on his spear or belt fang.

The elder was patient and content, and he watched well out of long habit, peering this way and that into the night often, and listening, always listening.

For all his diligence, Bhiilu's eyes and ears were old and failing. He never saw the young Fleetfoot warrior creep carefully behind a nearby overturned stump and settle down behind its cloaking leaves where he could see the old elder and the trees the Fallingstar women slept in.

Thorn fell asleep seeing Stoneskull name him a warrior before all the tribe, putting into his hands the long, heavy, carved war spear that was a gift from the tribe and a sign of the elders' regard for him. Soon. *Soon.* In his slumber he patted the haft of his short hunting spear and smiled grimly.

"This place is . . . not good," Bhiilu growled, looking down at the tangle of vines below. "Anything could be down there. I'd best go down first, to—"

"You'll stay here," Shal said firmly, taking one of his arms in a tight grip while Aereth took the other. "You're *old*, Revered Elder. A fall could slay you, where one of us could get up and go on. Stay." Shal rose to follow Duara over the edge of the ridge.

"But I—"

*"Stay,"* Aereth hissed, wrapping her arms around him and kissing him. Startled, Bhiilu pushed at her.

"This is . . . not right," he protested. "You're uncloaked . . ."

Aereth chuckled and ran her fingers through the few strands of hair he had left on his head. There was more on his chin. "Which means I've never been so close to any man before. I just wanted to see what it was like."

She laughed at the puzzled look he gave her and added, "And I was an uncloaked she of the Fleetfoot tribe. I'm a woman of the Fallingstars now."

Bhiilu nodded thoughtfully as Shavvara and Shal climbed slowly back into view. Shal carried the spear that Bhiilu had given to Duara and insisted that she take down into the place of vines, but Shavvara was struggling proudly up the rocky slope under the weight of four stone axes.

Duara came up behind them, and at one glimpse of the

bone sword she held proudly aloft, Bhiilu gasped and went white.

Aereth turned to him, puzzled, as he leaned forward and barked, "Did . . . were those in a stone cairn?" He made a pyramid with his hands and added, "As tall as two warriors?"

Shal nodded, smiling, as she clambered up onto the ridge beside them. "It was broken open," she said, "just as Duara said."

Bhiilu looked up toward where the top of an old black-bark tree hid the sun and said hoarsely, "Great Altos, forgive us! This was done by innocents who meant no ill! If a life must be the price, take mine! Hear me, great Altos!"

Shavvara started to laugh and then saw Bhiilu's face. She dropped to her knees and joined him in prayer, and Shal and Aereth echoed his calls to the god in the sky.

They all fell silent, shocked, as the bone sword blazed with sudden blue fire in Duara's hand. As she joined them on the ridge, the strange glow slowly faded.

"Are . . . are you well?" Bhiilu asked anxiously.

Wonder was in Duara's eyes as she replied, "More than well. All the small aches and hurts I bore are gone, and their pain with them."

"A sign from Altos," Aereth said quietly, and Bhiilu nodded fervently.

"Yes! The god smiles upon us!" he cried.

"So he does," Thorn whispered aloud from where he watched behind a plana bush. He shook his head in wonder as Duara flourished the bone sword one last time before her companions crowded around to look at it. "She spoke truth," he said slowly. "Perhaps this safe place does wait for her." He turned to whence the sun rose and looked into the trees of Araunra, and his face was troubled.

Two sunrises had passed since they'd gone around the place of the tombs, and now it seemed to the Fallingstar Tribe that Araunra did have an end and did not stretch on forever, as the Fleetfoot elders had taught them. The land was rising and the trees thinning out; rocks were strewn everywhere, and not all of them bore the carpet of moss and creepers that always cloaked such stones in the Fleet-foot part of the forest. The day was drawing to its height when Duara pointed excitedly ahead, over a ridge, at the peak her dreams had shown her. If all held true, they were nearing the safe place.

"This land seems empty." Bhiilu nodded uneasily as they pressed on.

Shal bent and picked up a long, curved bone. "Not as empty as all that," she replied, holding it up to him. "This must be from a gruntears—one larger than I've ever seen, too!"

Bhiilu nodded again as he watched her toss the bone back onto the ground, but the frown did not leave his face. As they went on, and the forest gave way to rolling wilderlands cloaked in shrubs with only a few stands of trees, they saw more bones—many bones, strewn over the land. All sorts of creatures had died here, it seemed. They even saw the toothed skull of a deathfangs, and it was frighteningly large. Of what had slain them, there was no sign. The Fallingstars began to look around uneasily as they went. Once Shal thought she saw something large trailing them, darting from bush to bush, but when they halted for battle, nothing emerged, and they turned and trudged on as the day spent itself slowly around them. Bhiilu sniffed at the ground suspiciously and poked it often as they went along.

"Seeking crawling ones?" Duara finally asked quietly, and he nodded.

"All these bones . . ." The elder looked up into the sky, peering around in all directions, and at last shrugged, hefted his spear, and strode on.

Soon they could hear a whisper in the distance—a whisper that soon built into a hissing, and then a roar. Broadleaves, tripfoot vines, and stunted manybranch trees began to grow thickly, and the Fallingstars had to slow their advance, picking their route with care and watching for snakes and small scurrying things that might be hiding under the leaves. The ever-present roaring grew deafening.

And then Shal, who was in the lead, cried out and threw up her hand for them to halt. "Come," she said, "but slowly. Everything falls away."

They joined her on the rocky edge of a cliff that overhung the river of Duara's dreams and looked down at it. Swift it ran, splashing and hurling up spray as it plunged from a high shoulder of the mountain peak and raced down, down to a green land that lay to their right, in the same direction as the Hot Forests of the saurans.

"A river that runs with all the fury of the gods," Aereth breathed, and Bhiilu nodded approvingly.

"Well said," he agreed. "I'd not want to try to cross it here." He peered doubtfully up at the rocky heights it was falling from, as if he was unsure that they could even climb to its source while staying safe on this bank. "The day draws down," he said, sounding relieved. "We dare not go on until next sunrise."

There was a murmur of agreement, and they looked

about for a place to camp, choosing a height among all
the greenery. Dusk came swiftly, and with it something
rose from the banks of the river, like tendrils of black
smoke.

"What is that?" Aereth asked, pointing.

Bhiilu frowned. "I know not," he said slowly, peering
down into the river mists at the dark, rising wisps. "It
almost looks like the darkwings that fly in the Hot
Forests at nightfall, but . . ." And then his voice rose,
sharp with alarm, and he turned and shouted, "Beware!
War! War, all!"

The women stared at him, bewildered. Then they
looked to the sky and saw death rise up and then swoop
down on them.

Hundreds of darkwings flapped in the golden sky of
sunset; large, leathery, and dusty brown, their eyes like so
many hungry, glittering red coals. They dove down upon
the Fallingstars, uttering tiny, cold cries. And then there
was no sky any more, only a cloud of slashing talons and
biting fangs.

The Fallingstars shrieked and roared and hacked frantically at things that bit and slashed and then were gone.
They swung their weapons over and over again, trying to
keep their eyes from harm. The bright pain of fangs bit
into Duara all over until she fell onto the rocks and rolled
about to try and crush some of them, catching at the flapping things and hammering small biting bodies against
the increasingly slippery stones beneath her.

A stone axe rang off stone somewhere nearby, and she
heard someone scream—a high keening that rose and
went on and on, until at last it died away in a horrible wet
gurgling.

By then, Duara was on her feet, her hair wound around

her head to protect her face against talons and fangs, slashing out blindly with the bone sword. It seemed to sing in her hands, warm and light, and she seemed to *feel* where the biting things were in the air around her with each slicing pass of the blade. A long and panting time passed before she realized it was blazing with the god light again.

Duara tore away some hair and risked a look at it as she swung and hacked. She gaped in wonder.

The bone sword was flickering with a pale white light, like the dapples of moonlight on moving water, and all the darkwings seemed drawn helplessly down to it, milling about her in a spiral of wings and talons and dark, leathery bodies that she could not help but strike.

All of the bats were whirling around her, now, and beyond their swirling she could see her friends—or what was left of them.

Someone who was so covered with blood and her own matted hair that Duara could not recognize her lay draped over some rocks, panting, a broken stone axe in her hand.

Ildra lay faceup on the rocks beyond, her eyes and throat torn out, and a little way off to the left Bhiilu stared at the setting sun, his tongue and one eye gone. The spear in his hand glistened with dark blood and the twisted remnants of transfixed darkwing bodies. Their old teacher was stretched protectively atop Aereth; all that Duara could see through her rising tears was one bloody hand, its nails sunk forever in the last bat her friend had slain.

A rage rose within her. She screamed her fury and hit out at the flapping things again and again, until only one wobbled in the air around her, squealing in pain and fear but unable to draw away from the glowing sword.

Duara turned, and turned again, moving always to face it as it flapped desperately about, trying to get behind her. And as she turned, she seemed to see a ring of watching, grinning human skulls floating in the air all around.

"Do . . . do you approve?" she panted at them, her voice trembling with anger as she swung the bone blade savagely, cutting the last darkwings almost in half.

It fluttered to the trampled leaves in front of her. She took a step toward it and almost fell. The light of the blade was fading swiftly, and with its waning, pain and weariness rushed in, almost overwhelming her.

Then the skulls faded away. Duara Fallingstar shook her head to set free the last of her tangled hair, set her teeth grimly, and in the last rose red moments before night came down on a world much emptier than it had been a few breaths before, forced herself to look again across the field of heaped darkwings and her dead friends.

The bloody figure with the axe was on its feet, staggering to meet her. It limped heavily as it came, but it could only be . . .

"Shal?" Duara asked uncertainly, lowering her blade. "Are . . . are we the last?"

Her friend shook her head helplessly and dissolved into tears. They fell into each other's arms, sobbing in fear and sorrow, as twilight stole across the land.

And from atop a high rock up the edge of the gorge above them, Thorn watched the women weep. One of the two below had seen him earlier in the day, and as the trees grew thinner he'd been forced to fall back to avoid being recognized; old Bhiilu wasn't as blind as the warriors thought he was. Or rather, Thorn corrected himself wryly, he hadn't been.

The gathering darkness had made moving quietly difficult, and it had been a long, slow climb to reach this height above them—just in time to see them die, one after another, under the claws and jaws of those clustering darkwings. Thorn shook his head in remembered wonder at the sight of that glowing sword Duara had wielded. He must have it!

There were only the two women left now, covered in blood and crying out their terror and grief; it was time—and past time—for him to take them back to Stoneskull now. Then Thorn Blackskull would be named a warrior and could claim this Duara as his own. By Altos, but she could fight!

Much of that may have been whatever god power was in the sword. But he'd seen Duara leap about, duck away from swooping darkwings, and swing as savagely and swiftly as any veteran Fleetfoot warrior. Win her, and the sword would be his also. He smiled in triumph, turning to go down from the high rock where he stood—

And with a growl that was even more triumphant, a deathfangs sprang out of the bushes at him, claws out and its great jaws gaping wide!

Duara's head jerked up at the sound of the growl above them. She and Shal looked up in time to see a great forest cat pounce on a man on the very edge of the gorge, raking at him. The man twisted and rolled on his back, kicking out desperately—

And a moment later the high rock where the man had been was empty, as man and cat both tumbled head over heels through the empty air, down toward the river far below.

The two women clung to each other in astonishment and fear long after the bushes hid the falling combatants from view.

"Was that . . . a man of the Fleetfoot?" Shal asked, her voice rough from weeping.

"I fear so," Duara said grimly, her deep green eyes locked on the rushing waters far below. "I fear so."

Then she sighed, shook herself, and added wearily, "That deathfangs may have a mate, and there's too much blood here not to draw carrion eaters. We must go."

Shal looked down at their dead friends, and her face twisted. "We can't just *leave* them . . ."

As if in answer, someone moaned. The two women looked at each other and then clambered hastily over heaped darkwings toward the sound.

Shavvara lay on her side behind a rock. All of her save her legs was covered with dead bats, but when they uncovered her it seemed she would live—at least, she still had both her eyes and could move freely, but she mumbled dazedly and was covered with open, bleeding bites.

"We've got to get her away from here," Duara said fiercely as they lifted Shavvara up onto a rock. She hung limp and heavy in their arms. "The others are in the arms of Altos now; let him look to them."

Shal looked up, lips parting to protest her harsh words, but saw the tracks of fresh tears running down Duara's bloody face and said only, "There is no place to hide where we walked today. Where shall we take her?"

Duara jerked her head to indicate the high rock where the man watching them had been, up the gorge.

"Down is easier," Shal said, shaking her head, "and the land below has trees, and berry bushes, and—"

"And no safe place," Duara replied. Beside her on the rock where she'd set it down to help Shavvara, the bone sword flashed with sudden light. Both women stared at it in awe, and then at each other. As that eerie radiance faded, Duara looked up into the rocky heights and said softly, "The refuge of my dreams has rock walls, and caves in them, and streams running through it. Those things can only be up there."

Water struck him like a hand of rock, and then he was plunging through its roiling depths, air rushing out of his shocked lungs in a bright webwork of bubbles— and something large and sleek was pawing the waters behind him.

Thorn's foot scraped on a rock, and he kicked out desperately, reaching for where the water was bright as the swift flow of the waters swept him along. Up, up he went, lungs burning and with the deathfangs close behind him, up and—into air! Gasping for breath, he churned the water in frantic haste, struggling to get out of the deep river.

Altos smiled on Thorn; almost immediately, his feet found sharp stones and the mud of the shallows, and he was able to stand. Hastily he stumbled toward the bank, clapping his hands to his sodden belt to be sure his stabbing fang was still there.

It was, Altos be praised! Then a thrashing of the waters and a deep-throated, angry roar told him that Altos was smiling on the deathfangs, too. Thorn sloshed hastily downstream out where he could stand knee-deep in the rushing waters, on rocks but with soft mud in front of him for the great cat to wallow in—and there he turned grimly to face it, his belt fang in hand. A tree limb lay half in the water nearby; Thorn bent and plucked it up, and when the great claws reached for him, he smashed them away. On the backswing, as the cat surged on, he caught the wood solidly between the cat's jaws. It snarled and shook its head to spit the wood free, and Thorn lunged in to slash at the inside joint of one foreleg and then bury his fang deep in the eye nearest him.

The world exploded in shrieking pain and rage, and a blow that broke something in Thorn's side flung him helplessly away from the stricken deathfangs, away into the rushing waters.

The Fleetfoot youngling flailed away at the waters, twisting in pain but determined to keep hold of his fang until he was scraped along the outside of a bend in the river and was able to slip and stumble into the shallows once more.

Peering upriver through the water running down his face, Thorn saw the great cat buck and writhe, raking the mud and the rocks around it in its pain. It was a long time before its rage subsided into snarls and it found the riverbank—the far bank, thank Altos—and bounded away. Thorn let out his breath in a rush and discovered two things: that doing so brought a fresh stabbing of hot pain in his ribs, and that he was shaking from head to foot like a leaf dancing in a gale. He sat down suddenly on a rock and never knew when the night claimed him.

The sun rose over the plains beyond the peak and fell across the faces of the sleeping Fallingstar women. They came awake quickly, stiff and aching, and sat up feeling for their weapons. But in all the bright morning, nothing offered menace. Duara and Shal looked at each other—and then at the pale, bloodstained Shavvara lying between them—and tried to smile at each other. Then they rose in silent accord, hauled Shavvara—who half roused to stumble along between them mumbling to folk and things that she must be seeing in dreams—upright, and began the hard climb up along the edge of the gorge to the place from which the river spilled. They'd slept only a few paces below the high rock where the death-fangs had found the warrior, but they had found no traces of man or beast on the curving stone as they passed.

All morning they climbed beside the falling water while feathered ones whirred and called around them and the day grew warm and bright, as if Altos was pleased with all things.

And then at last came the moment when there were no more rocks to climb, and they stood at the edge of a broad, beautiful valley where dew made the leaves of the trees shine, and the river wound laughing through a lush sweep of vines and ferns and as many longbarks and olbols as at the heart of Araunra.

Shal laughed aloud in delight. "The safe place, just as you said!" she cried. "Your safe place, Duara!"

But Duara let go of Shavvara, who sagged against Shal, and took three quick strides into the creeper leaves and then stood still, staring—and as if by magic, the bone sword was in her hand. She was staring down at something that wound among the vines.

"What is it?" Shal called softly, knowing that something was wrong by the set of her friend's shoulders. "What can you see?"

Duara pointed, mutely, and Shal stumbled ahead with Shavvara leaning on her shoulder until she could see it, too: a trail. Someone else had found the safe place first. Duara looked slowly around at the trees, feeling the sudden, cold weight of watching, unfriendly eyes.

The cold water lapping at his ankles and the warm sun on his face roused Thorn, and he looked around in wondering pleasure before remembering how he'd come to be here and feeling for the fang he'd thrust into his belt the night before. It was there. He looked grimly up at the thick brush on the riverbank above him, and then began to climb. It was a long way up to the top of the river, and the deathfangs could be lurking anywhere.

"These deaths were . . . not long ago," Duara said grimly, rising from the gnawed bones of a man who'd stood a head taller than she before something had torn him apart.

It was the third eaten human they'd found along the trail as they followed it into the heart of the safe place. Shal was clutching her axe and looking uneasily at the trees around them.

Duara watched her grimly, knowing just how she felt. The chuckling waters were never far away as they'd walked, and the valley was even more beautiful than Duara had hoped. But death could be lurking anywhere, and the name she'd called it by for so long was a mockery.

"Enough," she said suddenly, rising and hefting the bone sword in her hand. "Enough skulking and fear and creeping about waiting to be eaten! If you're here, let there be war between us! By all-holy Altos, *attack*!"

Her words had risen into a shout that rang back at her off the trees around, and she had one glimpse of Shal's startled, frightened face before something exploded out of the trees to her left.

Duara spun to face it, holding the sword out before her, and the deathfangs crashed into her and flung her sprawling, the blade spinning from her hand. She came to a dazed stop against a tree, with a roar ringing in her ears. The cat had twisted aside from the sword's edge in midair to avoid being impaled, and so she still lived, but . . .

She looked wildly around for her weapon, clutching at her belt for her puny sharpstone—and saw the cat loping through the brush toward her, head down, coming for the kill.

And then Shal ran in from one side, shouting and slashing at it with her axe. The cat snarled once but ignored her, coming for Duara with death glimmering in its eyes . . . No; in one eye, Duara noticed as she darted toward where she thought the bone sword might lie. The other was milk white and blind.

As blind as she'd been, her blade was right *here*! She snatched it up and without pause dove headlong away from the claws that were reaching for her. A snarl of rage rang in her ears as she rolled to her feet to face the deathfangs. It had turned with awesome speed and was bounding toward her. Duara waited for it to spring, and when it was in the air, she ducked behind a tree, leaving the edge of her blade behind for it to feel as it stormed past.

The bone sword cut a ribbon of blood down the cat's flank, and it roared again and twisted, trying to snap at her, though its own charge had carried it well past her. Duara set herself to meet its next charge and swallowed as she saw it turn in frustration, rake Shavvara open into bloody ruin with one swipe of its cruel claws, and then start back toward her.

*It is playing with us,* she thought angrily, and swung the bone sword to loosen her arm as the deathfangs rushed to meet her.

It sprang high this time, rearing up in front of her to bat the blade aside with one paw and tear her open with the other. It might have been successful if Shal's axe hadn't struck the side of its head with savage force, with all the strength of her own hurtling body behind it.

The cat snarled and spat as it went over on its side, rolling with Shal and snapping at her. Duara leapt after them both with desperate speed, determined not to see her friend slain before her eyes, and stabbed down at the sleek musky hide again and again, trying to make the beast turn away from the bleeding thing in its paws. Shal screamed again and again as the weight of the great cat rolled over her. When it sprang up, she half rose in the trampled leaves—and then fell back and lay still.

Rage and grief rose to choke Duara once more as she faced the deathfangs, close enough to breathe each other's air, the woman and the cat. And then it sprang, and all her dreams of a safe place and a happy life there were whirled away in an instant as she stabbed and stabbed again, feeling her blade bite deep. And then one paw smote her arm a numbing blow, and her fingers were open, and the sword was *gone*!

Duara stared helplessly at those gleaming fangs as the cat slapped her back into the dirt and then strode up her body, raking her mercilessly with stone-hard claws. She screamed as the burning pain blossomed in her savaged midriff. Then those paws bore down on her arms and shoulders, pinning her into the damp earth, and the cat smiled at her, slow and triumphant, as its fangs dipped to her defenseless throat.

And then there was a rustle of leaves and a flash as the bone sword thrust deep into the deathfang's remaining eye—in to its hilt—and was held there by a man almost as scratched and torn as she was, as the cat spasmed and sprang away, trembling from fangs to tail, twisted once, and then fell on its side, twisted, and died.

She knew this man, Duara realized slowly, as she lay on her back wet with her own blood, too weak to move. A bright-eyed youngling of the Fleetfoot, not yet a warrior. A handsome one that she'd looked over once or twice across the fires. He was looking down at her now, the bone sword in his hand, red with blood. Duara tossed her head, shuddering at the pain the movement brought. She knew what she had to do.

"My life is yours," she said formally, but the words turned into a gasp of pain. By Fleetfoot law, a warrior who saved the life of an uncloaked she could claim her as his mate—and whatever his standing in the eyes of the elders, any man who slew a deathfangs had to be fairly counted a full warrior.

The dark-haired man knelt and clasped her hand. "Let us walk together, then," he said softly, giving the formal response of one who intends to wed. Then he lifted his head to look around. "Are you the last?"

"Aye," she told him bitterly, remembering Shal's laughter, and Aereth teasing Bhiilu, and Ildra's skillful backrubs. "My dreams brought only death to the others." She tried to lift herself on one elbow and could not. "What are you called, and how came you here?" she asked, through teeth clenched in pain.

"Thorn, I am, and Stoneskull sent me," the man

told her slowly. "To prove myself as a warrior, I am . . . was . . . to bring you . . . all of you . . . back."

"And will you?"

Thorn hesitated and then growled deep in his throat, much like the deathfangs had done, and looked down at her, his eyes bright. "I have seen your wisdom at work, Duara," he said slowly, "and now I have seen your safe place. I would wrap you in my cloak and dwell with you here. I'd rather have you lead me than Stoneskull."

And he put the bone sword into her hand. "Teach me to dream," he said softly.

Duara smiled up at him then, through her pain, and said softly, "I dream of a new tribe in the Staglands—a tribe whose home is the safe place, and whose revered old ones are Thorn and Duara."

Thorn's embrace was gentle, yet firm. "I would learn to share your dreams," he said, "elder of the Fallingstar Tribe. Lead me, Elder."

Duara shook her head. "We will stand together, as equals."

He smiled. "You can't even stand by yourself!"

Duara glared at him and tried to push herself up but fell back, shaking, at the pain. And then she stiffened as she heard a moan that was not her own.

Shal! Shal lived! "Go to her," she snapped, clutching at Thorn's arm. He grinned down at her as he rose and spread his hands. "See?" he said, delight in his tone. "Lead me, Elder!"

Duara fell back and stared at the sky with his laughter bubbling in her ears, and then her own laughter joined his, laced with tears, before the warm, waiting darkness claimed her.

She fell asleep murmuring, "Not much of a safe place, friends, but we will make it serve."

His laughter became a cloak around her as it swept her down to the place where there was no pain, and the bone sword blazed.

# The Ultimate Weapon

## Christie Golden

*T*here it was, glinting in the sunlight, and the Godtalker's heart lifted at the sight. The Sacred Pool, the means by which great Altos made His wishes known to His priests. Like all members of the One Tribe, Khamil Arc had heard of it; unlike the others, he had even been granted a vision of Altos as part of his initiation ceremony. But he had never before been called to witness a revelatory vision in its cool depths.

Hardly breathing, he stepped cautiously closer, reverently laying aside his weapons before he knelt on the soft grass beside the pool. Sunlight sparkled on its shiny surface, making the young Godtalker's eyes water, but he did not look away as he rummaged through his pouch for the calling stone. This stone looked much like any other that sat at the bottom of a lake or river. It was gray brown, smooth to the touch, and fit easily into the palm of an adult with a comfortable, pleasant balance.

But the calling stone created the ripples that formed themselves into the visions by which the god spoke with his people. No other stone would create such a doorway between one world and the next.

The tall, slim Khamil rubbed the stone with his thumb as it rested in his palm, and he began to sing. He closed his eyes, let the song fill him, and at the precise moment, as his dream had instructed him, he flung the calling stone into the air as high as he could, perched on the bank, and waited.

It seemed to take forever to fall into the pool, with a loud *plunk* and splash. Quickly Khamil blinked the blessed water from his eyes, straining to see what the ripples from the stone would have to tell him.

They spread out swiftly, then more lazily, and suddenly before Khamil's eager eyes they became not ripples in a disturbed lake but shapes and images.

The circle elongated, becoming more oval than circle, and the clear liquid turned yellow white. Khamil realized he was looking at an egg. More shapes appeared as the vision solidified. The egg was alone in a nest of soft earth, surrounded by what looked like a wall of green. A pair of hands entered the picture, then Khamil was looking at himself. By the size of the egg, he realized that the Godtalker in the vision cradled not an innocent bird egg, but the egg of one of the dreaded saurans!

*To what purpose?* he wondered, but did not speak. All would be made clear, he was certain.

The vision expanded, and Khamil saw himself walking toward Eom, chieftain of the One Tribe, and presenting the large egg as a gift. Khamil nodded, a lock of ebony hair falling across his forehead for an instant before he absently wiped it away.

*Clearly, a ritual slaying,* he thought.

But then Eom did something unexpected. After listening to something Khamil said, he nodded, then took the egg into his own dwelling, placing it near the fire but not in it. The egg hatched, and the ugly, mottled thing that emerged was greeted with affection, not anger and murder.

Khamil was utterly baffled. Was Altos really instructing his Godtalker to take in a *sauran*?

Then the vision began to speed up. Before his eyes, Khamil watched the sauran grow to adulthood, loved by his "family," initiated into the tribal mysteries—in all ways treated like a human. Then suddenly the scene shifted, to the young sauran in the midst of a sauran encampment, treated now like one of them. Khamil blinked but continued to watch. The scene shifted again, to a ferocious battle in which the saurans fell, like leaves when the cold time came, before the might of the One Tribe. From the carnage, the young sauran emerged and was made welcome.

The vision faded, and Khamil was left staring only at what seemed to be an ordinary mountain pool.

He sat back, trying to make sense of what had been revealed to him. Then comprehension dawned, and a smile split his face. Of course! Oh, Altos was wise indeed! What better way to learn about the saurans' weaknesses than to have one of their own betray them? What better tool—what better weapon—could there be, than a human-loving sauran!

He laughed as he shed his clothes and dove into the clear pool to search for the calling stone. It took several dives, and he surfaced with many false rocks. But finally, when his hand closed on a certain stone that tingled in his fingers, Khamil shot to the surface, his mind already on when he would make the trip to find a sauran egg.

He would return with what looked like a simple egg, but would actually be the ultimate weapon.

\* \* \*

Umala fidgeted, played with her unfamiliar and uncomfortable clothes, and blew noisily through her mouth. Her mother shushed her, but the effect was only temporary. The six-year-old shifted her weight in the cramped, formal boots and began again to pluck at the confining head-to-toe garb.

She was the daughter of the tribal leader Eom, and since the ritual that was about to be enacted involved the family, the little girl was forced to stand beside her father and mother as the Godtalker brought her new little brother or sister.

Umala watched, bored to death by the whole thing, as Godtalker Khamil Arc—a man who never *would* let her play with the pretty baubles he wore—now marched up toward her father Eom. Eom was decked out in full ritual regalia. He and his mate Sharin wore not the simple, functional clothing of day-to-day life, but the white leather, bleached with animal urine, that had been beaded and decorated over many long moons. Feathers, bits of bone, horn—all weighed down the head family of the One Tribe. And Umala didn't like it, not one bit.

Khamil Arc knelt before Eom. He carried a bundle wrapped protectively in warm furs. "From the farthest southern jungles, I have returned," he intoned. "I bring you the ultimate weapon of the People of Altos, the certain triumph over the dreadful saurans, the . . ."

Umala ignored him as he droned on; ignored her father the same way when he began to reply. She'd managed to work an ursu claw loose from her leggings and now held the huge, hooked claw in her small, brown hands. She was just about to put it in her mouth to nibble on in the absence of something better to eat when her parents, holding the bundle carefully between them, turned and presented it to her.

"Umala, meet your hearthsibling, Lasaric," they said together. Blushing, Umala dropped the claw as surreptitiously as she could and reached to touch the bundle. Under her questing hand, a corner of the furs flopped open. She was staring at a large, smooth egg.

Her thin, brown brows drew together in annoyance. "You can't fool me," she retorted. "Babies come from Mama's stomach! That's just an egg!"

Umala's statement caused ripples of laughter to run through the assembled tribe. Even more annoyed—Umala couldn't stand it when people laughed at her—the chieftain's daughter replied in a louder voice, "Well, it *is*!"

"Of course it is, Umala," the Godtalker soothed in his condescending voice. "But it is your new hearthsibling, too. This is the egg of a sauran—a kind sauran," he hastened to add as he saw her green eyes widen in horror. "He will be your friend. He will be a friend to all the tribe."

At that moment a tiny noise distracted Umala. A quiet sound, barely heard over Khamil's voice and the shifting, coughing sounds of the hundreds of people standing in attendance. It was a soft little *crack*, and Umala glanced down.

And gasped.

There was a thin, dark line marring the surface of the ivory-colored shell. As Umala watched, a small piece broke loose, fell to the grassy earth.

"It's hatching!" she yelped.

Umala was almost knocked over in the ensuing rush. Khamil cried, "To the hearth! It must be kept warm or it will die!" and "It must see the family when it hatches, to bond with you!"

The strange egg was whisked away from Umala's sight, and the little girl found herself staring at backsides and waists of her fellow tribesfolk. She felt trapped, closed in on, and began to fight her way to breathing space much as her "hearthsibling" was fighting its own way out of its shell.

At last she shoved her way out, stumbling forward and almost tripping on the pile of furs beside the hearth fire. Her mother shot her an angry look.

"Watch where you step, clumsy!" she scolded. "You almost stepped on the sauran!"

Mortified, Umala hung her head. "I'm sorry, I'm—" and then she stopped in midsentence, wonder stealing her words.

The crack had widened now, and a tiny arm, clawed and fragile, only about the length of Umala's shortest finger, reached out. It closed on air. Without thinking, Umala knelt down on the furs and extended her own hand. The little clawed hand brushed her palm, fastened onto her finger.

The sauran's head pushed through the hole. It was a tiny, perfect miniature of an adult's head, save it had no teeth and the slitted eyes held no expression of malice. Umala saw confusion there as the creature—no, her hearthsibling—blinked, trying to clear mucus and other fluids from its vision.

Dimly, Umala heard murmurs behind her.

*"It's so small!"*

*"So ugly, just like all its kind."*

*"I say we kill the cursed thing now. It's stupid to imagine this would be our friend."*

*"Remember the howlbeasts? They go hunting with us now and lie at our hearths."*

She ignored them. She watched as her hearthsibling's tiny chest hitched as it took its first breath then turned its wondering gaze toward her.

Her heart skipped a beat, and a smile of awe and love touched her lips.

It was a sauran. It was a totally alien creature, from a race of beings that, it seemed, lived only to murder humans. But this small, fragile thing had hurt no one, had looked at them and seen only friends.

"Hello, Lasaric," Umala said softly. "Oh, hello, my hearthsibling."

Lasaric stared at her for a moment, then his mouth opened and a soft, mewling cry escaped.

From that moment, Umala and Lasaric were as bonded as two hearthsiblings could be. It was she who carried him in a special sack next to her skin, so that he would never take a chill. And, she admitted to herself, so that she could feel his tiny little heart thumping as rapidly as that of a longear's next to hers. When, at the end of the summer, Aussasaur streaked across the skies, burning what was left of the crops, it was Umala who punched any playmates who blamed Lasaric for the stellar curse. And throughout the long, dark winter that followed the comet's autumn appearance, it was Umala who kept Lasaric warm, wrapping him in furs and warming him with her own body's heat at night while he slept like a dead thing.

He grew faster than a human, and by the next time Aussasaur burned its cruel way past Tethedril, bringing its heat that so invigorated little Lasaric's kind, the young sauran was able to communicate.

"Umala, why do I look so ugly?"

"You're not ugly, Lasaric. You're different, that's all. But you are still a member of the One Tribe."

"Why am I different?"

"Because you're a sauran."

"Why?"

"Because you're not a human."

"Then why am I here, and not with the saurans?"

"Because we adopted you."

"Why?"

"Because Khamil Arc told us to."

"Why?"

Umala once complained to her mother about her hearthbrother's seemingly unbounded curiosity. Sharin had merely stared, then convulsed with laughter. Umala tried to wait it out, but every time Sharin seemed to calm down, she would look over at her daughter and begin to laugh again. Finally, Sharin gasped, "A little of your own medicine, hearthdaughter!" and would say no more.

Though the Godtalker repeatedly urged the tribe members to welcome Lasaric openly, acceptance was a long time coming. But he was a good-natured, open creature and, except for the fact that cooked meat seemed to make him ill, he behaved as those around him behaved.

The years passed. Umala grew into a tall, strong, lovely young woman, with her mother's beauty and her father's level head. From some distant ancestor, though, she seemed to have inherited a quick temper and sharp tongue. Her friends—those who accepted and played with Lasaric—knew she would die for them. But those who denied her hearthbrother his proper place in the tribe, by look or gesture or muttered insult, Umala shunned. These, fortunately, grew fewer over the years.

Six years after Khamil Arc saw the vision that would lead to the adoption of Lasaric, the One Tribe's affection to the strangest member of their number was put to its most demanding test.

The assault was complete unexpected. The tribe knew to beware during the spring and fall, when Aussasaur's heat often stirred the blood of Her children, bringing them north to wage war against the children of Altos. But winter was always a safe time, and rarely had the saurans attacked in summer.

Umala, Eom, and three other tribesmen were returning victorious from the hunt. The faithful, sharp-nosed howl-beasts that hunted with the tribe had managed to flush an unwary cloven. The strong bowing poles had launched their deadly, barbed missiles, and the cloven, with a faint bleat and rolling of its large, brown eyes, had tumbled to the earth. Now it was strung on a stick, its striped brown-and-black body limp, its graceful neck lolling. It would provide a good meal for the tribe tonight.

Eom did not see the threat until they were almost at the campsite. He paused, shielding his eyes from the sun to get a better view—to confirm his deepest fears. Then he cried, "Sauran attack!" and dropped his end of the pole. The fat cloven lay where it had fallen, forgotten. The howlbeasts, their noses scenting prey, gave voice and charged ahead of their human masters, their short brown fur on end, their sharp ears flattened and equally sharp teeth bared.

Umala's heart leapt into her mouth. Even as her strong, long legs sprinted easily to keep pace with the other hunters, she knew shame. Their concern was for their tribe—their people, their way of life. Her one, over-whelming anxiety, riding her like a burr rides a cloven, was for Lasaric. What would the saurans do to him? He was none of their kind, for all his cold blood and slitted eyes and scales. He was her hearthbrother, and as human in his spirit as . . . as Khamil Arc!

She whispered a soft prayer to Altos to protect His weapon—her brother, the dearest person in the world to her.

It would seem Altos was in a benevolent mood that day, for even as the little band of hunters charged onto the camping grounds, they could see that the group of saurans was small and already defeated. Two lay dead, their heads bashed in by solid blows from equally solid clobbers. The remaining, a pitiful six, had taken flight. Only one human had been hurt, a young man named Kathin who had been lavishing unwanted attentions on Umala. Still, she was sorry that he had been wounded. Khamil Arc was already there, chanting over the youth's bloody arm.

"What happened?" Eom demanded as they rushed up.

Sharin ran to him, embraced him quickly, then replied. "Eight saurans. They came from across the Silver River."

"Weapons?"

"Spears, whipcords mostly. They seemed very disorganized."

"Probably just a wandering group of raiders," commented Eom. Such were not unheard of in recent years, at least not during the times of the comet. This was the first a raider band had attacked outside of that limited time frame, though. "No poison?"

Sharin shook her head, and everyone breathed a sigh of relief. The dreadful poison with which some of the saurans tipped their spears and darts was their most powerful—and deadly—weapon.

Beside her father, young Umala had been fairly jumping up and down with anxiety. Now she burst out, "Where is Lasaric?"

Kathin overheard her query, and pain made his tongue sharp. "Your cowardly lizard brother hides in the shelter with the children," he spat, his blue eyes angry. "You will find the sauran there, shaking and shivering!"

A hot retort burned in Umala's mouth, but before she could utter it, she received help from an unexpected source—Khamil Arc.

"I told Lasaric to hide himself," the Godtalker chided Kathin. "He is no good to us at all if word of his presence spreads among the saurans. They will mistrust him when he comes among them to steal their secrets, and his usefulness will be lost."

Kathin nodded his understanding, but a second type of anger swelled and burst in Umala's heart. "He is nothing to you but a weapon, a means by which to destroy the saurans! Doesn't anybody care about Lasaric for who he *is* besides me?"

Tears of rage clouded her vision. Without another word, ignoring her father's attempt to soothe her with his calming voice, she fled and ran into the shelter.

She found him cowering beneath the furs, his whole body trembling. Gently, Umala pulled back one of the concealing hides. With a little cawing sound, Lasaric drew away until he saw her face. Then he launched himself into her arms.

"They were dreadful!" he whimpered. Umala hugged him tightly. "So ugly, so cruel . . . and I am one of them!" The thought clearly appalled him.

Umala hugged his slim, sleek body tightly. "No," she

soothed. "You're one of *us*, Lasaric. And you always will be."

"They looked at me—Kathin and the others did—as if I would desert them, run to be with the ... sssssssss-sauransssss!" The hated word emerged as an angry hiss. Lasaric's speech deteriorated when he became emotional. "Umala, I would never betray you—never!"

"I know you wouldn't," she soothed. "I know. And soon, you'll get a chance to prove it."

"That moment may come sooner than you think," a male voice interrupted. The hearthsiblings both gasped, startled, and looked up to see Khamil Arc standing in the doorway. The light behind him cast his shadow on the floor in front of him, a shadow that was long and seemed very dark indeed to Umala. "You are both to come with me. I have had a dream, and we must—all three of us—visit the Sacred Pool."

Fear and excitement surged through Umala. Usually, the only one to ever glimpse the Sacred Pool was the Godtalker and his successor. Ordinary people never even saw the pool, much less saw visions in its depths. But then, as she felt Lasaric's frightened shivering start to abate within the warm, comforting circle of her arms, she knew that they were not ordinary people.

"Get what you need to climb Godtalker Mountain," Khamil Arc instructed, "and come with me."

The climb took a full seven sunrises. Umala had no trouble keeping up with Khamil Arc; she was in the prime of her youth, had been athletic all her life, and had energy to spare. During the warm daylight hours Lasaric, too, was able to keep pace. In fact, his reptilian body and clever three-toed appendages enabled him to climb even faster than the humans. But when the sun sank behind the gentle, rolling hills of the west, Lasaric's body temperature dropped with it. He began to grow cold and sluggish, his pace slowing until they were forced to camp. He would eat their evening meal, then fall fast asleep until dawn came to warm him again.

At last they reached the little plateau, where the winds and sun had been merciful and carried tiny seeds to take root. There was grass here as well as moss, earth as well as stone. And here, most magical of all, was the Sacred Pool.

Umala and Lasaric were silent, though they automatically reached for each other's hands as the Godtalker began his musical invocation. Khamil Arc waved them forward, indicating that they should kneel beside the pool, and they obeyed.

The Godtalker's song reached a crescendo, and he hurled a fist-sized stone high up into the air. It fell into the pool with a splash, and the three—holy man, chieftain's daughter, and child of the enemy—stared, fascinated, as the ripples twisted and turned into comprehensible shapes.

Lasaric's heart slammed against his ribcage as he watched the scene unfold. He knew he was witnessing the mighty battle between Altos and Aussasaurian, as the powerful human struggled to escape the coils of the mammoth, copper-colored serpent. Altos' face was noble, handsome, determined; the snake with which he battled hissed and spat, twisted, crushed. Yet She, too, was lovely in a primal sort of way.

The scene dissolved. Suddenly Lasaric saw himself, bleeding from an injury clearly delivered by a powerful blow from a clobber. The rough scratches along his side could have come from no other weapon. He frowned as he watched. Who had injured him? Why? As far as he knew, the members of the One Tribe were the only ones who used that particular weapon.

He saw himself being welcomed by other saurans, and he shuddered at the sight. Surely, he was playing his part—being the ultimate weapon, as he had been hatched to be; infiltrating the dreadful enemy, ferreting out their secrets.

But . . .

He did not seem to be working under a false mask of camaraderie in the vision. Lasaric watched himself in the pool, saw genuine concern for the saurans on his ugly, so-familiar features. And then the scene shifted, and he watched with horror as he sprang at Umala, his hearth-sister, the dearest person to him in the world, and clawed savagely at her beautiful, beloved face.

Then the image was gone.

Lasaric heard his companions sink back on their haunches, but he continued to stare at the pool—though now it only reflected the bright blue sky and clouds sailing overhead. The pool never lied. He knew that. Slowly, he turned to face Umala.

She was smiling, and reached a loving hand to brush his shoulder. "I saw you succeed!" she cried happily. "I saw them take you to them, as if you were really one of them! I saw you giving me their secrets!" She turned her radiant face on the Godtalker. "Honored Khamil Arc," she said with a solemnity that Lasaric had never heard from her, "I confess that I doubted the wisdom of your vision. I thought we were sending my hearthbrother to his death. Now, I know that you saw truly. We will succeed!"

Khamil Arc permitted himself a thin, supercilious smile. "Yes, I knew of your doubt. But now the pool has allayed any fears, hasn't it, child?" She nodded eagerly.

"And what of you, Lasaric?" the Godtalker queried. "What did you witness in the Sacred Pool?"

Lasaric's mouth was dry. His flickering, pointed black tongue cleaved to his throat. Then he found the words.

"I saw the first great battle between Altos and Aussasaurian," he said. That much at least was true. "I suspect it was because I am both tribe member and sauran." He waited, his heart racing, praying to—to whom?—that they would pry no further. He could tell a partial truth to his priest and his sister. He could not tell an out-and-out lie.

But they were nodding, satisfied. Not even Umala noticed his discomfiture. Lasaric was confused. The pool never lied. Then how could it reveal such different visions? Which was the real truth—the actual future?

Lasaric shivered, and not just with cold. The sun was setting, and the Sacred Pool began to turn crimson and purple with its colors. They camped that night not far from it, and Lasaric was haunted with nightmares in which he repeatedly murdered his dear Umala.

The wound inflicted by the clobber blow ached with inflammation. It had crusted over with the passing of three days, but Lasaric had not tended it. The idea had been to make the wound even more convincing, but now he wished he had done something. The poison of infection had seeped into his bones and was now beginning to affect his mind as well.

He had left three days ago, to a hero's send-off peculiarly combined with a clobber blow. Alone, his side aching, he headed due south, following the sun and never wavering. He drank where he could, but spared no time for hunting food. And, of course, he carried nothing human-made.

The blazing heat and increased moisture in the air felt good to the young sauran. If only he were not feeling so weak, so ill, he might even be enjoying this part of his mission. But it was all he could do, as the hours wore on, to put one clawed foot in front of the other.

He began to have waking dreams, dreams in which Umala was walking beside him, alternately chatting happily or weeping with fear. Of course, he knew that Umala was shadowing him, keeping well out of sight—such had been the plan—but she was certainly not beside him.

Lasaric, moving like a thing constructed and not birthed, shuffled on. Altos and Aussasaurian Themselves now fell into step beside him, one on his left, one on his right. They were squabbling as easily, as comfortably, as Eom and Sharin did, completely ignoring Lasaric. He was confused. He had thought them violent enemies, not quarrelsome siblings.

And when the small horde of saurans came out of the green wall of growth almost directly in front of him, Lasaric merely stared, wondering why they didn't interact with their goddess. It was only when the clawed hand closed over his own forearm in a steadying gesture that Lasaric realized that these were no hallucinations, created from infection and lack of food, but real beings. He started, then remembered his purpose and tried to speak. Gibberish flowed from his mouth, the earth rose up to meet him with startling speed, and he knew no more.

\* \* \*

There was softness beneath him. Warmth surrounded him. Cool, gentle hands stroked his brow. Hushed voices whispered concerned words.

For an instant, Lasaric wavered between wakefulness and sleep, content to believe that the whole incident had been nothing but a bad dream, that the softness beneath him was furs, that the cool hands belonged to Umala, that the concerned voices were those of his fellow tribe members.

Then he opened his eyes.

Four saurans, their bodies various combinations of green and blacks and browns, stared down at him with slitted eyes. Their tongues flickered in and out. Lasaric found them hideous to behold. "We thought Aussasaurian had claimed you, stranger," said one sympathetically. "Your wound was very serious. Another day or two without care, and we would have lost you."

The softness beneath him was ferny vegetation, springy and comfortable. He was in no shelter, but lay open to the sun and sky. The sauran who spoke seemed to be in command. His scaly body was mostly green, with only a few dapplings of black. He wore colorful paint and bore jewelry of a sort not dissimilar to that worn by the tribe. A robe of sorts draped his body, and he leaned on a staff carved out of a wood Lasaric had never before seen.

Lasaric knew that the saurans had their own priests, who prayed to and worshiped Aussasaurian as the humans followed Altos. They were called *shamans* and knew the secrets of healing—and killing. He suspected that the dignified individual before him was this group's shaman.

The pain that had raged through him was gone. Only

the ache of injured flesh remained, and that would pass with time. "You . . . healed me," he whispered. His throat was dry. He could not help himself but felt shame as his own black tongue flicked out, scenting those around him.

The shaman gestured, and a gourd of water appeared. Strong, clawed hands helped Lasaric sit up, steadied him as he drank thirstily. The water tasted odd. Did they know what he was? Had they cured him only to watch him die in front of them? Such a thing would not be unheard of, not from the treacherous saurans.

"I have put herbs in the water, to help you regain your strength," the shaman said, answering Lasaric's unasked question. "I am Kullais, the shaman of the Kindred. And you are . . . ?"

"Lasaric," he replied, drinking more of the water that quenched even the deep, inner thirst. Kullais frowned.

"A strange name. I have never heard of it before. Where are you from, friend Lasaric?"

This was it—the most dangerous moment of all. Lasaric said a silent prayer to Altos, that He would protect His weapon, and replied.

"I do not remember," he said haltingly. He gestured to his injury. "The humans . . . I know they attacked, they hurt us . . . but all memories are gone. It is a frightening feeling."

The reptiles that surrounded him nodded their understanding and sympathy. Only Kullais kept watching him, his eyes sharp and alert. "How did you know how to find us?"

This, Lasaric could answer. "I saw a vision of Aussasaurian," he replied. For he had, both in the pool and while he was delirious. "I suppose She must have guided my footsteps, directed me to you. For surely, alone, I would have died. Thank you for your kindness to a stranger."

Kullais' eyes searched Lasaric's, then the old shaman nodded. "I believe you. Welcome to our tribe. Are you hungry? My wives have prepared food for you." He gestured, and six smaller saurans tentatively approached. They each carried crudely fashioned bowls of raw meat. Unbidden, Lasaric's black tongue flicked out. The fragrance made Lasaric's mouth water.

"It smells wonderful." He smiled as he reached for the first bowl, chunks of dark red flesh swimming in herbed blood. He ate, surprised at how hungry he was, how sweet the meat tasted. At least, he mused grimly, he would not starve during his sojourn among the enemy.

Strength seeped back into his body as he ate the healthful raw meat, imbibed the herb-laced water. His mind cleared, and he was better able to be alert for carefully worded traps—and avoid making dangerous mistakes of his own. Lasaric and Kullais talked quietly, Lasaric learning trivialities about day-to-day sauran life that would mean the sun and the moon to his true—though not of the blood—people, until the sun was low on the horizon.

"The golden orb goes to rest," Kullais said, his voice somber. Of course, Lasaric realized. Night was especially dangerous to saurans. Another useful tidbit to report to Umala. "We will bear you to the sleeping place. My own wives," and here the older sauran bowed deeply, clawed hand to his chest, "will keep you warm tonight."

Lasaric was carefully carried a distance away to the mouth of a cave. Others remained behind, gathering up embers from the fire and putting them into earthen pots— pots, Lasaric recognized, that had been stolen from humans. The coals glowed redly. All the saurans headed for the cave, where they curled up in groups of seven or eight, each group clustered around a pot of life-giving warmth.

As he entered the cave, his slitted eyes adjusting to the darkness far better than those of a human, Lasaric got the fright of his young life.

The walls were moving.

He gasped and jerked in startlement, reinjuring his wound so that it throbbed painfully. One of the saurans who bore him followed his gaze.

"Your people must have lived closer to the jungles than we," the sauran commented. "Have you never shared a cave with the warmwings before?"

Lasaric continued to stare, shaking his head in denial. Now that he looked closer, he could see that it was not the wall itself that moved, but rather the thousands of small animals with long, membranous wings that perched upon the surface of the cave walls. "I have never seen these before," he said, then amended hastily, "that my memory recalls."

Lasaric was gently laid down, wrapped in a covering of ferns. The precious pot of embers was placed right next to him—a position that denoted his honored place as an injured stranger, he suspected. The six wives of the shaman curled up beside him, draping him and each other with their bodies. Lasaric felt sleep stealing upon him. "If the warmwings serve such a valuable function," he said to Mila, who lay next to him, "then why don't the s— the Kindred tame other warmbloods to keep them warm? The humans have tamed the howlbeasts, who hunt alongside them."

Mila hissed in surprise and drew away from him. "The

howlbeasts are dreadful—they hurt and tear and feast upon our flesh! *Hssssss* . . . how can you even speak of such a thing?"

Lasaric felt a sudden stab of fear that he had gone too far. "Not the howlbeasts, of course, but perhaps something smaller, something that would not mind sleeping with you, something that you could breed and eat." Even as the words left his lips, he wondered about them. Why was he suggesting this? What did he care about sauran warmth in the darkness? If his mission here was a success, every one of these creatures would die, while his own tribe would know how to defeat the Kindred's dreadful poison. Giving the saurans advice on how to live better and longer was hardly part of the strategy. Yet the suggestion had come, unbidden. And he found he did not wish to retract it.

A chuckle sounded in the darkness. Lasaric recognized the voice as belonging to Kullais. "What a strange one you are to be sure, Lasaric. If you wish to stay with us, I am sure that the Kindred could only benefit from your . . . imagination."

The words were slightly condescending, but there was warmth behind them. Lasaric smiled to himself. "Kullais, I would be honored to stay with the Kindred."

He had gotten in, been accepted, and learned valuable things about the saurans, all within the space of a single day. Surely, Altos must be smiling upon him. Wouldn't Umala be pleased!

A half mile downwind of the sauran encampment, Umala huddled in the safety of the natural shelter she had found. She did not dare light a fire to cook her food or to warm herself. The tribe thought the vision of the saurans weak enough, but their sense of smell was unnaturally sharp. They would scent a fire within minutes.

It had been agony to the young woman to watch her hearthbrother struggling with his pain and sickness from such a distance. She had ached to help him but knew that in order for the daring plan to work, he must appear genuinely wounded and sick. She herself, sobbing, had been the one to strike the blow with the clobber, had watched him walk off, then followed. Umala had been forced to be a silent witness to his pain, had done nothing when the small group of the hated enemy found him, tended him, took him back. She had been fortunate to find this natural shelter of stone and concealing vines, and had made it her camp. It gave her a clear view of the saurans; and Umala had an even clearer connection with her brother.

She carefully unwrapped the bowl given her by Khamil Arc. Closing her eyes, she whispered a prayer to Altos and then poured a small amount of water into the sanctified bowl. This was precious liquid indeed, not for drinking save in a life-or-death situation. For this water was from the Sacred Pool itself, and as she watched, her dark reflection in the bowl shimmered and vanished, to be replaced by an image of Lasaric.

He lay, talking quietly to a decorated sauran who was clearly a being of note among his people. For a moment, Umala was startled to realize that she could understand the saurans. They had wondered if communication would be a problem. Lasaric was clever; he'd have picked up the language and invented some sort of story to explain away his ignorance. Apparently, though, he didn't have to—and the fact that Umala as well could comprehend what was said was an unlooked-for good omen.

She listened as they talked, learned about their cave with the warmwings, and smiled. "Well done, my hearth-brother," she whispered although she knew he could not hear. Already, he had made wonderful progress. She was certain that soon, they would return triumphant to the waiting tribe, bearing with them the seeds of sauran destruction.

She rose, picked up her spear, and went to find food—fruit or vegetables if she could find them, animals if she could not. She was strong; she could eat the meat raw. There was a spring in her step. The night was safe from saurans, at least, and that much, she knew from her clever hearthbrother.

Dreams of the coppery-scaled Aussasaurian haunted Lasaric's sleep at night, and the unexpectedly gentle ministrations of the saurans filled his days. He reasoned, with truth, that it was only because he himself, unfortunately, was a sauran. Had he been a human, these apparently caring beings would have torn him apart. He'd seen them fight. He knew what they were capable of. Whenever he found himself smiling in gratitude at Kullais or his wives, or laughing at the antics of the playful youngsters, he would remember that they were monsters, that they were the enemy—and that he, Lasaric, together with his silent and unseen partner Umala, was born to be a weapon of vengeance.

It was becoming increasingly hard to do.

He concentrated on learning everything he could, knowing that what he saw, Umala saw. She knew now, through him, about some of the sauran vulnerabilities. She knew their numbers. And the more Kullais responded to

Lasaric's seemingly innocent questions, the more the shaman unwittingly damned his own people.

So it went for two weeks. Lasaric kept fearing that somehow the saurans would discover Umala's hiding place, but she remained safe. He wished that he could see her, as she could see him. It would be a comfort—and an increasingly desired beacon, to help him see his way. For despite his better judgment, he was growing to like the saurans. He played a game with himself, just before drifting off to sleep each night. He constructed a scenario where Kullais and Umala sat beside a fire and chatted like friends, while he, Lasaric, watched with delight. Umala listened to the wise words of the sauran, her dark hair glinting in the firelight, her beautiful, human face alight with interest. And in turn, she told exciting and humorous stories to the sometimes too-grim shaman, and Kullais laughed, his mouth open and his tongue lolling as he *hssssssssed* with mirth.

It would be wonderful. Perfect.

It would never happen.

Lasaric healed. He became more and more a member of the Kindred, learning their legends and tales and history. His time for departure, when he would steal both poison and antidote and escape with Umala, back to the tribe, grew nearer. Each night he glanced at the moon before heading into the cave. Finally the night came when it was three-quarters full.

He forced himself to stay awake by sheer will. Fortunately, it was heading into the end of summer; Aussasaur would be coming soon, and the temperature was already starting to rise. Lasaric waited until he felt sure all were asleep, then extricated himself as unobtrusively as possible from the tangle of limbs, tails, and bodies.

He knew where Kullais kept the things most precious to the Kindred: beneath a stone at the foot of a huge, gnarled tree. The scent of poison—of danger, of death—hung about the stash. No animal would venture near. It was safe enough, Kullais had thought.

*Safe from everyone except the ultimate weapon,* Lasaric thought to himself. For the first time since he had been old enough to understand the word, the thought of himself as a weapon gave him no joy.

Quietly, his senses alert for danger, either from an awakened sauran or jungle creature, Lasaric heaved the stone aside. There they were, in stolen jars that were identical save for the telltale color. The blue jars—earthenware stained with blue pigment—housed the counterpoison, a carefully mixed combination of deadly taiperserpent venom and other essences distilled from plants. The black jars contained the milky secretions of pure venom.

Lasaric swallowed, glancing back at the cave entrance. He could return to the cave now without anyone knowing. He could leave the poison and counterpoison untouched. If humans had this deadly advantage, they would wipe out the Kindred.

*But if the Kindred are permitted to keep it,* wailed Lasaric to himself, *they will wipe out the tribe!*

Indecision gripped him, rendered him paralyzed. What to do? Who were his true people—humans or saurans? Was he One Tribe, or Kindred?

"Who am I?" he asked softly, staring at the little jars of death and life.

"You are Lasaric, of the One Tribe—and hearthbrother to Umala," came a soft voice.

Lasaric knew the voice but jumped all the same.

"Umala!" he gasped. "What are you doing here? I was supposed to come to you. It's dangerous for you here!"

"The saurans sleep in the cave." She laughed softly, staring down at him in the moonlight. "I have watched them slumber for many days now. Only you and I are awake here—you, and I, and the jaguar," she amended, glancing about. "Come, Lasaric." She knelt down beside him, then impulsively reached to hug him. "I have missed you—but I am so proud of you! You fooled them completely, just as it was prophesied!"

But Lasaric was stiff in her warm-blooded embrace. Her words brought back his own vision. He saw again the genuine concern for the Kindred—the saurans. And worst of all, he saw himself leaping at Umala, ripping her pretty face to bloody ribbons. He shuddered at the recollection. The first vision had come true—would the second?

"Lasaric," Umala said. "What is wrong?"

Desperately, he stared at her. "Umala, my time here among the Kindred has taught me much about them."

She nodded, her dark curls bouncing with the gesture. "Of course. You've learned their weaknesses."

"No, no, I . . . How can I explain?" He, too, sat down, leaning back on his reptilian hind legs. "They are not a faceless, hated name. They are people, just like the tribe."

"How can you say that?" she asked, shocked. "You've seen what they do to us!" Hurt and confusion sat on her face.

Lasaric buried his face—his ugly, sauran face—in his clawed hands. "I know, I know, but . . ."

He made his choice. Taking a deep breath, he picked

up the blue jars. "Here," he said, placing them in her sack. "Take these. This is the counterpoison."

Umala started to smile. "I knew you would not fail me, hearthbro—"

"And these are the jars of poison," he interrupted. He could not permit her to say the word. If she did, he would not be able to resist her. "But I cannot let you take them." He moved to replace the stone.

"But we decided!" yelped the girl. Her voice rose with her anxiety, carrying in the clear night air. "We needed the poison to destroy the saurans!"

"We are not going to destroy the saurans!" hissed Lasaric. "Umala, I love you. I love the tribe. I cannot sit by and let the Kindred decimate the people who cared so much for me. But the saurans—they don't deserve death, either. Not all of them—not for no reason other than their appearance. I cannot give the means for their destruction into the hands of their enemy. Please, go. Take the counterpoison, and leave me with my people!"

Even in the dim light of the moon, Lasaric saw Umala grow pale. "No," she whispered. Then, louder and with increasing volume, "No, they've turned you against us! No, I won't let them!"

Out of the corner of his eye, Lasaric saw movement. Someone, awakened by Umala's frantic denials, had emerged from the cave. Lasaric knew what he had to do.

Hissing furiously, he gathered himself, then, propelled by his powerful lizardlike back legs, he launched himself at Umala. His right forearm lifted, descended. Sharp claws bit and tore the soft, yielding, human flesh of Umala's left cheek. He missed puncturing her eye by only the barest margin.

Umala's scream of betrayal, fear, and pain slashed the

night's silence as her hearthbrother's claws had slashed her face. Lasaric's heart ached for her, for the lost beauty and deep trust that he himself had utterly destroyed.

"Go!" he hissed, his sharp ears hearing the Kindred cry their concern. "I will keep them away from you, but go now!"

With a last, horrified look that Lasaric knew he would remember until his dying day, Umala fled into the darkness.

"This way!" Lasaric shrieked, taking the Kindred who were now catching up to him off in a totally different direction than that in which Umala had gone. They had seen him attack her. They had seen him fighting alone, to protect the Kindred's possessions. They had no reason to mistrust him, and they followed at once. Again, Lasaric's heart ached, for he was now betraying them, as he had moments ago betrayed the person he loved best in the world. But he knew this was the right course.

After a short time, it became clear they had lost the dreaded human's trail. Defeated and panting, unused to expending so much energy on a comparatively chilly night, Lasaric and the Kindred returned to their campsite.

They found Kullais sitting at the foot of the old tree. "What is missing, shaman?" someone asked.

"The counterpoison is gone," the sauran mourned. Murmurs of regret rippled through the group. "The human must have been watching, waiting to steal it. I find it odd, though," and now he turned to look directly at Lasaric, "that she did not take the poison—something that would avail the humans much more, in the end."

Lasaric met the shaman's slit-eyed gaze steadily. "I'm sure she intended to," he replied. "But I heard the noise she made and interrupted her."

For a long, long moment, Kullais held Lasaric's gaze. Suddenly he smiled, and Lasaric went cold inside. *He knows,* he thought. *Altos and Aussasaurian save me, he knows!*

"Then it is indeed fortunate that you have come among us . . . to *stay*," Kullais said, putting emphasis on the last word. "Isn't it, Lasaric?"

A heavy burden fell away from the sauran's heart. Yes, Kullais knew. He knew everything—and understood everything. And he was going to keep the secret. Lasaric was Kindred now.

"Yes, Kullais," the being who had been born to be the ultimate weapon said in a humble voice. "I am glad I am here . . . to stay."

# *Blood of the Lamb*

## Mary H. Herbert

*H*e was trapped—as surely and irrevocably as a buffalo driven to the edge of a precipice. He could not move forward or he would plunge off the headland into the turbulent surf so far below. He looked left and right, but he knew there was no help there. He was on the center point of a three-pronged peninsula that stretched out into the great bay like an eagle's talon, and there was nothing to either side but cliffs, partially submerged rocks, and deep water.

The man slowly straightened to his full height and thrust back his shoulders. For a moment his clear gold eyes stared north to the smoky line on the horizon that divided the sea and the sky. That pale insignificant line was Tharos, a rolling land of meadows and woods his people had once called home. There had been a time when the man prayed to the god Altos to guide him home, but he realized now his prayers had been answered a different way.

He heard a sound behind—a distant, roaring, hissing cry of triumph—and he turned on his heels to face his hunters. They came bounding up the slope toward him, their mottled green and yellow skins glowing in the light and the heat of the afternoon. Their forked tongues flicked in his direction.

The man swallowed hard. By Altos, he hated saurans! Vicious, ugly, cunning lizards! They were slender and short and quick as whips, and their malice had killed over half of his people. His hand crept to the sheath of his precious bronze sword and stayed there, more for comfort than any idea of defending himself. He had left his sword in a safe place, knowing there was little chance of fighting these heavily armed hunters. Nor was there really any point. This time, at least for now, they wanted him alive.

Hissing and cackling with pleasure, the saurans charged toward the man. Perhaps twenty paces away, they halted and raised slender blow tubes to their mouths. The man made no attempt to dodge the stinging darts that flew at him. Three of the thorn-sharp points found their target in the man's shoulder, chest, and thigh, and their sedative flowed into his blood like a hot, melting tide.

The man felt his limbs go numb. With his last strength, he fought to stay upright long enough to turn his back on the saurans and look again at the distant rim of the bay where the shores of Tharos hung between water and sky. Then his muscles failed him, and he collapsed to the rocky ground. His thoughts passed into silence as the brilliant daylight mercifully faded to darkness.

Across a wide inlet on the northernmost claw of the peninsula, Caerleon shaded his eyes with a hand and looked north as well. He was a young man, barely into his twenties, thin and sinewy, with fair hair bleached by the sun, and eyes of stormy gray. Although he knew the landscape and the water that surrounded it by heart, he sat on a tall rock and studied it again, detail by detail, to distract his mind from the worry that was mounting by the moment.

The three-clawed peninsula lay at the southern end of an enormous bay called the Chaldron. To the north lay the fertile fields of Tharos, where families of humans hunted, farmed, and struggled to survive. To the east lay a boundless sea, and on the western side of the bay lay the Thunderborn Mountains, a narrow but sheer range of peaks that rose like blue gray giants between Tharos and the jungle realm of the saurans to the south. It was this mountain range that had been the beginning and the cause of the disaster.

From a distance the peaks looked innocuous, almost lovely as their flanks gleamed a dusky green in the sun and their snowy tops shimmered against a vivid blue sky. But their beauty was a trap, Caerleon thought bitterly as he gazed at the distant mountains, and their riches were bought at too deadly a price.

The young man tore his eyes away from the mountains and shifted on his vantage point to look across the toe of land toward the broader foot of the peninsula. Here on the northern claw his family, the Damrani sect, had built their homes among the tumbled boulders and sand dunes of this lowest point. The crude village was deserted now, for most of the people had gone into hiding, in terror of the sauran hunters. Only Caerleon and a few men remained behind.

"Where is he?" Tesar suddenly snapped. "Do you see him yet?" The young man paced a few steps and violently pitched a rock at a hovering seagull.

"Have patience, Tesar; he will come," Cantii said, shifting slightly on his seat. Cantii, the oldest surviving

Damrani in the village, had learned patience through wisdom and tragedy. He had lost his wife and son, his brother, and too many good friends to the saurans. There wasn't much left he could lose.

"How can you be so sure?" Tesar replied hotly. "Some mishap may have befallen him. Already the hunters draw near."

"Because I know the eldol. Our chief will come unless he had good reason not to."

Caerleon, on his perch on the outcropping, flinched as if stung, but it was Tesar who looked at the older man in consternation. "What reason would he have not to hide with us?"

"I don't know, but we will wait until the last possible minute," Cantii answered reasonably.

Tesar lapsed into silence and continued to pitch rocks at passing birds. Caerleon remained quiet, his eyes pinned to the strip of land where his brother, the eldol, should appear. Of course Acteon would come. He wouldn't be stupid or careless enough now to be caught by the saurans. Even death by their poisons would be better than what they intended at this time of year.

Suddenly a lithe figure appeared, racing through the scrub and sand hills toward the little village. Caerleon lifted his fist in salute; then his hand fell in dismay when the face became clear enough to recognize. It was only Haldan, the point guard.

"They're coming!" he bellowed. He charged up to Caerleon's seat. His face was pale and hollowed, and his nondescript clothes were soaked with sweat. "Twenty or thirty saurans," he reported. "Closing fast. And they already have a prisoner."

Caerleon leaped from the stone outcropping and

clutched the man's shoulder. "Who?" he shouted, although from the man's stricken face, he already knew the answer.

"The eldol," Haldan said miserably.

Tesar and Cantii gathered around, their weathered faces appalled. "We have to go now," Cantii urged. "To the caves before the saurans capture any more."

*"No!"* Caerleon howled. He would have bolted for the distant sauran hunting party if the three men had not held him back and dragged him out of the deserted village.

"We can't just leave him. We have to get him away," Caerleon begged. He struggled against the implacable hands, but his friends refused to free him.

"We can't go," Cantii said with tears in his voice. "We don't stand a chance against their weapons, and you know it! Would Acteon want you to die in a vain attempt to save him? Not here! Not now. Wait! Later there may be a chance. Come with us now, and wait."

Caerleon bit back his fury and his bitter retorts and calmed down enough to follow his friends to their hiding holes. Cantii was right. But when the hunt was over, there were still three days before the comet came and three days before Acteon would be sacrificed to the sauran god, Aussasaurian. Much could happen in three days.

Slowly the afternoon faded to evening, and the harsh light of day aged to a dull bronze. The Damrani in their tiny caves and hand-dug holes whispered their prayers and sweltered in the soaring heat as they waited for the saurans to leave. At sunset, the hunting horns sounded once in victory, and the lizard people returned to their own camps.

In the dim evening light the Damrani crept forth and returned to their tiny village. The news of the eldol's capture had somehow traveled to all the scattered groups, and they gathered around Cantii and Caerleon looking shocked and frightened.

"How could this happen?" several asked. "Did the eldol wish to die?"

"I don't know," Caerleon said miserably. "I just don't know."

"Well, we cannot let the eldol die while there be breath among us. We have already lost our Godtalker. We will not survive without the eldol!" Tesar cried above the murmurs of the other people.

"Caerleon, for once I agree with Tesar," Cantii said. "I know the saurans will be hunting again, but somehow we must get the eldol out."

The young man did not answer them, for his mind was too troubled for words. Blindly he pushed his way out of the circle of people and walked to the tiny stone hut he shared with his brother. For three years they had been forced to live in this hovel while they struggled for survival and fought to escape this prison.

It had been only three years. But it seemed like a lifetime ago when the Godtalker, the priest of Altos for their sect, had a dream—sent, he thought, by Altos himself. Gathering all those Damrani who could travel, he led a large band into the Thunderborn Mountains to search for the veins of copper, silver, and gold he had dreamed were there. They thought to explore several valleys and be out of the mountains before the spring passing of the comet, Aussasaur, when the saurans left their warm jungle homes to cross the mountains and raid the human domain of Tharos. But the Godtalker delayed their return too long, and the saurans caught them on the wrong side of the mountains. Many Damrani were slaughtered, and the rest were driven like sheep onto the peninsula and left alone. There they paused gratefully to lick their wounds. It wasn't until they tried to pass back over the narrow neck of the peninsula that they realized what the saurans had done. At the thinnest section of land, where the path was forced to pass between two high cliffs of stone, the saurans had brought down two massive landslides that blocked escape as effectively as the tallest wall.

The humans were trapped on a barren, treeless claw of land with no means of escape. They learned to scrape out a meager living on berries, birds' eggs, shellfish, and the few small animals in the rocks and cliffs of the coast. At the autumnal passing of the comet they found out why the saurans had gone to such trouble to pen them on the inescapable projection of land. As the great comet approached, the lizards sent hunting parties onto the peninsula and captured seven Damrani. On the holy day of Aussasaur's passing, the saurans put the humans to death in a sacrifice to their god, Aussasaurian the Heatbringer. They had been doing the same thing every spring and fall for three years with each cyclic return of the comet, and of the eighty-four Damrani who had fled onto the peninsula, only forty-one remained.

There would not have been even that many if it had not been for the eldol. When their Godtalker died the first year, Acteon became the Damrani's only leader. Using all his powers of persuasion, he had urged, cajoled, and bullied his people into building the huts for shelter, experimenting with new foods, looking for caves along the rugged shoreline to hide in, making new weapons as their old ones wore out, and searching for any means of escape. He was their chief, their priest, their courage, and their heart. Without him, they would have given up in despair.

Caerleon leaned against the hut's wall, letting the stone

bear a little of his grief and fear. He wracked his mind
for possible solutions, but nothing seemed to explain
Acteon's strange behavior. The eldol knew the saurans
were coming; he knew the nearest hiding places and the
dangers of being caught in the open. He had no reason to
be out alone.

And what about rescue? Did they dare attempt an
armed raid against overwhelming forces? Also, as Cantii
pointed out, the hunting would continue for two more
days. Should the men leave the women and children
unprotected? Oh, Altos, what were they going to do?

From the tiny slit of a window on the northern side of
the hut, a gold beam of light slid through the opening and
came to rest on Acteon's stone chair. The comet, so close
in its northern trajectory, held night at bay with the
orange gold light of its burning for several more hours
after sunset. That light gleamed now on the polished
blade of a long sword that lay across the furred seat of the
chair. The gleam caught Caerleon's eye, and he gasped
with horrified realization.

Acteon never went anywhere without the precious
bronze sword. It was the badge of his authority and an
heirloom passed down from father to son. Forging
weapons like that one was still a skill only a few could
master. He would not forget the sword or simply leave it
behind—unless he knew he would no longer need it.

Caerleon stepped toward the weapon, but his hands
refused to touch it. Hopelessness and indecision crawled
into his mind. Acteon had always been there to council
him and urge him on. Now he was alone and terrified
of the decisions he would have to make. As the eldol's
brother and one of the most capable men left in the
sect, he would be expected to lead in his brother's

absence, but this was all too quick, too soon. Trembling, he grappled with the blinding fear of this leadership thrust upon him; then he forced his thoughts to Acteon and the two days that were left. His trembling eased, and he stared down at the sword the eldol had left behind. At last he knew what he was going to do—for now.

Swiftly Caerleon turned on his heel and went back outside. The sun was gone, but the comet blazed its fiery trail in the northern sky like a torch in the hand of the god. The young man faced his worried people and said, "The eldol has chosen to be captured, but we don't know why. Until we discover his reasons and make further plans for his escape, the Damrani people are the first concern. Let us eat and return to our caves. I will go to the eldol when I can and try to talk to him. Perhaps he will tell me why he has chosen this path."

The others nodded glumly. Like shadows dark and sad, the Damrani collected food and water, then followed Caerleon into the dim night.

During the next two days the saurans made halfhearted attempts to capture more Damrani for sacrifice, but the wary people remained hidden in camouflaged holes and caves around the peninsula. The saurans themselves were pleased with their valuable prize. They knew the value of the eldol to his people, and although the hunters were slightly disturbed at the ease of his capture, the rest of the attending saurans were overjoyed at this great portent.

They placed the man in a strong cage at the foot of a high bare hill near the towering mass of stone and earth that blocked the land bridge to the mainland. On the crown of the hill sat a huge, flat slab of stone that pointed north and overlooked the wide bay. It was this slab that the saurans

used for an altar every year. This time they had brought a
high shaman, the highest ranking priest in the sauran hier-
archy. After a special ceremony to reconsecrate the stone
altar, the high shaman had something new erected on the
stone: a polished bronze basin the width of a tall man's
height. He gave no indication what the basin was for, but
Acteon in his cage stared at it in horrified fascination.

In the skies to the north, the comet streaked closer, and
the heat of its coming scorched the stones and sand of
the peninsula. With the heat grew a tension of waiting that
was as palpable as the bright orange flow of the comet's tail.

On the evening of the second day, Caerleon could stand
the suspense no longer. The next day the comet would be
at its closest in its pass by the planet, and on the afternoon
of that day, the sauran high shaman would sacrifice Acteon
to their god and the comet that bore her name. This night
would be Caerleon's last chance to get close to the eldol.

He waited only until the comet passed over the horizon
and the darkness was at its fullest, then he bid a quick
farewell to Cantii, Tesar, and the others and sped on his
way. He hated to leave them behind, but he knew their
prayers went with him and besides, it was too dangerous
for so many. He had a rather selfish reason, too, to go
alone. He realized he might not be able to convince his
brother to abandon whatever plan he had in mind. This
could be the last time he talked to Acteon.

For two days he had imagined what it would mean to
have Acteon dead. The other Damrani liked and
respected Acteon, but he was the last of Caerleon's
immediate family. No one else shared the deep relation-
ship he had with his older brother. To lose him would be
as if someone ripped away part of his life and left it

empty. Caerleon shivered at the possibility. He had to get Acteon out somehow!

With his determination pushing him on, he hurried through the darkness, clambering over the rocky terrain with the skill of three years' practice. Soon he reached the main body of the peninsula and slowed as he carefully angled his way toward the hill where the bloody stone pointed to the approaching comet. He knew the saurans usually kept their prisoners in a cage at the foot of the altar hill, and he hoped they had not changed their methods. He could hear drums and the sound of revelry in the distance beyond the earthen wall, where the saurans celebrated the coming of the comet, the approach of summer, and the beginning of the killing season.

Like a shadow, Caerleon slipped around to the bay side of the altar hill. The hill was really the tail end of a tall ridge that formed part of the narrow neck of the peninsula. On the bay side, the hill dropped in a series of sheer cliffs, slender ledges, and jagged rock faces into the deep water of the bay. Caerleon took advantage of the treacherous slope to work his way unseen around the back of the hill to the western side.

Cautiously he lifted his head over the edge of a rock, and a wave of relief swept over him as he spotted the secluded cage placed in a broad, level clearing. A solitary figure sat in the center of the cage, his head up and his posture alert.

Caerleon stayed still and stared at his brother. He wanted to run forward and grab him, to tell him how much they needed him, to shout some sense into his obstinate skull, but he couldn't do it. Only careful planning and logic would save the eldol now, not irrational hysterics.

Deliberately he peered into every nook and dark shadow

around the clearing. There were no guards to be seen, but
that did not mean they weren't there. The saurans' mottled
hides could be very difficult to see in the darkness, and
some guards excelled in staying invisible until it was too
late for the hapless victim. The way seemed clear, though,
and Caerleon was about to move when he saw a hint of
movement at one end of the clearing. He froze in place as a
sauran guard paced slowly toward the cage.

The lizard paused by the cage to make certain the prisoner was still inside, then he hissed softly and walked out
of sight toward the earthen wall.

From the edge of the hill, Caerleon crept forward to
the bars of the cage. "Acteon!" he whispered.

The wooden cage, built by sauran standards, was too
short for Acteon to stand upright, so he pushed himself
backward until he reached his brother. For a few brief
seconds they clasped each other through the bars, laughing and crying in turn. At last the eldol pushed his brother
away. "By Altos, it is good to see you," he whispered, but
a strong sense of urgency hardened his next words.
"Caerleon, you fool, get out of here! I don't know when
the guards will return."

The young man shook his head. "No. Listen to me, my
brother! I beg you, come with me. Save yourself while
there is still time."

"No."

The tone was so adamant, Caerleon was shocked.
"Acteon, please! Why do you do this? You are the eldol
of our sect, the only leader we have left. Without you we
will not survive."

The eldol paused, his face obscured in the darkness. A
brief shudder seemed to run through his powerful body
from an inner pain he feared to disclose. He had known

before he would have to tell his brother, but the fore-warning lent him little strength for the difficult task.

"Caerleon," he murmured at last. "Do you remember the day the Godtalker died?"

The young Damrani nodded impatiently. He remembered that day two years ago all too well, when the Godtalker led the men on a bloody raid to free several prisoners taken by the saurans for sacrifice, but he wasn't sure what that had to do with the eldol's wish for death.

"The Godtalker was my friend," Acteon went on, "and as he lay dying in my arms, he told me how guilty he felt for bringing us to this disaster. He wanted to do something to atone for his mistakes, something to help his people. So he gave me his magic."

"What!" Caerleon gasped.

"Not the knowledge to use it, not the herbs, or the words, or the skill to control it," Acteon explained with an edge of bitterness to his voice. "He put the magic into my mind and body. He said I was to release it some day at great need, and the magic would do something to help us."

Caerleon could scarcely believe what he was hearing. "Do something?" he repeated, aghast. "Release it? How?"

Acteon sighed, a sad breath of resignation. "The only way I can release the magic is to die."

Appalled, Caerleon sank to his knees, trying to hold back his tears. "Oh, no, no," he groaned. "You must be mistaken."

The doomed eldol knelt beside the shaking form of his brother and gripped his hand fiercely. "No, Caerleon, I am not mistaken. Do you think I want to die? I have known of this power for some time, and I have run from it while others died in my stead. No longer! Altos has chosen me to save our people, and I will obey."

"But Acteon, if you die as you say you must, who will

know what to do with this magic? Who will lead the people?"

"You, my brother."

Caerleon jumped to his feet and stared at the kneeling eldol. "I? But I am not fit to be the eldol. I have neither the age nor the wisdom." It was one thing, he thought, to make a few quick decisions when needed, but it was something entirely different to be responsible for an entire sect of people. The thought terrified him.

The older man looked at his brother with sympathy. "Age doesn't matter, and you will have the wisdom when you need it. Have faith, Caerleon. The magic is there. I feel it growing stronger within me." Acteon continued kneeling, his head lifted to watch his brother pace in a frenzy outside the cage. The night was nearly over, and already the sound of drums heralded the rising of the comet. There was very little time left.

Caerleon, as if realizing the approach of doom, frantically grabbed his brother's sleeve. "Acteon, I cannot let you die. I beg you, defy this fate and flee with me now. Save your life while there is still time."

The eldol pushed away the hand and proudly faced his pleading brother. The light of the dawning comet gleamed in his golden eyes and shone on his light hair. "Caerleon, listen to me once and for all. I have seen my doom as clearly as a vision in the Sacred Pool. My fate lies on that rock up there, and yours lies in the green fields of Tharos. Between us we shall bring our people out of this prison and lead them home."

When at last the full meaning of the eldol's words sank into his understanding, Caerleon leaned on his brother and wept.

The time for tears quickly passed. With their duty clear

before them, the two men set their plans and bid farewell
for the last time.

The sun was rising above the trackless sea when Caerleon climbed back around the hill and headed for his village. He raced over the rough and barren ground, trying
to outrun the grief and fear that clung to his heels. Even
the bright light of morning could not ease the darkness in
his heart. He accepted Acteon's belief that what he was
doing was right, but his own faith was not so certain. All
he could think about was that his brother was about to die
an excruciating and needless death, and he could do
nothing to stop it. He ran until his lungs burned and his
legs quivered from the exertion. At last he glimpsed the
stone huts of the village through the scrub pines ahead.

With a final burst of speed he plunged headlong
between the huts and into the central clearing. Startled,
several men jumped to their feet as the rest of the people
crowded around the eldol's exhausted brother, everyone
quiet as they waited for his news.

"He will not come," Caerleon managed to gasp
between great lungfuls of air.

Cries of astonishment and grief burst from their lips. In
confusion they pressed forward, imploring him to explain
their leader's choice for death. A sweep of Caerleon's hand
silenced them, but their eyes continued to plead for answers.
Quickly and painfully he told them of the magic and
Acteon's willing sacrifice. When he finished, the people
looked at one another, too shocked to know what to do.

Cantii grasped Caerleon's shoulder. "We cannot let the
eldol die by the saurans' hands. We must do something!"

Caerleon shook his head, his fair face dejected.
"Cantii, you most of all know we do not have strength or
the weapons to free Acteon from the saurans' grasp."

"But what about this magic?" another man asked. "What is it supposed to do?"

"The eldol didn't know. He only said it would help us escape this prison."

"This is ridiculous!" Tesar snapped. "How can he throw his life away for the word of a dying man? It's too uncertain!"

Something flickered in Caerleon's gray eyes like lightning in the heart of an approaching thunderhead. He straightened to his full height, his head thrown back in a gesture similar to his brother's, and he replied, "You may call the eldol's faith ridiculous, but I saw the conviction in his eyes. He believes what he does is right for us. Therefore, I am going to watch the sacrifice and show the eldol my love and respect." He turned on his heel and strode into his hut. He came out a moment later carrying a bundle and, without another word, jogged back up the trail toward the main body of the peninsula.

Cantii, Tesar, Haldan, and the others exchanged glances; then every man, woman, and child fell in behind Caerleon and followed him toward the altar hill.

The day was rising toward noon as the saurans began their procession to the altar rock. Caerleon, hidden in the scattered rocks on the crest of a nearby hill, watched the lizard people chanting rhythmically as they paced slowly along the road from the earth and stone wall. Rank after rank of armed saurans led by their high shaman approached the hill and came to a standstill in the wide clearing. In the sky overhead, the comet and the sun combined to bathe the peninsula in a brilliant, metallic light.

The chanting and singing ceased, and the saurans watched in reverent silence as their high shaman and his attendants moved to the barred cage. Acteon was dragged out and forced to lie prostrate on the ground before the high shaman. A slow drumbeat began, its sound reverberating through the bare hills. The high shaman, in his cloak of human skin, raised his arms to the bleached sky and began a series of prayers to Aussasaurian, the Heatbringer.

Although the Damrani, waiting in the soaring heat, could hear his deep, sonorous voice, they could not hear his words. To them, the rite sounded strange and harsh. Caerleon could only stare at the altar rock and the great bronze basin that sat on the stone's rim. He had seen two sacrifices before and thought the whole ceremony was horrible, but the burnished basin was something new, and he wondered what the saurans would do with it.

"Maybe the magic will kill all those saurans," Tesar growled fiercely beside him. The eldol's brother said nothing, for he did not trust himself to speak.

At last the service was over. Drums, shakers, and whistles burst into a wild song of celebration, and the saurans began to sway and chant. Rough hands hauled the eldol to his feet to face the high shaman. Acteon's face was calm, and his head was held with pride as the high shaman reached out with a clawed hand, grasped the front of his tattered tunic, and ripped it off, leaving the eldol wearing only his leggings.

Step by step, the high shaman and his attendants escorted Acteon to the top of the altar rock. As the drums beat and the saurans below watched avidly, the shaman sprinkled the man with oil to purify him for the sacrifice to their god.

At that moment, Caerleon lifted the great bronze sword of his fathers over his head. Like a beacon, the polished blade caught the sunlight and sent it flashing in a signal across the hills.

Acteon saw the flash and understood it for what it was. He smiled in gratitude. That brief burst of light lent him strength and courage for what was about to happen.

The high shaman saw it, too, but he merely sneered and nodded to his attendants. The saurans quickly poured oil into the bronze bowl. One spark set it alight, and the basin erupted into a huge bowl of flame.

The high shaman stepped forward, drew out a three-pronged dagger, and plunged it into the eldol's belly, ripping it upward toward the man's heart. He smiled in pleasure as blood gushed over his hands.

A great cry of rage and grief rose from the nearby hill and echoed over the rocks and cliffs. "Acteon!" Caerleon sprang to his feet, uncaring now if he were seen.

But if the eldol heard the cry he gave no sign, for in that instant, the high shaman picked up the man and hurled his body into the basin.

A silence as deep and complete as Caerleon had ever witnessed settled over the peninsula. No drum beat, no bird cried, no voice spoke, while every eye stared at the bronze basin and its towering flames. The Damrani held their breath and waited in grief, in regret, in horrified fascination for what felt like an eternity.

"Come on," Caerleon cursed between gritted teeth. "Come on. Where is the magic?"

The saurans broke the silence first by bursting into a wild song of celebration. Their drums began again, and the reptiles leapt and danced at the culmination of their holy ceremony.

Because he was so close, and perhaps because he was not expecting anything unusual, it was the high shaman who first noticed the change. His slitted eyes narrowed, and he drew back from the basin. The other attendants saw his agitation and looked worriedly at the flames. The fire was beginning to smoke. Not the usual, expected exhalation of a burning substance, but a sudden gout of dense black vapor that climbed into the sky in a thick, heavy column.

Startled, the saurans below faltered to a stop, and the shamans quickly retreated from the altar rock. The smoke rose rapidly upward until it reached high above the peninsula; then the dark vapor began to spread out across the sky. In what seemed like a matter of moments, the smoke covered the sun and the comet and formed a thick gray canopy over the bay. An eerie twilight fell over the land.

Without the heat of the celestial orbs to warm the air, the temperature began to drop. The saurans' cold-blooded bodies felt the change immediately, and they hastily regrouped and marched back to the wall. Using the rope ladders they brought every year, they clambered back over the earthen barrier to their camps, taking their shamans and their guards with them. The humans were left behind with the smoking basin.

The smoke continued to pour from the basin for a while longer, then as inexplicably as it began, the black vapor stopped. The fire burned out, and the basin lay scorched and empty on the altar rock.

The Damrani watched and waited long into the dim afternoon, but nothing more happened. Although no one was crass enough to say anything, Caerleon heard their words as clearly as if they had shouted, "Is that all?" He felt their disappointment as poignantly as his own, as well as an aching sense of outrage. Was this all Acteon had died for? A column of smoke? It had changed nothing! The wall still blocked their way; the saurans still lived; the deep treacherous waters of the bay still surrounded them. Nothing useful had been left behind, and no revelations had been granted. True, the saurans had left without further killing, but they would be back in the fall when the comet returned.

In twos and threes the Damrani finally took their disappointment and sadly went home, leaving Caerleon alone on the hill.

Cantii, one of the last to go, tried to find some words of solace for his friend, but one look at the young man's face stilled all the feeble phrases he could find. He finally squeezed Caerleon's shoulder and followed the others back to the village.

When evening came and the comet passed over the horizon, the gloaming beneath the cloud of smoke turned to true darkness. Caerleon hardly noticed. He remained on his vantage point, staring over at the altar rock and the bronze basin. He lost sight of them in the thickening night, yet he could still see them permanently etched on his mind's eye. For hours he stayed on the hill, too sick at heart to abandon his vigil.

Midnight passed, and the darkness seemed to intensify even more until the man could no longer see his own hand. To the east, far away over the forbidding sea, a flicker of lightning illuminated the low-slung clouds. A breeze skittered by, stirring the grass and shrubs. Caerlcon lifted his head and saw another flare of lightning. Thunder rumbled with the deep, heart-pounding throb of war drums. The breeze suddenly strengthened to a stiff wind, and the lightning moved perceptibly closer.

Caerleon thought briefly of returning to his hut, then dismissed the idea. It wouldn't matter if he got wet—nothing mattered very much at that moment.

In just a few minutes the storm roared overhead. Its wild winds tossed and whirled the canopy of smoke into a maelstrom of black vapor, and out of that seething smoke came the rain in huge, heavy, pelting drops. The rain fell so hard and so heavily that it took Caerleon several moments to realize that something else was falling with the rain. He put his hand out, and a small round object dropped into his palm. It was hard and black and looked very much like a nut.

Caerleon stared at it in astonishment. A nut? Acteon died for a column of smoke and a mysterious kernel of black stuff? Other round balls were falling around him like hail, but Caerleon curled his fingers around that one nut, threw his head back, and laughed a sound closer to a wretched howl of despair than any human noise of hilarity.

At last, soaked, cold, and miserable, he retreated down the side of the hill, curled up in the shelter of an outcropping, and drifted to sleep, the black nut still clenched in his hand.

*"Caerleon!"*

The shout echoed through the rocks and startled the sea birds in their cliff nests. Caerleon heard it and chose to ignore it. He screwed his eyes shut tighter and wished the shouter to go away!

*"Caerleon!"* The call was closer this time, and something frantic in the tone of the voice caught Caerleon's attention. There was something else, too, a note of excitement perhaps, or confusion.

He blinked blearily and winced, for the smoke cover was gone, and the sun shone in a brilliant sky of blue. Groaning irritably, he sat up and discovered he had been sleeping on the bronze sword. He muttered a curse as he rubbed the sore places on his chest and stomach.

"There you are! Thank Altos!" Tesar's voice cried overhead.

Caerleon looked up to see his friend standing on the outcropping that formed the meager shelter he had slept under. "What is it?" he grumbled.

Tesar leaped down and pulled his friend to his feet. "I can't tell you. You wouldn't believe it. You'll have to come see for yourself."

Just for a heartbeat Caerleon considered staying where he was, but that tone in Tesar's voice piqued his curiosity. Tesar sounded dumbfounded, a quality Caerleon had rarely seen in the pragmatic young hunter. Interested now, he allowed himself to be led back up the hill to their vantage point of the day before.

"Look," Tesar said, and he turned Caerleon around to face the three claws of land stretching out from the peninsula.

Caerleon felt his jaw drop. As far as he could see, from the main body of the peninsula down each toe of land to the sheer cliffs at the points, rose a forest of trees. The short, scruffy scrub pines, willows, and oaks that had dotted the barren land had been replaced by a tall, healthy stand of silvery gray trunks and wide, majestic crowns. The trees were in full leaf, and their opulent foliage gleamed emerald green in the heightened light of the sun and the retreating comet.

Caerleon could only gape. Tesar looked at his face and laughed. "Overnight! Can you believe it? They grew overnight!"

Awed, Caerleon opened his hand and looked down at

the hard black nut still resting on his palm. "It fell out of the smoke and the rain last night," he murmured.

"Yes, well, come on," Tesar said insistently. "The others are waiting for you." He pulled Caerleon down the trail toward the village. He slowed only for a minute when they entered the new woods to let Caerleon fully appreciate the unexpected beauty of the changed landscape.

Caerleon slowed and stared around at the trees in delight. A fresh, pungent smell filled the air, and the light that filtered through the green leaves was cool and soft. The trees seemed to sigh and whisper with a pleasant conversation all their own. Caerleon felt at home among these trees and strangely welcomed. He was loath to hurry on, but Tesar grabbed his arm and hustled him back to the village.

Caerleon almost didn't recognize the village at first. Trees grew around the huts, softening the crude rooftops with dappled shade. Cantii and the others were standing in a small clearing looking up at the lofty foliage with mixed awe, surprise, and a little fear.

They crowded around as soon as they saw Caerleon, their voices a babble of questions. He tried to answer them, but he couldn't quiet anyone down long enough to listen. "Silence!" he finally bellowed. In the sudden quiet he nodded his thanks and climbed up on a rock where everyone could see him.

"This is the eldol's magic, isn't it?" one woman asked.

Caerleon held out the black nut he had caught the night before. "No mundane tree grows from smoke and rain and lightning," he said loudly. "These trees are Acteon's legacy." Somehow, he thought, the trees were appropriate. As strong and enduring as Acteon himself, they challenged the Damrani to make their own magic.

"So what do we do with them?" the realistic Tesar asked.

Cantii looked thoughtful. "Dare we do anything with these trees? They have sprung from a magic we know nothing about."

"Of course we shall use them," Caerleon said firmly. "The magic came from our Godtalker and our eldol, who gave their lives to help us. Now we must decide on the best way to use their gift so we do not shame their memories."

"We could have a decent fire tonight and cook a hot meal!" one woman suggested. The others laughed. It was a simple idea but a good one to people who had been rationing wood for so long.

Caerleon grinned. The Damrani were beginning to come alive and show more enthusiasm and union than he had seen in a long time. "We will do just that. And while we hunt and cook and eat this day, think of ways we can use the wood to go home."

The word *home* was a promise in their ears. For the rest of the day, the Damrani cut tree branches for firewood, hunted birds and animals for the fire, and cudgeled their brains for every idea, silly or sensible, they could imagine. After a delightful feast that night, they gathered around a large fire and aired their ideas.

Many suggestions were made and discussed, including ladders, a bridge, and even floats. But it was Cantii who said, "Why don't we make a dugout?"

"A what?" Tesar asked.

"A dugout," Cantii explained, "is a hollowed tree trunk shaped into a boat. I saw one many years ago when I traveled to the great river. Another sect built them and used them to fish in deep water."

Several woman paled. "A boat?" one said. "But we can't swim."

"I hope you won't have to," the old man said easily.

"Won't it take many of these dugouts to carry all of us off this peninsula?" another man said dubiously.

Caerleon suddenly raised his eyes to Cantii's, and clearly in his mind he heard Acteon say, *You will have the wisdom when you need it.* "We could do it with only two dugouts!" he exclaimed. The idea grew in his mind even as he found two thick pieces of a branch and laid them on the ground parallel to each other. Next he carefully laid a platform of smaller sticks across the tops of the two. "We could lash two dugouts to a platform big enough to carry everyone. We don't need to go far, only past the mountains. We can walk from there, so the craft does not need to be complicated. Rowers could row it across the bay."

"We have so few tools. Do you think we will have time to finish this . . . dugout before the saurans come back?" Haldan wanted to know.

Caerleon looked at each of the Damrani in turn, and he nodded. "We will if we all work together."

And so it began. For people who had little knowledge of the water around them, almost no tools, and only a rudimentary knowledge of boat building, they plunged into their task and learned a great deal in a short time.

Caerleon organized them and encouraged them as they began the difficult task of cutting the trees for the dugouts and the platform. He chose a small beach in the inlet between the northernmost and the central claws of land and there set the men to work at the painstaking chore of hollowing out thick tree trunks under Cantii's direction. They ruined several trunks before they discovered the art of controlling small fires to burn slowly through the inner wood.

The women, meanwhile, fed the workers, preserved food for the journey, sewed water skins, and helped trim and shape the platform logs. An older woman hanging her laundry to dry thought of making a sail for their craft. With Caerleon's urging, she and her helpers gathered every scrap of fabric and leather left in the village to stitch a rectangular sail.

Slowly the boat began to take shape, and the Damrani's excitement grew as the summer passed. Caerleon, too, grew stronger and more capable in his role as the Damrani's new leader. Usually an eldol was chosen by a sect after proving himself in battle and in competition with other contenders, but the survivors never considered another possibility. Unbeknownst to him, Caerleon had assumed many of the traits and habits of a good leader he had learned from Acteon. From the moment he saw Acteon die, he had struggled to fulfill his brother's wish that he be a good leader for his people, and whether he knew it or not, the Damrani were proud of him.

Late summer arrived all too soon, and one day two sharp-eyed boys spotted the first pale sign of the returning comet. Its approach meant the saurans would be journeying back over the mountains to escape the cold weather of autumn. The men knew they had barely any time left until the saurans came over the wall for another hunt. Caerleon placed spotters on the highest hill to keep a watch for the saurans' return, and work on the dugout raft moved ahead.

It took several days to figure out how to lash a mast to the platform and attach the patchwork sail. That done, the entire sect helped push the heavy craft down rollers into the water and cheered when it floated on the tide. It became immediately apparent, though, that the craft needed a steering mechanism, and another two days were spent designing and rigging what Cantii called a rudder. At last everything looked ready. The Damrani packed their meager belongings, brought their supplies to the beach, and prepared to take the craft on its first practice voyage around the inlet. They never had a chance.

That day dawned hot and clear, and overhead the comet drew its fiery tail across the path of the sun. While the women fixed breakfast and the men checked over the dugout raft, Caerleon jogged to the hill to check on his sentry. By now he had become accustomed to the tall trees, and he barely gave them a second glance as he trotted along the path. He had nearly reached the edge of the forest when a swift movement caught his eye. Just beyond the green and brown of the woods, he glimpsed several green and brown mottled hides. He slammed to a stop and ducked behind a large tree just as an advance party of five saurans, carrying the body of his sentry, halted to stare quizzically at the trees.

Caerleon did not hesitate. He wrenched loose the small horn he carried on his belt and blew a long, frantic warning signal. The saurans dropped their prey and sprang after him. The young eldol sprinted down the trail toward the beach and the waiting boat. He blew the horn again and again and prayed the Damrani had heard. Behind him the agile sauran hunters came leaping and racing after him. He could hear their feet beating the forest floor, but he did not turn to look. Something buzzed by him, and he dodged around a tree as a second dart flew by his cheek.

Desperately, Caerleon ran harder. Ahead he saw the trees thinning out, and he knew he had to run across an open stretch, down a rocky slope, and onto the beach in the inlet. He blew his horn one more time. *Oh, Altos, let them hear!* he prayed.

The hunters were nearly upon him when he cleared the trees and came charging into the open. They shouted with glee when he turned to draw his sword, but their pleasure abruptly changed to fear. Ten Damrani men and boys hurled themselves out of the cover of the trees and fell on the saurans with nothing but clubs and rocks. Three years of pent-up anger and grief turned their attack into a slaughter, and before Caerleon could catch his breath to come help his men, the five saurans lay in bloodied heaps on the stony ground.

Tesar grinned at Caerleon, then raised his club and shouted the Damrani war cry. "There will be more coming, eldol! It's time to go."

Scrambling down the hill, the men reached the beach. As quickly as he could, Caerleon took a quick head count and was relieved to see that everyone was there frantically loading the craft.

Sauran horns sounded on the heights. The Damrani looked up and saw lizards on the skyline on both points of land and many more streaming out of the woods.

A woman screamed, and the children bolted onto the raft.

"Let's go! Let's go!" Caerleon shouted to the rest. The rowers took their seats; the women unfurled the sail; and the remaining men, with a strength born of desperation, pushed the ungainly craft out into deep water. The dugout craft floated well, but it hesitated under the unskilled, frightened movements of its masters.

On the shore, the saurans jeered and shouted at the

loaded craft and threw spears at the struggling people. Several waded out, intending to swim to the dugouts.

Caerleon hauled himself out of the water and grabbed for the helm. He straightened out the rudder, thrust it into Cantii's hand, and reached for an oar. "Together!" he bellowed, dipping his oar into the water.

The Damrani were fortunate that day that the water was smooth and the tide was running out. Ever so slowly, the raft turned toward the opening of the inlet and began to gain speed. With each dip of the paddlers' oars the craft moved closer to open water. The saurans on shore saw what was happening and screamed with rage, but the raft was too far away to hit with blowguns or spears. They threw rocks from the cliffs that splashed harmlessly near the craft until at last they could do nothing more than watch the humans go.

The dugout craft reached the mouth of the inlet and cruised slowly into the great bay. Away from the stone cliffs, the wind found the ragtag sail and stretched it tight against its ropes. The craft seemed to leap forward. With a steady hand, Cantii angled the rudder to steer the boat north by northwest. The tree-shrouded peninsula fell away behind them, yet there was not one Damrani who did not look back at least once.

Caerleon laid his oar aside and turned to look one last time at the tree-clad hills. He lifted his hand in salute. He did not know what would become of the trees that sprouted from smoke, rain, and lightning. Perhaps they would continue to thrive on the barren, rocky soil as tribute to Acteon; perhaps they would wither and die now that their purpose was served. Whatever became of them, Caerleon gave thanks for their service, and in his tunic he carried one small black nut to be planted in the green fields of Tharos.

# The Greatest Gift

## Mary Kirchoff

**M**elinas Fori had never considered herself a brave woman. She was hard working—the corded muscles in her arms and back from years of hauling nets heavy with shrimp attested to that. She was dutiful even, though many would question the last if they could read her thoughts on this warm, dark night. Pitching herself into the sea could hardly be considered dutiful to the village. Somehow she had to find the courage tonight. A brisk sea breeze blew the dark strands of hair from her face as she took a shuddering pull on the bitter but fortifying zinnerberry cider she'd pilfered from Gillin's larder that afternoon.

"Come and break bread with my family this night," her friend had insisted. Melinas knew the reason—and the meaning—of the first invitation she'd received to break bread with others in exactly thirteen lunar cycles. Her official mourning period was over today. Not only would she be allowed to rejoin the flow of life in Hamildan, it would be demanded of her on the morrow. Another mate and more children were her duty to the village that had supported her for the thirteen cycles since Aquas had seen fit to take her family in a tempestuous storm.

"Don't you fret, Melinas. You're a fine-looking woman. If only you'll let yourself get over Zedil, you'll be wed in no time, what with those brown eyes and lashes and perfect pale skin," Gillin had said. "There aren't many of us who've kept our figures so well after bearing two babes," she'd added enviously. Gillin often looked with regret from her own stout form to Melinas' slender, strong figure in the traditional loose white blouse and apron over a long, colorful skirt. The young widow knew her good friend meant to be kind, but Melinas' looks were the last thing on her mind.

In fact, Gillin's expectation that she would remarry immediately and bear more children for the sake of the village was the very thing that had brought her to the sea tonight. Women worked the fields or hauled the shrimp nets for their men between birthings, but with the exception of the childcatcher, the only actual job for village women was to bear children. That, and being the fire-woman, the witch who lived just beyond the village, but no one wanted that job. Hamildan lost several handfuls of people every year to the sea, and those people needed to be replaced to keep the village alive and running.

Like all dutiful and devout villagers, Melinas had come to accept the water god's will about her family. The people of the island of Sidenia were a deeply spiritual folk who bowed humbly to Aquas' whims to call his followers to him during the region's frequent storms. Death was a part of the cycle of life, however short that cycle might be.

In truth, the young widow's grief had dulled around the edges some time past. Death not only robbed you of your loved ones, but it also blurred your memory of them over time. She missed her children's presence dearly every day—warm and funny Rork, gentle and pretty Ameia—but in truth she found it more and more difficult to remember what they had looked like. If she still mourned her children, still clung to any part of Zedil, as Gillin believed, it was for the memories of their faces.

And if she longed for those memories, who could blame her? Unlike most of the women of Hamildan, Melinas had known love in her first marriage. She and Zedil had been together since her own birth, had run in the fields and splashed in the sea. Though Zedil gave lip service to the structure of their society, in secret he had taught Melinas the written Word. Their village was isolated, and few travelers came from across the sea. But Zedil, a fisherman, had taken every opportunity to bargain for scrolls, manuscripts, whatever he could acquire from the few who made the trip.

Reading was a love they shared, under darkness of candle in a cove before they married, then behind shutters in the home they built when they fulfilled everyone's expectations and wed. Together they read of lands no one in Hamildan had ever heard of. And they dreamed of the day they would see them together.

How could she settle now for a man who did not share her dreams? There were no men of marriageable age in tiny Hamildan to compare with her warm, open-minded Zedil. Young and old, she knew them all. With every one she would have to deny her ability with the Word, for it was not tolerated that women should read. Without the Word, her dream would die, as irretrievable as her family.

Accepting Aquas' will, she had hoped a solution to her dilemma would present itself during the mourning period, but nothing had changed. Sometimes, as her old grandpere claimed, there were problems without solutions. This must be one of them, Melinas felt forced to conclude now, since tonight time was up. She loved Gillin and the other women who had supported her, but she was not like them. She could never be.

"I should have been on the ship with Zedil and the children," she muttered aloud, her voice sounding slurred by cider even to her own ears. But the thought had not sprung from depression or drink, for, despite the occasion, she was not morose, only resigned. There were places on Tethedril where women could think for themselves, but she would never see them now, not without Zedil.

Why would Aquas spare her, only to kill her dreams with the same fatal storm?

If she stayed in Hamildan, she would be forced to remarry or starve. The villagers would no longer support her after tonight, and a woman alone was not allowed to make a living, only aid in her husband's trade. She'd thought of stealing a boat—Zedil's had been smashed on jagged rocks in the storm—but where would she go? Besides, she hadn't the seafaring skills or supplies to survive such a trip. There were faster ways to kill oneself.

And smarter ones. Legend held that if you succumbed to the waves, at the precise moment between your last breath and death you could hear the voices—even see again—loved ones taken to Aquas. If Melinas could not escape by sea, at least she could touch water that had lapped at other lands, water that had taken her children and husband from her one year ago. She would see them again.

Melinas took her last sip of zinnerberry cider and wiped her mouth determinedly. She had chosen this lonely stretch of sea near Point Mequis, removed from the village, deliberately because the remains of Zedil's boat had beached here. Raising her long apron and cerulean skirt with shaking hands, Melinas walked reverently into the sea as if to an altar. The cold, lapping water pulled her skirts from her fingers, their weight slowing her down. She slogged on until the water splashed just below her bodice. Melinas turned and looked her last at the distant, twinkling torchlight of Hamildan and sank without regret to her knees.

Her head bobbed beneath the waves. The sounds of Sidenia's flora and fauna slipped away until she could hear only her own troubled thoughts. Chilly at first, the water grew surprisingly warm, lapping at Melinas' chestnut hair, sending it out in water-blackened waves. She held her breath out of reflex. Realizing it prevented the inevitable, she forced the air from her lungs in a gust. Whirlpools of small bubbles engulfed her head. As her vision grew dark, Melinas' last thought was that legend was wrong. She was dying, and she had been denied a last glimpse of her loved ones.

Melinas felt something tickling her fingers. Thinking it seaweed, she drew back, only to be greeted by giggling whose sound was not affected by water. Her eyes didn't open, yet suddenly Melinas could see two petite, thick-winged creatures taking her hands to draw her farther below the waves. Pulled weightlessly in their wake, Melinas gaped in wonder at the oddly beautiful, blue green creatures. They were thin and small boned, but with long, graceful fingers and large eyes. What Melinas had first thought were wings were actually folds of skin under the creatures' arms, which they seemed to use to propel themselves while swimming.

The sea sprites led her around a shelf of orange coral,

and her heart, true to legend, literally stopped. Frolicking with a handful of younger sprites were her children as she had last seen them. They smiled when they saw her, young Rork's grin warm and welcoming, Ameia's shy and white as fresh milk. Between them stood her beloved Zedil, an arm protectively draped around their shoulders. Her dead husband gave a jerk of his head, as if to say "come with us," and Melinas took an eager step forward.

Suddenly, Zedil's plain but loving face wrinkled with concern, and he drew the children back, his gaze focused beyond Melinas. The sprites abruptly fled her side like frightened ants, but not before one pressed a cluster of sharp items into her hand. Melinas hadn't time to look at them before she caught a flash of another face struggling above hers, a man she didn't recognize. The light, teasing pull of the sea sprites had been replaced by an iron grip on her wrists. Her lungs abruptly pounded with unbearable pain. She struggled against the grip, to throw herself deeper into the waves, not caring if she struck her head, not caring how much water she gulped.

But Melinas was losing the fight, and she knew it. Holding tight to the items piercing her palm, she stole one last despairing glance back at her swiftly fading family before she gave in to the pain. Then Melinas saw nothing at all.

"Thank Altos you're alive," Melinas heard someone breathe. Her eyes were closed, and she left them that way while she tried to make sense of the time and place. Her last waking image came back in a rush.

"Zedil!" she cried abruptly, pushing herself up to look around. With a sinking heart she instantly recognized the deserted shoreline near Point Mequis. There was no hoping she was with her family now. They were gone, Zedil, Rork, and Ameia. Maybe forever.

In their place was a stranger, on his haunches before a small fire. He was a rugged sort, who perhaps had been handsome in his youth. But too many battles or too much hard living and exposure had left him weathered and scarred. His clothing, too, was simple and workmanlike: a loose shirt and baggy trousers tucked into soft boots, much like the garb of the foreign sailors Melinas sometimes glimpsed near the quay.

"The name's Khurri," he corrected her. "I pulled you from the sea last night and frankly didn't think you'd survive. You must have a strong will."

"If that were true, I'd be under the waves right now," Melinas muttered, more to herself. She straightened up with difficulty, her head and lungs still aching. Raising a hand to push back her damp, straggly hair, it came away gritty with sand. Her clothing was cold and heavy with old water, despite the small fire Khurri had built between them.

"You were trying to kill yourself?" he asked, eyeing her incredulously.

"It's not that simple," she said, but didn't follow with any explanation.

Khurri shrugged. "I guess it's pointless to expect any thanks, then, but I'll settle for your name."

"Melinas Fori," she responded without enthusiasm.

Neither spoke for some time. Melinas, who had never been alone like this with a man other than her husband, was acutely aware of the stranger's analyzing gaze while he prepared food over the flames. She curled in upon herself, as much from cold clothing as embarrassment.

Khurri dished up a portion of fish poached in green leaves and handed it to her. She declined it at first with a turn of her head, but her stomach rumbled when her nose caught wind of its delicious scent. Peeling back the leaves, she separated the pungent meat from the oily fish skin and popped it into her mouth eagerly with the practiced ease of a fisherman's wife. Khurri's rugged face drew up with pleasure at her expression.

She regarded his dark, curling hair, longer by far than the men of Sidenia wore. "I know everyone from Hamildan, and most everyone from the island, for that matter," she remarked between bites. "You're not from around here, are you?"

"Hardly," he said with a chuckle. "I've traveled by sea for months, looking for this island. I anchored my boat just beyond Point Mequis and was wading to shore when I came upon you under the water."

"Did you see the sprites when you pulled me from the water?" she asked anxiously.

He seemed puzzled by the question. "I saw nothing but a young woman lying lifeless and nearly dead."

"They were there, I know it," Melinas muttered firmly to herself. "They must have been frightened away by your sudden arrival."

"I don't know what you think you saw," he said, "but I've heard that dying people often hallucinate just before the end."

A distantly remembered image burst through the fog of Melinas' melancholy. "I was holding some things in my hand when you pulled me from the water. Where are they? Did I drop them?"

Khurri snorted. "Not hardly. I could barely pry your fingers from around them. It's amazing you didn't cut your hand." He fished around in a leather pack. "Here they are." Squinting, he held the objects up to the sunlight to examine them. "They don't look like much more than a string of odd-shaped seashells to me, but I saved them anyway."

Melinas lunged forward and snatched the string from between his leathery fingers. It was, indeed, three shells strung together like pearls. When she held their iridescence up to the sunlight, she could see the faces of her lost family as clearly as if they were standing with her on this very beach. The beloved images of her family had been returned to her by the water sprites, their shells serving as a channel. She felt certain her memories would never be taken from her again, as long as she had the shells. Melinas' palm shook, and tears of gratitude flooded her eyes.

"What are they?"

Melinas' head jerked up to see him watching her curiously. She did not wish to share this miracle with anyone, let alone a stranger. "Just something from my family that means a lot to me and no one else." She slipped the string of shells into a small pocket sewn into the waistband of her bright blue skirt.

Khurri seemed to take her answer at face value. "Speaking of family, yours must be worried sick about you. When you've finished eating, I'll escort you back to Hamildan." He looked to the distant shingled roofs and fully timbered buildings nestled closely in the small, meticulous village on the edge of the sea. "I was headed there anyway," he assured her.

"There's no one," Melinas said softly. "No one I care to see, anyway."

"No mother or father? No husband, even?"

"No," she said with simple finality. "That's part of the problem. If I go back to Hamildan, they'll make me marry."

"You're an odd girl, fearing betrothal," he remarked, eyeing her over a fresh mug of steaming tea.

She straightened determinedly. "I don't fear it," she returned, with a bite to her tone, "I just don't want it."

"That's obvious, if you're willing to kill yourself to avoid it." He looked at her with mild sympathy. "Was the one they selected that bad?"

"There's no one yet," she began, then gave up. How could she explain to one not of the village? "You wouldn't understand our ways," she finished, with a despairing shake of her head.

"Suit yourself." Khurri turned his back and stirred the fire. "I don't intend to be here long enough for your ways to affect me."

Melinas seemed only then to realize fully she was speaking to someone who had seen places beyond the sea. His manners were strange to her—a man from her village would never have served a woman food—as was his clothing. Most unusual of all were the iron and leather armor, and the gleaming sword hilt Melinas had glimpsed protruding from his rolled-up blanket.

"Where do you come from?" she asked.

"Jakda-Mava," he said simply, as if she should know of it.

Melinas leaned forward eagerly. "Tell me about this city." She nearly mentioned she had seen the name in her readings, then thought better about revealing that dangerous skill. "What does it look like? Do many people live there? Is it very far away?"

Khurri was clearly surprised by the barrage of questions. "Has no one from Sidenia ever been there?"

Melinas' dark head shook. "Not that I know of. A few sailing ships have come here, but women were never allowed to speak with the crewmen. My husband told me what he heard about other lands, though."

Khurri cocked a brow. "Husband?"

"He died," Melinas responded in a clipped voice, indicating she would tolerate no further questions on the subject.

Khurri took note of the pain in her eyes. "To answer your questions, Jakda-Mava seems very far away to me now," he confessed. "I've been gone for more than two hot and cold cycles: Trees have lost and gained their leaves twice over."

"The trees drop their leaves where you're from?"

He looked at her strangely. "Of course. Every six and a half lunar cycles, when the comet makes its streaking pass and the frigid ice and snow descend. Have you never seen the comet?"

"Yes," she said, recalling the fiery white ball that slashed the distant sky twice a year. "We have a rainy season because of it, but aside from that the weather seldom changes on the island."

Khurri seemed barely to hear her. His eyes had a far-away look. "I've traveled far and wide, and I still believe Jakda-Mava to be the most beautiful of cities. It is lush and green in the warm season, thanks to its place at the mouth of the fertile Silver River and the hard work of its several thousand citizens."

"Several thousand." Melinas gasped. "How can so many live in one place?"

"There's plenty of room for everyone," Khurri replied, amused by her childlike reaction. "There are grand streets as wide as this beach, lined with tables where merchants sell wares from far and wide. There's a plaza where people gather to hear speeches and watch acrobats perform. And, of course, the river is filled with ships of every size and shape imaginable, all brightly painted and flying banners of different colors."

Melinas' sight rested wistfully on the horizon, where blue sea met even bluer sky. "It sounds as wonderful as I've imagined it." She smiled slyly. "Except the snow part, though that might be interesting to see."

Khurri chuckled his agreement. "A new snowfall is beautiful beyond description. Cold as Aussas' heart, though."

"You said you were at sea for months searching for Sidenia. If you love Jakda-Mava, why have you left it for so long just to come here?" Melinas asked boldly, curiosity getting the better of her usual reserve.

Khurri looked mildly uncomfortable. "I tracked to Sidenia an ancient bracer, legendary among my people for many centuries. It means a great deal—everything to me."

She eyed him with new respect. "You must be someone very important to your people."

Khurri stood, his jaw set with determination. "Not yet. But one day I will be," he vowed.

Melinas looked away, and Khurri's sight joined Melinas', locked on the horizon. She watched his strong, determined profile from the corners of her eyes as he seemed to be considering something. Khurri tossed back the last of his warm drink, then turned to her abruptly, a decision made.

"What will you do, if you don't return to your village?" he asked.

The question startled her at first, but she gave him a wry look. "I thought I'd found a solution to that. Now I don't know."

"Then let me offer you a job."

Melinas looked wary. There *was* one other profession for the women of the village . . .

"I'm not talking about *that*," Khurri put in quickly, seeing Melinas draw back. Whether he was red from anger or embarrassment she couldn't be sure. "What I offer is fair and honorable," he assured her. "Be my guide here on your island and help me retrieve the item I seek. In return I will take you with me to Jakda-Mava when I leave. In this way both our goals are reached."

Melinas hesitated. "What would I have to do, exactly?"

"A woman who goes by the name Mistress Fea has the object I seek."

She drew in a breath. "The firewoman!"

"You know of her?" Khurri asked, leaning in eagerly.

"Who on Sidenia does not know of the witch? She settled here some years ago, a rare event, worthy of notice. I have never actually seen Mistress Fea," Melinas hastily amended. "But I have spoken with people who've sought her skills at her hut of bones outside Hamildan." She blushed. "I confess, I considered consulting her myself this last year."

"Why didn't you?"

"Magic is feared and the people who use it frowned upon, since its spells are given by the lizard goddess Aussas."

Khurri nodded in agreement. "It is the same in Jakda-Mava."

"Besides," Melinas continued, "I bowed to Aquas' will. He would have provided a way out of my dilemma, if He meant for me to escape. The one I chose for myself was denied me last night when you pulled me from the sea."

Melinas froze as she heard her own words. Her hand strayed to trace the outline of the shells in her waistband. The water sprites had given her back the faces of her family. She could take them with her wherever she went. Perhaps it was possible Aquas *had* found a way to save both her memories and her life after all.

Melinas stood, straightened her dried skirts, and set her slight shoulders with determination. "I'll do it. I'll help you find the firewoman who has your bracer."

Khurri regarded the reserved young woman washing her face in the shallows of the sea. Pale as porcelain, she also appeared to have its strength as well. He remembered her fevered thrashing in the sea, how difficult it had been to pull her from it. He couldn't imagine the horrors that had led her into its depths last night. Must be some terrific demons, he thought. He had enough of his own to understand that.

At this very moment, he was trying with only partial success to choke down his own sense of panic. The truth of the matter was, he was running out of time. It had taken him far longer to find Sidenia than he had planned. While he had high hopes now that he had recruited Melinas as a guide, he had all he could do to keep from yelling at the somewhat skittish woman, "Hurry up!" He knew with certainty that to push her was to lose her.

His time line had been set in stone by the god Altos Himself. Khurri had been a not particularly devoted legionnaire for the forces of Jakda-Mava when a powerful energy within him guided him to the Sacred Pool, where Godtalkers of all tribes had found their visions since the beginning of Tethedril. Though many of his profession spent their whole lives seeking the location of the fabled pool and the promise of its riches, Khurri had been content with the odd but ordinary treasure hoard.

Khurri may not have sought the knowledge, but he had

been powerless to deny the call. Looking into the wondrous pool of sacred water on Godtalker Mountain, Khurri was given a vision that instructed him to retrieve the millennium-old bracer once worn by Kassis the Cowardly, as the high shaman of the saurans had been known among Khurri's people for nearly one thousand years. Legend held that Kassis had worn the bracer during the fatal battle with Rasha Arc of the One Tribe, from which the people of Jakda-Mava were descended.

In the vision Altos gave Khurri two hot and cold seasons to retrieve the ancient bracer and return with it to the Sacred Pool. Now the mercenary had just enough time to return there by ship—*if* he set sail within the week, and *if* he had no problems at sea. There was no time for error. But then, Khurri reminded himself, there would be no life for him if he failed the god's directive anyway. It was a sobering thought.

"Are you ready?" he asked Melinas.

"I'm prepared to leave," she said. "Does the fire-woman know you're coming to see her?"

Khurri snorted. "Not from me she doesn't."

"Then how are you planning to retrieve this item? Surprising or stealing from her is almost impossible because of her magic. What's more, she's protected by guardian lizards."

Khurri frowned. "I should have considered these possibilities, but I've just been so intent on tracking Mistress Fea to Sidenia, I never got past the shoreline in my thinking." Pondering that now, he scratched his curly head. "You must have heard something about her, how she works. What do you suggest? I haven't any time to waste with missteps."

"It is said she requires as payment the item she senses most valuable to the client," Melinas said.

"I did anticipate the need for coin," Khurri assured her, thumping another of his leather sacks.

"Then the fastest approach would be to offer her everything you have of value, and hope she accepts it." Melinas cracked an ironic smile. "At least she will not kill you straightaway."

Ignoring the woman's attempt at humor, Khurri frowned, unwilling to abandon the warrior's option of surprise. "It would help if I could think of any way to use the nearby landscape to my advantage."

Suddenly, Khurri recalled something. He dug through a leather sack until he found a scroll. "During my travels to find your island, I met a man who stayed here briefly. He sketched out a map from his memory, but unfortunately he knew nothing of the firewoman." He slipped the ribbon from the scroll and unfurled it before Melinas. "Perhaps you could point out the location of her camp on this map."

To his surprise, the young woman blushed and averted her face from the map.

"What's wrong?" he asked, then thought he knew the answer. "Can't you read?"

"That's just the problem," she admitted reluctantly, her pale face crimson. "I can. Women on Sidenia are not allowed to know the written Word. My husband taught me in secret."

Khurri began to understand a little more about the demons that drove her into the sea. "You'll be happy to know that in Jakda-Mava, the women are the teachers. You will not have to hide your skill there."

Melinas beamed her pleasure. She pointed to a wooded area appropriately labeled "The Dense Forest," directly west of the village, northwest of their current location. "It isn't far, since we needn't go near the village."

Melinas hitched up her skirts to strap on rope sandals she'd left on the beach the night before, while Khurri settled his gear. The young woman led the way from the shoreline and into a broad hedge of shrubs. Sea scent gave way to the darker green notes of conifers when they burst from the thicket and into a forest unlike any Khurri had ever encountered. As far as the eye could see there was no low-growing vegetation, only distantly spaced massive red tree trunks, each thicker at the base than the average half-timbered home in Jakda-Mava. Khurri's eyes followed one trunk to far above him, where the canopy of furry, olive green pine boughs seemed high enough to touch the sky. Filtered light prevailed.

"What manner of trees are these?" he breathed.

"Rubywood," she said, mildly surprised by the question. "Are there none in Jakda-Mava?"

Khurri's pale head shook. "I've seen none like them anywhere I've traveled."

"It's an extremely hard wood," she explained, "perfect for building homes exposed to the sea."

Khurri chuckled. "I should think one tree would build an entire village!"

"There's some truth to that," Melinas agreed. "And a good thing, too. Rubywood is inhabited by spirits of the forest. Chopping one down requires a four-day ritual of fasting and offerings to the forest to appease the spirits. It's fortunate, then, that our houses seldom need repair. What's more, there's very little new building, since few newcomers venture to our shores."

Melinas stopped suddenly and cocked her head. "The spirits are listening. They can be quite prankish if bored or provoked. We should observe silence until we leave their domain."

They walked for some time through the forest. Khurri expected to come upon a road, or at least another human. He asked her about this when they departed the ruby-woods and entered a sunlit meadow of sweet-scented, knee-high grass and purple coneflowers.

"There is a road through Hamildan, and one to the smaller village of Normildan," she explained. "However, most everyone lives within the protection of the two villages. What use is there for more roads? Where would we go?"

Melinas' voice dropped as she squinted at the nearing tree line. "We're nearly at the bone hut."

Khurri glanced at the corded arm muscles below her short, gathered sleeves. "Can you handle a weapon?"

Melinas looked alarmed. "Will I need to?"

"That depends on Mistress Fea," he said wryly, noting her concern. "Look, I'm just being honest here."

She nodded. "I wield a butcher knife with great accuracy when gutting fish. Does that qualify?"

For an answer, Khurri pulled a short-handled blade from his belt and offered it to her. She stopped short in the meadow and took the weapon, its jagged edges gleaming in her palm.

"I'll feel better knowing you can defend yourself. Tuck it into your waistband," he advised.

The truth of the matter was, Khurri was unused to needing anyone's help. As useful as Melinas had been, he regretted having pushed the innocent young woman into helping him. He didn't like the responsibility of it. Perhaps it was enough that she had led him to the firewoman. And yet if he left her behind, he couldn't be certain of linking up with her again to fulfill his promise of taking her from the island. Chances were good that he would be forced to leave the witch's hut in great haste. Besides, how could he leave her in the woods unprotected, where any manner of beasts could lie in wait? No, he shook his head wordlessly, best to keep her where he could keep her safe himself.

Wordlessly they crossed the meadow. Khurri's eyes scanned the tree line constantly, looking for any sign of movement, for shadows of the wrong size or shape, for any of the dozens of other signs that would alert him to danger. But nothing was amiss.

Then they passed through the thick vegetation at the edge of the trees and once again stepped into the coolness of the open woods. Melinas pointed slightly to her right. "There it is."

Khurri had seen it even before Melinas pointed. The hut was strikingly out of place in the soft, cool woods. True to its name, it was a hideous, dome-shaped monstrosity of bleached white bones so large they could only have come from auraks. The huge, mastodonlike creatures were reputed to live exclusively in the lands far north of Jakda-Mava. Only powerful magic—or a vast ship—could have transported them so far over sea.

Enormous leg bones linked curved-plated hip bones; emerald green moss grew in the cracks, serving as contrasting mortar to the whiteness of the bones. Matted hides were draped haphazardly over some sections, creating the impression of an enormous carcass. As they approached slowly, Khurri was surprised to see that no door hung from the arched entryway, though the open portal revealed that the bone walls were stacked as thick as his arm was long. Still, the entire hut was smaller than the base of the smallest rubywood.

Melinas and Khurri exchanged wary glances. Could the hut be as unprotected as it seemed? Where were the fierce guardian lizards? Perhaps Altos was helping him and had sent Mistress Fea away. She had to leave the place sometime, didn't she?

Drawing his sword with his right hand, leading Melinas behind him with his left, Khurri advanced on the hut cautiously.

"Don't stand out there gaping."

Khurri nearly jumped from his skin, then held perfectly, anxiously still, his eyes darting everywhere at once. He could feel Melinas' hand grow cold in his.

"Yes, you!" the crackling, high-pitched voice said with obvious impatience. "I've got my eyes on you. Put that sword away and come forward."

He peered more closely at the hut and noticed for the first time a pair of glowing pinpoints in the midst of the gruesome bones. Was it possible they had been there before and he just didn't notice? Khurri had his answer in a moment, when the dull lights disappeared. The soldier did as he was bade and slipped the sword back into its sheath.

However, Khurri must have hesitated just a little too long for the firewoman, for he felt himself literally pulled through the arched threshold of the bone cave, Melinas in his wake.

The hut was unexpectedly dark and hot, and it took his eyes a moment to adjust. Staring down, he focused on the wool rugs covering the rough dirt floor: Rich, earthy tones had been woven into elaborate patterns.

He looked up and blinked in disbelief. The smoke-blackened bone walls of the dim hut were farther away than he'd imagined, farther than physically possible, considering the building's small exterior. And yet when he reached out a hand, the walls seemed no nearer.

Magic. A chilly finger traced Khurri's spine at the realization of how little he knew about the art inspired by Aussas. He had never before faced an enemy with the skill; its use was so rare. How could he hope to succeed against a woman of magic, when he had only his eyes, so easily duped, to guide him? Melinas was right: He would just have to offer Mistress Fea payment for the artifact up front.

If only he could locate the firewoman. Was she even in the hut, or were they just hearing her disembodied voice?

"I am here, you blighted human," she growled as if reading his thoughts. "Come and ask your question before I grow tired of your presence."

Khurri followed her voice to the left, where a gauzy, crimson curtain hung from the ceiling in a semicircle. The curtain was slit in the center, the edges drawn back, creating a pie-shaped opening to an even darker area beyond. He could see nothing there but a brief flash, like metal catching a ray of light.

"Go to her before she changes her mind," Melinas whispered softly behind him. "She's known for a capricious nature."

Khurri approached cautiously, circling around stools and low tables and taking great care not to disturb the jumble of pots, sticks, and bones decorated with string and paint that were scraped into piles on the floor. Every warrior's instinct cursed his foolishness for walking to the witch like a lamb. Yet what option was left him? He was fairly sure she would strike him dead with magic if he even considered raising his weapon against her, and that was the legionnaire's usual method for dealing with foes. Khurri kept his hand on the hilt of his sword just the same.

At last he crossed the distance and stood at the parted curtains. There he got his first glimpse of the firewoman. He could just make her out in the still-dimmer light of the curtained area where she reclined on a round, cushioned dais covered with a flood of floral pillows. She was a small, thin woman, wiry but not brittle, under a loose black caftan and fringed shawl. Fine, ebony hair was coiled into a loose bun atop her delicate head. He nearly gasped aloud at the sight of her oddly yellow red eyes, which reminded him of a low-burning fire. A nudge from behind by Melinas, who must have sensed his distraction, reminded Khurri of his purpose here.

"I have come to purchase the Bracer of Kassis," he announced, controlling his voice with great effort.

Mistress Fea's hand rose from her lap, the ringed index finger pointing like a talon to her left. A glow ball appeared from thin air and drew his gaze away from the witch on the cushioned dais to a pedestal made of a single stout aurak leg bone. On the eerie platform, spotlighted by the glowing globe that hovered above it, was the object Khurri had long sought. He had seen it only once, a shimmering, wavy image in the Sacred Pool, and yet it was too distinctively primitive to be mistaken for anything else.

Adorning a simple, braided black leather strap was the mummified head of an ancient, poisonous taiperserpent. The bracer was distinctive: The interesting, sarcophagus-shaped head gave the illusion, almost, of slithering continuously after the braided band, and glittering red garnets had been placed in the serpent's small eye sockets.

Khurri had seen many flashier items, gem- and metal-studded, but none that evoked a greater sense of historical import.

"What payment do you require for such an item?"

Khurri prepared himself to hear an impossible sum. "I have brought enough coin to—"

"I have no use for coin from another land," Fea retorted before he could finish. "Or for weapons or armor, or anything else you may offer me. I sense that you carry nothing of spiritual value to yourself, only possessions."

Khurri blinked in surprise. "Is this your way of telling me the bracer's not for sale?"

"Only to you." The firewoman's clawlike hand raised again, this time to point around Khurri to Melinas. "*She* has something of value to me, however."

Khurri felt frustration spark his temper. "But *she* does not want the bracer!"

Fea arched a brow. "Then why is she here with you?"

Khurri scowled. "Because I want it, and she is helping me to get it," he explained, clamping his teeth over his irritation.

"Wouldn't she be helping you to get it if she paid me?"

"Indirectly, yes!"

"There, you see!" the firewoman crowed victoriously.

Melinas had hung back behind Khurri, but now she stepped around the big warrior. "I have nothing, Mistress Fea. Only the clothing on my back and the ability to read. Surely those things are of no use to you."

"Are you sure you have nothing else you value?"

Khurri saw Melinas' face grow red with a light of understanding he did not at first comprehend. Then her hand flew to the pocket at her waistband, and he knew what the witch was after.

"But they're just seashells!" Melinas protested. "The beaches on Sidenia are rife with them. I will go myself and bring you baskets full, if shells are what you seek. But these three can mean nothing to you!" Melinas drew back, protecting the shells at her waist with a hand, Khurri thought, as a mother would shield her children.

The firewoman smiled, an ugly sight. "But they mean everything to you. And that is why I want them."

Melinas cried aloud, a sound wrenched from her soul.

Khurri took her arm and spun her away from the witch's hearing. "I don't know why those shells mean so much to you, Melinas, but please believe that I don't expect you to give them up. This was not part of our agreement. I'll think of another way to get the bracer," he hissed over his shoulder, as if to defy the witch.

"Think again about your chivalrous offer, man," the witch cut in. "Only the shells will buy you the Bracer of Kassis."

Her hand still curling at her waistband, Melinas looked Khurri squarely in the eyes, her own tear-filled. "What will happen if you fail to retrieve the bracer?"

"That's not your concern," Khurri said curtly, but not before his eyes revealed the answer. Melinas understood that he was as good as dead, even if she didn't know it would be at the hand of Altos himself.

Her mouth trembled as she pulled the string of shells from her hidden pocket and held them up to the light of the glow ball. Khurri had seen men die in battle, but never had he witnessed such pain in another person's eyes. He struggled with himself, wanting to tell her not to give them to the witch, while at the same time hoping she would. But in the end, he knew it was her decision to make.

Melinas mumbled a strange thing to the shells themselves then. "Thank you," she said softly. The words appeared to help her gather herself so that she held out her palm to the firewoman. Fea snatched the string of shells from the young woman's hand with a victorious cackle.

"You'll be damned for your greed!" Khurri cursed the firewoman.

"No more than you will be for bearing the bracer," Fea said mysteriously, unmoved by his venom.

"*I'll* be damned if I'll listen to your wickedness one heartbeat longer," Melinas said fiercely to Fea. "I have paid for the bracer with my blood. Take it, Khurri, and let's be gone from this evil place."

He reached out toward the macabre pedestal. Highlighted by the glowing ball above them, strong fingers paused, then closed around the fabled Bracer of Kassis. The digits tingled but felt no pain. Khurri snatched the bracer from the pedestal. "Let's go," he rasped hoarsely to Melinas, turning to leave.

But she had already gone.

A strong sea breeze blew across the gunwales of Khurri's small sailing boat, stretching the sail and scattering Melinas' hair about her face in a dark whirlwind. Yet inside, the young woman was more serene than she had felt since . . . ever, she realized.

The man who watched her now with curious, concerned eyes might never know what she had given up. Her family, so newly returned to her, was gone forever with the passing of the shells.

But now she understood they would never really be lost to her. The memory of her family's last and greatest gift—the opportunity of freedom—would keep them alive in her heart. Melinas strained forward eagerly from her perch at the bow, as if she could hasten the journey— and the start of a new life beyond the sea.

# *The Sleeping Sauran*

## Elaine Cunningham

**S**lowly, soundlessly, the hunting party crept toward the valley where the aurak had been spotted. It had been many years since an aurak had been seen in the grasslands of the One Tribe, many years since winter had been harsh enough to drive the giant creatures this far south. The few humans who had seen an aurak described it as twice the height of a man, clad in tough hide and thick wooly fur, and armed with two long, curving tusks that were sharper than a sauran's spear. The hunters—six men and two women—were eager to see this wonder with their own eyes.

Not only was the aurak immense, it was fast, wily, and keen of hearing. The hunters knew their only hope of taking such a creature would be to surround and surprise it. This was no easy task—on such a night, so crisp and cold, the smallest noise would make the aurak take flight like a startled bird. Only the most silent trackers, the most skilled hunters, dared to hunt the aurak. Even so, some of them would probably die this night, trampled by feet as broad as the base of an eldercactus or gored by those deadly tusks. Yet as they followed the trail, their spears and javelins at the ready, the hunters' thoughts were not of danger. The mighty aurak would feed their people for many days.

Sember, the chieftain of the One Tribe and leader of the hunt, stopped suddenly and pointed with his spear at the ground ahead. Several paces away was a pile of sign, so fresh that wisps of pungent steam rose from it toward the cold night sky.

One of the trackers—Zeeta, a young woman so thin and taut that she brought to mind a drawn bowstring—went up to the steaming pile and crouched down for a better look. At once her hand flew up to clasp at her mouth, and her shoulders began a silent, rhythmic heaving.

The men froze where they stood, dismayed that Zeeta might alert the aurak and horrified by her sudden, inexplicable sickness. Such a thing usually indicated that sauran poison was at work. But no—at this season the lizard people were in the warm lands to the south, many days' walk from this place. What else could such a thing be? An evil omen, perhaps? No, the new Godtalker, Terka Arc, had assured them that Altos had blessed the hunt!

Only Kiri understood the ailment that had overtaken the other woman. She herself knew such sickness each winter, before the child within her quickened and grew large. Any strong smell, even the good odor of smoked fish, could bring it upon her. So Kiri took the woman's arm and hauled her to her feet, led her quickly downwind. After a moment Zeeta nodded and wiped her streaming eyes. The tracker squared her shoulders with determination and pointed her spear in the direction the aurak had taken.

But Kiri was taking no chances. She dug into a pouch hanging from her belt for a sprig of dried herb, and she indicated with signs and gestures that Zeeta was to chew it as they walked. When the woman hesitated, Kiri broke off a bit of the herb and popped it into her own mouth. After casting a furtive glance toward the men, she laid one hand on her flat belly, the other on Zeeta's.

The tracker looked puzzled for a moment; then her eyes grew wide with wonder and delight. She had not known that she was carrying a child! It did not occur to her to ask how Kiri knew. Kiri was the childcatcher, adept in the mysterious ways of birth and blessed with healing power by Altos Himself. Kiri knew what she knew.

Even Sember, the strongest and wisest chieftain that the One Tribe had known throughout its five generations, bowed to Kiri on matters of healing. When she indicated through the silent hand talk that Zeeta was fit and strong, the chieftain did not hesitate to resume the hunt. He even sent Zeeta ahead with the two other trackers, whose task it was to surprise the aurak and drive it toward the waiting hunters.

The chieftain motioned Kiri to his side, for of them all hers was the keenest aim. He and other men would slay the aurak with their long-handled spears, but they trusted Kiri's javelins to slow its charge.

Kiri took her assigned place, her eyes burning with eagerness. She was glad of this hunt, and her enjoyment was made keener by the knowledge that it would be her last this winter. A plump sliver of moon lit the sky, growing ever fatter with the approach of the winter solstice. And when the solstice came, so did the winter babies. Many women would give birth during this solstice moon, more than Kiri could count on the fingers of both hands. The childcatcher would soon be too busy to hunt.

A shrill roar split the silence, a trumpeting like the blast from many bonchetta shells blown at one time.

Then came Zeeta's high, undulating cry and the whoops of the other trackers as they herded the beast northward. The ground shook beneath the waiting hunters as the aurak rolled toward them like summer thunder.

Kiri sprang to her feet, a javelin up and back. Her first glimpse of the aurak stole her breath, and her grip went lax as she stared at the charging beast. She had expected it to be big; she had not imagined that anything so big could move with such speed. On four thick legs it ran, faster than a desert cat and effortless as a child at play. Behind it the churned dust rose into a cloud thick enough to capture the timid moonlight.

The woman quickly rallied. Taking aim at the aurak's neck, she hurled with all her strength. Before the first javelin found its mark she threw another. There was no time for a third. Wild with pain, trumpeting its rage and confusion, the creature veered and charged straight toward her.

Kiri fell to one knee. Bracing the butt of her long spear against the ground, she raised the stone point to a deadly angle and waited for the aurak to come. She heard Sember's voice shouting at her to move and saw the other hunters rushing forward with ready spears, but only as she might have noticed the hum of a small insect. For her there was only the aurak. Its scent—the smell of musk and blood and terror—flooded her senses. She felt the rhythm of its pounding charge in her bones. She gripped the spear with a determination that matched the aurak's strength, and she held firm while the aurak bore down on her like a storm.

There would come a moment—one no longer than the span of a single heartbeat—just before the spear met the creature's woolly breast, yet not so late that the heavy stone tip would fall useless to the ground. Kiri knew that moment's measure, and when it came she let go of the spear and flung herself to one side. She rolled wildly, following the same will to live that had plunged the aurak into desperate flight and into the waiting spear.

The aurak faltered as the spear sank deep into its chest, swinging its head back and forth as if in denial. Then the massive forelegs folded, and the beast stumbled to its knees. Sember ran up behind it, a long stone knife clasped in his two hands. Once, twice, he struck, cutting deep gashes into the back of the creature's hind legs. The aurak toppled and would not rise again. It trumpeted as it fell, weakly, sending forth a spray of bloody foam.

Instantly the hunters were upon it with their spears. But the aurak was not content to die. It caught one of the men between its tusks and sent him flying with a toss of its head. The humans were more careful then; darting in to thrust, dancing clear of the stubborn, sweeping tusks.

Meanwhile Kiri had found her feet and shaken the dust and the dizziness from her eyes. She took up the fallen man's spear and found a place in the ever-tightening circle. The trackers, too, had raced in to join the attack. Seven spears flashed in the faint moonlight, again and again. At long last the aurak's struggles slowed, and finally its massive head lay still upon the crimson soil.

The celebration would come later, around the campfires of the One Tribe. There were tasks to attend now, and the hunters promptly, wordlessly, set about doing what needed to be done: taking the hide and tusks, cutting the meat, stretching lengths of gut out to dry. Every scrap and sinew would find a use, just as each member of the hunting party had a task and a purpose. A white-faced Zeeta set out for the camp to summon others to the harvest. While two of the men stood guard—for the winter was hard, and night beasts would be drawn by the smell of death—the rest set to work on the carcass. Only Sember did not tend the kill—his task was to see to the wounded.

As the chieftain crouched at the side of the fallen hunter, the elation of battle fled from his face. The man was Tanthis, a friend, and his hurts were beyond Sember's simple warrior remedies. The chieftain stood and beckoned frantically for Kiri.

The woman hesitated only a moment, then wiped her hands clean on the grass and came over to the chieftain's side. A glance at the wounded man was enough for her.

"We knew it could happen," she said flatly.

But Sember was not ready to accept what his eyes showed him. "Is there nothing you can do for him?"

"Am I Altos?" Kiri demanded. She pointed to the wounds. "See how the jagged bone breaks the skin of that leg there, and again there? He will not walk again. Do you hear how the air whistles through his teeth? The bones of his chest are probably broken as well. He will not breathe long, and his death will be hard." She laid her hand on the grip of Sember's knife, which was still wet from the aurak's blood. "You are chieftain; it is for you to do."

Sember gazed down at the wounded man, struggling with his duty—and his doubts. He could easily believe that Tanthis would never walk again—and perhaps the hunter would prefer death to such a fate—but apart from the shattered leg, Tanthis did not seem to be so badly hurt. Yet if Kiri said that he could not live, it must be so. Sember knew that a quick death would be the gift of a true friend; nonetheless, it pressed bitterly on the giver.

Kiri's eyes softened as she took in Sember's silent anguish. "If you wish, I will release him."

The chieftain accepted her offer with a nod. Kiri pulled his knife from its strap and turned to kneel beside the wounded man. She reached into one of the bags at her belt for a pinch of herbs. Holding the leaves under Tanthis' nose, she rubbed and crushed them between her fingers. A nepenthe, thought Sember with a rush of gratitude: an herb that would dull the man's pain and ease his spirit into the realm of Altos.

But to his surprise, Tanthis stirred; his eyes flickered open, focused, and settled on the knife-wielding woman. Kiri laid aside the knife and began gesturing in the silent hand talk—explaining to him his hurts, no doubt, and perhaps saying farewell. Her back was to the chieftain, and Sember could not see the words she formed; but he saw the horror and disbelief dawning in the eyes of his friend. The chieftain frowned. Tanthis was no coward, to fear a well-earned death. He looked more like a man accursed.

An old story crept unbidden into Sember's mind, faint and insistent, like a whiff of wood smoke from a morning campfire stealing into his dreams and pulling him from slumber. He began to remember something that had happened several years ago, during the festival that preceded the autumn equinox. Seasons were important to the humans, no less than to the saurans, for the women were fertile but twice a year: at the new moon before the spring and autumn approach of the comet Aussasaurian. Altos had planned it thus for the well-being of His children. The young came in times of lesser danger: The winter children were born when the nights were long and cold and the saurans kept to their jungle homes; the summer children came before the worst of the heat settled on the land like a blanket, sapping the strength of the laboring women even while it rose the fighting frenzy of the saurans to a fever pitch. The cycle of childbearing allowed the women to hunt or harvest the crops—and to fight in battle, if need be—before they grew too heavy and awkward. Yes, Altos had planned well.

Sember remembered that Kiri's first child had been born that summer, the first year she'd come into season. Each year since she had added a summer child to the tribe—six in all, and she was yet young. Kiri had seen fewer than forty passes of Aussasaurian, and she had several more years of childbearing ahead. Many women died in childbirth, but Kiri carried her young with grace and brought them forth with almost indecent ease. It was plain that Altos had granted Kiri a special blessing, and it had become a matter of pride among the men of the One Tribe to sire a child upon her. Nor was it a hardship to take her as mate. Kiri was beautiful, according to the tastes of the One Tribe. Her hair was a tight cap of sun-colored curls, and her eyes captured the clear blue of a winter sky. She was small and sturdy, with muscled limbs and a proud, well-rounded haunch.

As Sember thought upon these things, he remembered the details of that long-ago conflict. Kiri had been little more than a child herself when she birthed her first baby—unusual, for few women joined the equinox festivities before their third or fourth season, waiting until they'd gained the strength to bear a child in safety. The women who'd attended Kiri had whispered of the oaths that the girl had sworn while in the throes of her pain, promising that she would never forget the manner of that begetting. The old chieftain—Sember's father—had questioned her, afterward, but she would not name her child's sire.

Now, looking into Tanthis' trapped and desperate eyes, Sember thought he knew what that name might be.

Kiri reached for the knife. Before Sember could cry out in protest, she sliced it cleanly across the man's throat.

Calmly, efficiently, she wiped the blade clean on the dry grass and rose to return it to its owner. She recoiled before the naked emotion on the chieftain's face. For a long moment they stood, their eyes measuring each other. Then Kiri dropped the knife and opened her arms to him, offering silent consolation for the loss of his friend.

Suddenly the chieftain was ashamed, deeply ashamed, of the path his thoughts had taken. He gathered Kiri close and buried his face in her golden curls as if to blind himself to his own dark thoughts.

After a moment, he put her gently away. "Zeeta left before she knew of Tanthis' fate. It is not right that his kin should hear some, but not all, or that they learn of his death from the sight of his empty body. We must return to the camp with word. The others will manage without us."

Kiri nodded and fell into step beside him, and their breath made small cold clouds as they walked. There was less need for silence now, so they took the shortest path back to the campsite—a small dry gorge that would come alive in the spring, when cold water from the northlands spilled down into the Silver River. Here the plants grew thicker than on much of the grasslands, and the dried reeds and brambles crunched under their soft boots as they walked.

Suddenly Kiri stopped and peered intently into a thick tangle of skyberry brambles. She stood silent for a long moment before beckoning Sember near. The chieftain crept to her side and followed the line of her pointing finger. When at last he saw what she saw, his hand flew instinctively to the grip of his long knife.

In the midst of the bushes lay a sauran. Its dusty, mottled hide, with its pattern of dull brown and green and black, rendered it almost invisible among the shadows of the thicket.

"Not dead," Sember noted, for although the lizardlike creature did not move, neither did it stink. Three moons had come and gone since the last sauran attack, enough time to rot the creature's flesh from its bones. The sauran must have been wounded in battle and left for dead by its treacherous kin. Somehow, the creature had survived, only to lapse into a state of torpor with the coming of winter.

Once again Kiri laid claim to Sember's knife. She crouched down and began to hack her way into the thicket. Of course she meant to kill the sauran; Sember realized that at once. Kiri was ever practical, and killing this enemy was without doubt the most practical course. The chieftain acknowledged that, even as his mind rebelled against the idea of slaying a defenseless enemy. But perhaps it would be better, more honorable, to let the creature sleep out the winter and await the will of Altos.

He suggested this to Kiri, but she merely shook her head and continued slashing her way into the heart of the skyberry bushes. Finally the woman parted the last of the thorny limbs and reached through to run her hands lightly over the dusty hide that covered the creature's body. "The sauran's time is near," she murmured.

"Perhaps so. Leave that for Altos to decide," he said piously, still thinking to let the sauran die on its own.

The woman responded with a derisive snort. "What has any male—even a god—to do with birthing? Help me get her out."

Sember rocked back a step, staring with astonishment as Kiri began to tug at the creature. "What do you mean to do?"

"The winter solstice approaches, and the sauran is heavy with eggs," the woman said matter-of-factly. "They have grown within her as she slept, but she cannot bring them forth. She needs warmth, and tending, or her young will die and poison her from within."

The chieftain's thoughts whirled as he struggled to sort through these things. He was dismayed by the realization that saurans followed birth patterns similar to humans, for he was accustomed to thinking that humans and saurans held nothing in common but their mutual hatred. Kiri's knowledge of such matters astounded him; he himself could not tell the lizard people male from female. That Kiri wished to tend a sauran was utterly beyond his understanding.

It was this thought that finally found words. "You would help this creature? You would help the saurans increase their numbers?"

Kiri settled back on her heels and met the chieftain's dumbfounded gaze. "You lead the One Tribe; you lead the hunt. Those are the tasks given you by Altos. Upon me was laid the task of bringing forth new life."

Without waiting for his response, Kiri continued to drag the sauran from the thicket. After a long pause the chieftain stooped down to help. It was no easy task, and despite Kiri's care, the tough thorns tore through the creature's hide more than once. Through it all, the sauran lay as if dead.

Sember found himself hoping that the sauran *would* die. There was something wrong, very wrong, about aiding one of these evil, treacherous beasts. Yet he could find no arguments that would stand before Kiri's dedication. She was the childcatcher, and he could not find it in his heart to fault her for following the voice of Altos as it spoke to her. Sember knew that some in the tribe— especially Terka Arc, the new Godtalker—might not agree. After all, Kiri was a woman, and only men were granted the vision in the Sacred Pool.

Following Kiri's instructions, Sember slung the sauran over his back. The thing was small, smaller even than Kiri, and thin from its long slumber. It felt light and dry, like an armload of tinder.

"There is a cave in the bluffs, to the morning side of the campsite," Kiri said as they strode along. "It is better that we take the sauran there. It is a safe distance from the camp. She cannot steal out and bring harm to the One Tribe while I sleep."

Sember shot a concerned look at her. "You will stay there, alone with this creature?"

"I will be safe enough," the woman assured him as she turned her steps eastward. "The winter bears down upon us, and the sauran will know that she cannot survive for long beyond the warmth of the cave. She will need me to provide food and fuel for the fire. Why would she strike me down, and bring death to herself and her young? The saurans are not fools, to throw away their lives without purpose."

This was true enough—although fierce and fearless in battle, the saurans were cunning and careful about the risks they took. But there were other questions gnawing on the chieftain's mind. "The winter children will soon come," he pointed out.

"And when they do, I will return to camp," Kiri said steadily. "The sauran's winter slumber will soon melt. Once the eggs are laid, she can survive well enough on her own. I will sleep in the camp, and visit the cave when I can to bring what is needed."

Sember nodded. It was good to hear that the child-catcher placed her duty to the One Tribe over the survival of this enemy. "And when the spring comes?" he persisted. "There will be nothing to keep the sauran and her brood in the cave. What then?"

"When spring comes, you will do whatever best serves the One Tribe, and so will I," Kiri responded.

There was no argument for that, and nothing that the chieftain could add. Although he was still beset by doubts, he bore the sleeping sauran to the cave and grudgingly left her in Kiri's care.

Kiri hummed quietly as she stirred the broth simmering in her stone cauldron. The plaintive, eerie melody echoed against the walls of the cave as it coaxed magic from the swirling herbs. The childcatcher knew little of the needs and nature of saurans, but she was certain of these herbs. They stoked an inner flame, the same flame that had seared the sauran's flesh with magic fire, sealing the battle wounds and saving the female's life. The night of the aurak hunt, Kiri had seen the dark scars on the sauran's hide, and she had recognized the fiery touch of the goddess. Perhaps no other human would have understood the significance of these wounds, but Kiri knew what she knew.

The woman bore similar marks on her own body, and

within it, too. The birth of her third child had gone hard with her; the babe had torn its way toward the light with a force that would have killed any other woman. But when deadly bleeding began, Kiri had called forth magic fire to cauterize her own birth wounds. And so she had survived, much as this sauran had survived. Theirs was a sisterhood that went to some mysterious core within them both.

But as Kiri prepared the healing broth she felt no sentiment, no real kinship for the laboring female. Desperation, determination—these were the things that sustained her through the days and nights of watching. If the sauran died, then so did Kiri's only chance to learn the truth of what she herself was.

Many years ago, when she was yet a child, Kiri had heard the call of the goddess, had felt within her soul the power of Aussas, the Heatbringer. The firemagic came upon her slowly, for it was hard for a woman alone to hear the voice of the goddess when every member of the One Tribe prayed to Altos. Kiri knew that her people would shrink from her in horror if they understood the source of her power. They thought her blessed by Altos—for what good thing could possibly come of a sauran goddess? There were times when Kiri wondered this, herself, and doubted the truth within her own heart.

But this sauran had also been touched by the goddess. Perhaps, for the first time in her life, Kiri could speak to another living soul of the firemagic, and the goddess.

Especially the goddess.

To the humans of the One Tribe, Aussas was the enemy, the betrayer, the treacherous sister of the more powerful god Altos. Altos was good, and Aussas was evil—that was the truth as humans knew it. Kiri suspected that the truth lay somewhere in between this truth and the holdings of the lizard folk. She saw the sibling gods as male and female, not human and sauran. True, the saurans worshiped Aussas—whom they had named Aussasaurian—and they had cloaked her image in the mottled hide of their own kind. But the truth of the goddess went far deeper, was linked to the mysterious cycles of heat and life and renewal. Altos was constancy; Aussas was change: Together they formed the pattern of the world. Humans were as much a part of this pattern as any sauran that drew breath, and Kiri knew this in her very soul.

As Kiri worked and sang, the sauran watched with unblinking eyes. Two days and three nights had passed since the aurak hunt, and the heat of the fire had finally melted the torpor imprisoning the sauran. The birth pains began almost as soon as the sauran opened her yellow eyes.

"It is night now, and the time of the solstice moon approaches," Kiri said quietly, hoping to restore to the dazed female some sense of her bearings. "Your eggs will come before the dawn. You will need my help, for you are too weak to bring them forth alone. I am Kiri, known to the humans as the childcatcher." She paused and lifted her head a little. "But they do not know me for all that I am. Like you, the goddess has marked me with her fire."

As proof of her claim and her good intentions, Kiri spooned up some of the fragrant broth and held the wooden dipper dangerously near the female's fanged snout. The sauran sniffed audibly and managed a weak nod. It was as Kiri had hoped: The female recognized the herbs and knew their benefit. Slowly at first, then avidly as hunger returned, the sauran swallowed the broth that Kiri spooned into her mouth. There was always a risk in giving food or liquid to a laboring female, but both realized that without nourishment the sauran would not survive the night.

At last the sauran turned away from the offered broth, ready to focus her energy on the task ahead. She allowed the woman to help her into position, let her catch the first large, speckled egg as it came from her body.

Kiri had prepared a nest near the fire, and she moved to place the egg in it. She stopped suddenly, acting on impulse, and held up the egg for the female to kiss.

The sauran did so, reflexively, and watched intently as the childcatcher gently tucked the egg into the mound of dried grass.

"How do you know so much?" she demanded in a voice that was little more than a weak hiss. "Have you held other saurans captive?"

"You are no captive," Kiri assured her as she stopped again, ready to catch the second egg.

"What, then?"

The woman did not answer at once, and for several moments the sauran had no breath for speech. At last Kiri held up the egg. It was a beautiful thing, and the leaping flames of the campfire gleamed on the creamy shell. The childcatcher's face became thoughtful as she studied the shadows within. At last she turned her attention back to the sauran's question.

"Let us say that for a time you will be the teacher, and I the student. You will teach me the ways of the goddess."

"I will die first!" the sauran said, and spat into the fire.

Kiri did not react to the show of defiance. Calmly she presented the egg to the mother for the ritual welcome, then she rose and walked over to the fire. Holding the egg in two hands, she lifted it directly over the flames.

"*You* will not die," she said meaningfully. "There is no need for *anyone* to die. If you do as I ask, I swear by the power of Aussas that you and your hatchings will return to your people unharmed."

The woman did not finish the threat. There was no need. Although no emotion registered on the reptilian face, not so much as an eyelid's flicker, a tremor passed through the sauran mother's body. Kiri noted this and understood. Her own little ones were safe and warm in the lodge where the young ones slept, under the care of the childtenders. If the roles were reversed, and if her children had fallen into sauran hands, there was little that Kiri would not do to ensure their safety. And so it would be with the sauran.

They were not so different, after all.

When the first rays of the sun stole into the cave, they touched a nest heaped high with eggs. There were ten in all, kept warm by the heat of the fire and by the blankets that Kiri wove from dried reeds. The sauran had spoken little during the night, but she watched carefully as the woman turned the eggs and tucked the fragrant mats around them. Kiri hoped that the creature was still too dazed to notice that she had examined each egg as it was laid, and that she had kept them separated into two groups.

"Ten eggs! Do all saurans bear so many young?" she said conversationally.

The female was still too weak to move much, but she managed to lift her snout in a proud gesture. "No. None have brought so many into the tribe as Moorgen."

"It is so with me, as well," the woman remarked. "I have had six summer children, and I am young enough that I might bear at least as many more. Is this part of the gift of Aussas?"

"Aussasaurian," corrected Moorgen.

"Aussas," Kiri repeated firmly. "The goddess takes sauran form for you. Who is to say that she does not appear to me as a human woman?"

The lizardlike female turned away, clearly disdaining to answer such a question. "The fire burns low," she remarked, "and the peat to that side has not caught flame. If you truly bore the mark of the goddess, you could kindle it with a thought."

Moorgen turned her yellow eyes upon the campfire. Instantly the flames leaped high, sending shadows against the walls of the cave. "I am firesauran," she said, "revered by my people, blessed with firemagic by Aussasaurian the Heatbringer. You could not begin to understand what that means."

"Tell me!" Kiri demanded, coming to crouch at Moorgen's side.

The sauran merely sniffed. For a long moment Kiri did not move. She held the sauran's gaze, letting Moorgen see the inner flame of her determination. Then she rose in one swift movement and snatched up an egg.

"Can you *quench* fire, as well?" she taunted, holding the egg over the leaping flames. "If you can, do it now, or I will cook this little lizard!"

"You will not. That is not the way of humans," Moorgen said, but her voice betrayed a note of uncertainty.

In response, Kiri dug both thumbs into the leathery shell and wrenched the egg apart. The contents slipped into the fire with a sickening hiss.

"Nine eggs," the woman said in a grim tone as she threw aside the empty shell. "How many children will Moorgen add to the saurans this solstice?"

Again she held the sauran's gaze, this time in challenge. For a long moment neither female moved, or even breathed. Then . . .

"Nine," the sauran said faintly. "Moorgen will bring nine children to the camps of the saurans. You have sworn to spare my hatchlings—by the goddess you swore it! If you are indeed a firewoman, may Aussasaurian consume you with your own inner flame if you are forsworn!"

Kiri nodded, accepting the curse gladly if such were the price of knowledge. She sat down beside the fire-sauran and listened intently as the first lesson began.

Sember's heart pounded as he slipped down the side of the bluff, and his mind reeled from the words he had just overheard.

When he finally had returned to camp on the night of the aurak hunt, he did not tell the others about the sauran. Sember had not intended to keep it a secret. Other matters had demanded immediate attention—the death of Tanthis, the harvesting of the aurak. When at last there'd been time for speech, he'd yielded to some instinct that prompted him to tell the One Tribe only that Kiri needed time apart before the coming of the winter solstice, time for her special magic.

The irony in this did not escape Sember. His own words rang in his mind now, over and over, and he fancied that he could hear echoing in them the faint, mocking laughter of Aussas.

From the first it had been difficult for Sember to accept Kiri's determination to play childcatcher to a sauran.

Although he'd found much that was admirable in her stand, he was also troubled by it—too troubled to let the matter rest. He'd crept up to the cave to check on Kiri's safety, yes, but also to try to gain some insight into the childcatcher's devotion, to a dedication to mother and newborn so strong that it would embrace even an enemy. The reality he'd just discovered was much darker, and far more disturbing, than anything he could have imagined.

Sember had known Kiri all of his life. At least, he'd thought he knew her, thought he understood her place in the life of the tribe. Now he wondered if he understood anything at all.

A human woman who carried the power of Aussas— was this possible? The answering thought—that perhaps a sauran could hear the voice of Altos—was too immense for Sember's mind to grasp. He thrust aside that puzzle for matters that laid closer to his scope of understanding.

Kiri wished to learn the ways of Aussas. To what purpose? Would she turn against her own people and side with the evil saurans? She'd certainly shown signs of typical sauran treachery, using the eggs as bargaining chips to force the female into revealing secrets of her goddess' magic. Had he not seen it with his own eyes, Sember would never have believed that Kiri's skilled and dedicated hands could take a young life. The sauran mother's silent agony as her young one fell into the flames had been chilling—and familiar.

Suddenly the chieftain stumbled, jarred to a halt by the remembered image of Tanthis' death—the man's haunted eyes, his own doubts. Perhaps Kiri was *already* in league with the evil goddess! Indeed, what else could turn human against human? No member of the One Tribe had ever deliberately, needlessly taken the life of another.

And how many other times had Kiri slain? Granted, since the time that she'd become recognized as child-catcher, there had been fewer deaths among the women. Her skills were undeniable, but now Sember found himself listing the women who'd died in childbirth, striving to find some pattern that might explain Kiri's vengeance on those particular women. He could find no explanation, but when had he ever been able to understand the evil of the saurans?

With a jolt, Sember remembered that it was Kiri who consumed his thoughts, not some lizard creature. But perhaps the enemy was not so easily recognized as he'd always believed. Perhaps the evil of the saurans had always slept within Kiri, and he himself was just now awakening to it.

Horror crept through him like a chill. Sember broke into a run, suddenly eager for the familiar routines of the One Tribe. Yet even when he reached the comfort of the campsite, he knew that he would never again look at his life—or his people—in quite the same way.

The chieftain was quiet that night at the campfire gathering. Many noticed and remarked on it. Usually Sember took great pleasure in the telling and hearing of tales, but tonight he had ears only for his own thoughts.

There was a heaviness to his silence that pressed upon them all. The stories and the songs were subdued this night, and most of the people sought the warmth of their bedrolls early, even before the half circle of moon crested the distant hills. The chieftain remained at fireside, unmindful of the early silence or the growing chill as the flames faded into rosy coals.

There were few humans still awake when Terka Arc

came over to the preoccupied chieftain. He squatted at Sember's side and studied him with a friend's concern.

"The autumn festival is not long gone, and most of the men are still merry and content," he said softly, and there was a teasing lift to his voice. "But perhaps the blood of a chieftain runs hotter than most, and already Sember is thinking fondly of the next equinox?"

The chieftain whirled to face the other man. "Do you accuse me of forsaking the ways of Altos?" he demanded.

Terka Arc sat back on his heels, astounded by his friend's vehemence. Of course no man of the One Tribe would lay with a woman out of season, nor would any woman accept a mate at any other time! This was not their way, or the will of Altos.

"It was a ribald jest, no more," Terka said in a conciliatory tone.

Sember took up a stick and poked viciously at the dying fire. "You are the Godtalker. Take care what you say, lest the people see in every idle word that falls from your mouth a vision from the Sacred Pool."

The silence between the two men was long and profound. Finally Terka Arc cleared his throat. "I am rebuked, and justly," he said in a strangled tone.

Sember looked up sharply and was pained to the soul by the expression on the younger man's face. Terka Arc had been Godtalker for less than a year. His first vision of Altos had confirmed the tribe's fears that Rasha Arc—the former Godtalker and Terka's closest friend—would never return from the sauran jungles. Young Terka had taken up his duties with fervor and dedication enough for two men. Sember often suspected that Terka Arc strove to be two men, to finish the work of a friend who had died too young.

"I spoke harshly," the chieftain said with genuine regret. "There is reason why I do not wish to remember the autumn festival, but it has nothing to do with you. Your jesting was not meant to dishonor Altos, but to lift me from my dark thoughts. For that I thank you."

But Terka Arc was no longer listening. The young Godtalker drew away, seeking the far shadows of the camp where he might dance and sing and seek a renewed connection to the god he believed he had offended with his lighthearted words.

Sember sighed heavily and turned back to the fading coals of the campfire. He was glad he had not spoken of the nearby sauran or of Kiri's treachery. It was a heavy thing to bear alone, but Terka Arc already carried burden enough. Sember could not place upon the young Godtalker the knowledge that there was a sauran among them, or his fear that there might always have been.

The solstice moon was not yet full when the first of the winter children began to seek the light. This was a good omen, a sign that the births to come would go well and that many would be added to the One Tribe this year.

Yet not all joined in the celebration. The strange darkness still lingered about the chieftain, growing deeper as the nights lengthened and the sun crept toward its yearly rebirth.

Not even the prospect of holding his first child seemed to lift Sember's spirits. Indeed, a sense of foreboding filled him when Ghilanna's labor began. She was a tiny woman, and this child was her first. He was not surprised that the birthing pains lasted throughout the night and long into the next day. Despite repeated requests, some from Ghilanna herself, he refused to summon the tribe's childcatcher. He feared to commit Ghilanna and his unborn child into Kiri's treacherous hands.

When the sunset colors stained the winter sky Zeeta came to him, her face grim. "Ghilanna will not see another sunrise," she said bluntly. "Her strength fails. If you will not get Kiri, I will."

Few women would challenge him so, but Zeeta was known to be stubborn and tenacious. The chieftain did not doubt that she would do as she said. Disaster would surely follow if Zeeta discovered the nearby sauran. After a moment's struggle, Sember yielded to the inevitable.

"I will go. Tend Ghilanna as best you can."

"And so I have, but I do not possess Kiri's magic," Zeeta muttered.

Sember thanked Altos for that blessing as he raced toward the cave. He met Kiri on the way, a bowing stick in her hand and a young hind slung over her shoulder. She had been out hunting to feed the enemy and was returning to the lair with her kill.

The woman pulled up short when she saw him. One look at his face was enough for her. She dropped the carcass and sped to his side. "Who?" she demanded.

"Ghilanna."

Relief washed over the childcatcher's deceptively beautiful face. "It is a first baby. There is time."

"There is no time. Her pains began this time yesterday."

Kiri's eyes widened, then blazed with rage. "Why did you not call me?"

"I saw you destroy the egg," he said bluntly.

The childcatcher recoiled as if he had struck her. She opened her mouth as if to speak, then she spun on her heel and raced toward the campfires of the One Tribe. Sember, despite his advantage of strength and stride, was hard pressed to keep pace with her.

Kiri ran straight to the birthing lodge, a small shelter built of peat blocks and kept warm by an herb-strewn fire. She brushed aside the hide covering that served as a door and ducked into the room. The situation was grave, worse than she had feared. Four women knelt around Ghilanna, trying to hold the tiny female down as she tossed and shuddered in the grip of childfever. Her flailing hands were curved into talons, the fingers swollen to twice their normal size.

Kiri knew a moment's guilt. Had she been there, she would have recognized the signs of trouble and spared Ghilanna much of this ordeal. But guilt was an indulgence she could not afford now.

"Get out," she said bluntly.

The women looked up, and identical expressions of relief washed over their faces when they saw that the childcatcher had come at last. They released Ghilanna gratefully and scuttled out of the lodge.

Kiri went to work at once. There was a poison in Ghilanna's blood, and only strong magic could draw it forth. She caught the woman's hands between her own, and held them firm as she began the chanting that kindled her firemagic and poured it into the other woman's body.

Never had she used her firemagic to heal another. Knowledge of herbs, insight into the mysteries of birth—these gifts of Aussas she had wielded for years. She had long known that she possessed firemagic but had never understood its use. Now she would learn how well Moorgen had taught her.

Suddenly Ghilanna went limp. Kiri let out a cry of grief. This woman was mother's daughter to her, and dear to her as her own babes. Sisters they might be, but Ghilanna did not have Kiri's strength, did not know the touch of the goddess. The firemagic was too much for her frail body to contain.

But Kiri refused to give up. Again she gripped the woman's hands, and again her voice rose in prayer to Aussas. The sacred fires rose hot within her, hotter than she had ever known. When she could bear no more, she began to draw Ghilanna's poison into her own body, so that she could burn away the killing fluids with her own strength and determination. Sweat poured down Kiri's face, and the tiny lodge filled with fetid steam, but the childcatcher did not care or even notice. All that mattered was that at last Ghilanna lay easier under her hands, and the rhythmic pains that would bring the babe had begun again. Weak with relief and exhaustion, Kiri released the magic. She rekindled the fire and threw soothing herbs upon it to sweeten the air and bring ease to the laboring woman.

Yet despite all her efforts, the babe would not come. Kiri knew of another magic that might help, the magic of a parent's voice calling the child into the light. Ghilanna was beyond speech, but perhaps the father could work the needed magic. Kiri wearily unlaced the door closure and crawled out into the bright moonlight.

Sember was there alone, pacing about the small clearing.

"The child will not come unless it is called forth," Kiri told him. "Who is the sire?"

He stared at her a long moment. The childcatcher's golden curls lay tight and wet against her head, and her face was ravaged with exhaustion. It appeared that Kiri was doing her best for Ghilanna. Sember remembered that the two women were children of the same mother. Perhaps that would be enough. Then, once again, he remembered the sauran's egg, and he decided the risk was too great. There was great honor in being mother to a chieftain, and great danger.

And then the chieftain of the One Tribe told the first lie he had ever offered to a fellow human.

"I do not know," he muttered. "Ghilanna has not named him."

Kiri threw up her hands and turned back to the lodge. Left alone in the moonlit clearing, Sember waited for the birth of his child and mourned the death of his honor.

Before the sun touched the distant hillsides, Kiri held the next firewoman in her arms. She herself had called the babe forth, for there was none other to do so. She had made her sister's child her own in ways that went far beyond claims of birth. This girl child had been pledged to Aussas, and when she was grown Kiri would teach her.

Ghilanna stirred then, and Kiri placed the baby at her breast. The new mother regarded the child with a mixture of wonder and sadness. "A girl," she whispered.

"A strong girl," Kiri said stoutly. "Her name is Kanji, and she will be childcatcher after me."

The new mother accepted this pronouncement with an indifferent nod. "I prayed to Altos for a son," she said.

"You will have other children."

"But I will not bear another child to Sember!" she mourned, and burst into faint weeping.

Kiri stared at the girl, startled by Ghilanna's revelation and by her grief. "Does it matter so much to you, to be mother of a chieftain?"

"It is not the honor, but the *man* who matters to me! I cannot stand the thought of bearing a child to any other!"

Slowly Kiri nodded, beginning to understand. There were but three hundred souls among the One Tribe, and since the Day of Reckoning no man had sired more than one child upon the same woman. All of the humans understood that this was in the best interest of the tribe, but it went hard on some of them. There were those who formed close attachments, who grieved to see their mates turn to someone else with the approach of another solstice. It saddened Kiri that Ghilanna was such a one, especially since Sember did not return her constancy. Kiri had taken her sister's child; perhaps she could give Ghilanna something in return. The firewoman did not know what the price for such magic would be—there was always a price for magic—but she would gladly pay it when the time came.

Kiri pressed a small bag into the woman's hands. "When the next comet nears and your season comes upon you, steep these into a tea and give them to your chosen mate. There is magic in them that will make him want none but you."

Ghilanna's eyes grew round with fascination and fear. "But the way of Altos—"

"Have you no mind of your own?" Kiri broke in tersely. "Think, Sister. A time will come when the One Tribe is great in number, perhaps large enough to form many tribes. When there are more humans than now, do you think it will be a needed thing for a man and woman to have but one child between them?"

"But Altos—"

"Altos gives us knowledge; we have made the knowledge into rules. Will we cling to the rules when their time is past? The time will come when humans are numerous enough to choose their mates as they will and keep them however long pleases them both. And why should that time not come soon? This year alone, we will add over forty winter children to the tribe."

"Some of those will die a-birthing. More humans will fall to the saurans in battle," Ghilanna said.

"Not this year, nor for several years to come," Kiri promised in a grim tone. "I will see to that."

There was something in the childcatcher's voice that brought hope to the other woman—a strength and a magic that she recognized even if she did not understand. She gave Kiri's hand a grateful squeeze, and then for the first time she looked fondly upon the child at her breast. Kiri left Ghilanna then, to give her time to savor the birth of a child and a dream.

Sember still held vigil outside the lodge, and in his eyes were many questions.

"Ghilanna lives. I have a daughter." Kiri announced. "Since no man claimed the child, I called her forth myself. She is sacred to Aussas and will be firewoman after me. What the goddess has done, no man can undo."

A long silence lay between them. Then words burst from the tormented chieftain. "What am I to do with you, Kiri? Slay you for your treachery? Banish you from the One Tribe?"

"Treachery? How so? You know that I follow Aussas, but in what way have I harmed any human?" she demanded.

"You killed Tanthis!"

"Tanthis was dying slowly. I did no more than you would have done, had he not lain so near your heart."

"But he was no coward," Sember persisted. "There was fear in his eyes before the knife struck. Perhaps you did not kill him needlessly, but certainly you cursed him before he died!"

"He might have thought so," the woman admitted. "I prayed for his spirit. I prayed to Aussas."

Understanding began to steal into the chieftain's mind. He himself was well and strong, yet knowing that a human followed the sauran goddess was nearly too much for him to bear. The horror that must have come upon poor Tanthis, hearing the evil goddess invoked at the moment of his death! Sember could not help but believe that this was deliberate cruelty, an act of vengeance. He spoke the question that had haunted him since the night of the hunt.

"Who was the sire of your first child?" he demanded.

Kiri lifted one eyebrow, mockingly, and Sember knew that she had discovered his lie. Shame burned his cheeks and fueled his growing anger. He seized the woman by the shoulders and shook her, hard.

"Name him!" he thundered.

The woman wrenched herself free and put several paces between herself and the angry chieftain. Her own eyes blazed blue fire as she faced him down. "I did not name him for fear that no one would believe! If none would believe me then, surely you would not listen now!"

"I will listen. I will believe," Sember promised. "I must know why Tanthis died!"

The breath rushed from Kiri as if someone had kicked her in the stomach. When she could summon enough air to speak, she whispered, "You think that I killed a man in cold vengeance. How can you think this of me?"

"I saw you slay the sauran," he said stubbornly.

"And I have seen you slay *many* saurans!"

"In battle, yes. *You* destroyed one unborn and defenseless."

Kiri's smile was bitter. "Would you have done any differently, had you followed your will and left the sauran to sleep out the winter? All would have died. And what of the choices you have made these two days past? What of Ghilanna and her babe? What of *mine*?"

The chieftain stared at her, shaken by the speaking aloud of the secret between them. "You carry my first son, who will be the next chieftain," he said slowly. "Whatever evil you might have done, I will do nothing to you that will endanger your unborn child."

She began to laugh then, and there was a wildness in the sound that frightened Sember. He closed the distance between them, and tried to take her in his arms. At once she fell silent, and as she pushed him away her eyes still blazed with a kind of madness.

"If you believe only what your eyes show you and your ears hear, then you are a fool," she raged at him. She spun and stalked off toward the east, and the sauran. After a few steps she faltered, swayed, and then she turned back to face him.

"Call me when the next baby begins to seek the light. This time, call me *before* I'm forced to choose between the life of another woman's baby and my own!"

By the time she reached the cave, Kiri knew beyond doubt that she would bring no summer child to the tribe this year. Like all magic, the fire of Aussas carried a high price.

The sauran glared at her as she stumbled into the cave. "You have been hunting a long time. The meat is almost gone, and the eggs are hatching. Soon there will be nine young demanding food!"

Kiri barely heard. She sank to the ground, exhausted and heartsick. The firelight dimmed, and the walls of the cave seemed to fold around her as she sank into the darkness.

She awoke to the scent of herbs and the high-pitched chanting of the firesauran. Her body no longer ached from the effect of Ghilanna's poison and the ravages of magic fire. A pleasant lassitude swept through Kiri as the magic of Aussas touched her anew, bringing not only healing, but affirmation.

After a time she focused on the chanting sauran. Moorgen sat cross-legged by the fire, her golden eyes closed and an expression of intense concentration on her reptilian face. This was a marvel, considering that six tiny lizard people capered about her, clambering up and down her still form as if she were a tree placed there for them to climb.

A weak chuckle escaped Kiri. The sauran opened her eyes and saw that the human was awake. She nodded with satisfaction. "Good. You will need to hunt again soon. The little ones are hungry."

Kiri pushed herself up on one elbow and studied the young saurans. They looked very much like the eggs from which they'd come: a pale hide sprinkled with brown spots. She assumed that they would develop the characteristic mottled markings as they grew.

"You have a fine family," she said quietly. "Aussas has blessed you."

"Three more remain to hatch," Moorgen said, casting a worried glance toward the nest. "They are slow in coming."

The woman waited for a long moment before answering. She knew the pain of losing a child. "There will be no more," she said at last.

Moorgen's yellow eyes settled on her, unblinking. "Nine children," she reminded her. "You swore that nine would leave this cave in safety."

"I swore that your *hatchlings* would leave!" Kiri retorted. "Four of your eggs had no chance of hatching. Hold one of those eggs up to the fire and look within. You will see what I saw."

The sauran did as she was bid, and she nodded slowly as the truth settled in. "I had to use firemagic to heal myself. That, and the long slumber, must have killed those four." She shot a quick glance at Kiri as something occurred to her. "Four. That means that the egg you destroyed—"

"Was already dead," Kiri finished. "Even so, I am glad it took only one to convince you to teach me the ways of Aussas!"

There was a moment's silence, then a dry chuckle came from the sauran. "Well done," Moorgen complimented her. "Such treachery speaks well for you. Firemagic is not an easy burden to bear, not even for a sauran. But you have not only the courage to listen to the voice of the goddess, but the wit to follow Her! For the first time, I do not regret teaching you the ways of Aussasaurian!"

"*You* will not regret it," the woman said softly. "But your people might, for many years to come."

Moorgen nodded, apparently not surprised by this declaration. "That will be as it may," she agreed. "But the spring will not come for two moons, and my six hatch-lings and I are hungry. Are you going to sit there for the remainder of the day, or are you going to hunt?"

The solstice moon came and went, enveloping Kiri in a blur of long nights and a blaze of firemagic. But through it all she kept her promise to Ghilanna: Not one of the winter children was lost; not one of the mothers died in childbirth.

The rest of the winter passed quickly, too, for when Kiri was not tending the new mothers or seeing to her own children, she hunted to provide for the nearby sauran family. Kiri had another promise to keep.

She and Moorgen seldom had words now, for they had little need of each other. Kiri had learned well, and there was little that the firesauran could teach her. Moorgen was strong enough to tend and teach her own brood.

Strong enough, perhaps, to venture from the cave. Kiri knew this, and she feared what the sauran might do. Soon the children of the One Tribe would play in the hills and valleys to the east, perhaps explore the very cave where the sauran lay hidden.

Nor was Kiri the only one to think such thoughts. Sember came looking for her the first truly warm spring day and found her gathering the herbs that grew at the edge of the Silver River. They walked together for a while without speaking, for a gorge had sprung up between them and words to span it did not come easily.

"The river is rising early this year," he said at last. "The water will soon cover much of the campsite. The One Tribe needs to move up into the bluffs."

Kiri nodded. They did so every spring, before the coming of the comet.

"It is time to hunt," the chieftain said, and leveled a challenging glare at the woman.

"It is time," she agreed.

They went into the bluffs that night, just the two of them, armed with bowing sticks and javelins. The night was warm, and the first stars of summer had begun to edge their way into the dome of the night sky.

"The time of the comet approaches," Sember said grimly. "The saurans will attack soon, and you and I have seen to it that their numbers are increased!"

Kiri shook her head. "The saurans will not attack this year."

"Their goddess tells you this?" he scoffed.

"*My* goddess," she said. "Humans and saurans are not the only creatures on Tethedril, and the gods watch over us all. You insult Aussas—and Altos, too, for that matter—in thinking gods can walk only in your narrow paths."

Before Sember could respond, she flung out a hand to warn him to silence. With the hunters' hand talk, she told him to circle around the base of the hill that rose up before them. She would go to the top of the hill and draw the sauran's attention away from his approach.

The chieftain did not trust Kiri to do as she said, but he nodded agreement to her plan and crept toward the east. She strode up the hill, her eyes toward the south and the sauran.

As soon as Sember thought she would not see, he doubled back and traced her steps. Soon the southern slope of the hill lay before him, and beyond that the mouth of the cave where the creatures had spent the winter in hiding. As Sember watched, Kiri cupped her hands to her mouth and sent a long, plaintive cry wavering over the valley. It was a perfect imitation of a night bird's cry, yet Sember knew it for a signal. His hand tightened on the grip of his javelin.

The sauran recognized the signal, too. Before long a mottled snout poked out of the cave, and the lizardlike creature slunk out of the darkness. Behind her came a string of smaller creatures, identical in their loathsomeness. Sember shivered as he studied the sauran brood. Already the young were nearly as big as their mother, and all were armed with spears. He did not doubt that they had been trained in their use.

That meant that they were two, against an enemy that numbered seven. Or perhaps he was one alone. Sember could not be sure. He would never be sure of Kiri again.

Yet the woman's javelin gleamed in the moonlight as she held it high, ready to hurl it into the valley below. He rose, silent, his own weapon in his hand, and sighted down the big female. The sauran was in the outer limits of his javelin's range, but he and Kiri were the best in the One Tribe. With all his strength he threw, and he knew at once that his aim was good.

Kiri's javelin also took flight. It struck the wooden shaft of Sember's weapon, knocking it harmlessly aside. The lizard people looked up, and the female raised a clawed hand in salute to Kiri as the enemies of the One Tribe scurried off toward the south.

The woman turned to Sember then, her blue eyes unreadable. He cursed her and took up a second javelin—there was just time to get off a second shot.

The shaft burst into flame in his hand.

Sember dropped the burning weapon and stamped the smoldering grass into ash. When the threat of fire had passed, the saurans were long out of reach.

The chieftain's long-held frustration erupted into fury,

and he bore down upon the treacherous woman. "Tell me why I should not kill you," he demanded.

Kiri was pale, but her lips thinned in a grim smile. "The saurans will not attack this year, nor for several years to come. Their chieftain is like you—it will take him that long to accept without fear that a human woman wields the magic of Aussasaurian!"

The chieftain stared at her for a long moment, trying to absorb the promise and possibility in her words. "What if the female does not tell them? She may not, for if she speaks of this they will think her a traitor."

"They might, but she will tell them regardless," Kiri said confidently. "Do you think that Moorgen will allow her people to march against us, knowing the magic that I now wield? The saurans are not fools, to throw their lives away needlessly!"

Sember glanced at the charred remnants of his spear. He could easily see the benefit of such magic. It could set weapons aflame and engulf attacking armies in a circle of killing fire.

"If the saurans have firemagic, why have they not used it in battle?"

"If we marched into their jungles and attacked their homes, Moorgen would use firemagic to hurl us back. And so will I, if the One Tribe is in danger." Kiri paused, and a flash of remembered pain twisted her face. "There is a price to be paid for firemagic, for whatever we do comes back to us threefold. Moorgen has told me what happened to her mother's mother, when once she wielded it in battle. The firesauran was consumed by her own flame."

"And you would do this, to protect the tribe?" he asked, disbelieving.

She laid her hand on her flat belly. By this time of year,

it should already have been rounded with her summer child. *His* child, Sember thought, his son—for Kiri bore only sons—who would have been the next chieftain. This honor she had sacrificed for the woman and child who were her rivals.

Sember nodded slowly, and the light of hope and joy began to steal into his eyes. Perhaps Kiri was as she had always been; perhaps it was even true that the gods were not limited to the roles he had been taught to assign them. He would never know that, and did not truly wish to know. For him it was enough that Kiri had taken her rightful place in the One Tribe, and that she was at his side.

"Let us go home," he said quietly.

The firewoman fell into place beside him. Although there was peace in the silence they shared, and though Sember's face showed contentment for the first time in many days, Kiri walked alone as she never had before.

Sember's glowing eyes held a fire that she knew, one she had last seen in the face of Ghilanna, her mother's daughter. Suddenly Kiri knew why the man had kept her secret, why he had been tortured so by the knowledge that she had left the accustomed ways of the tribe. She doubted that he himself understood his heart, for it had wandered outside the ways of Altos, where his eyes refused to follow. And Kiri knew with certainty that he would seek her out when the spring comet drew near.

The firewoman understood the price that she would pay for the magic she'd given to Ghilanna. Sember, if ever he came to know, would see such magic as a betrayal. And perhaps a betrayal it was. With this magic Kiri had led him outside of the ways of Altos. If the chieftain had been so tormented by the emergence of a firewoman in the One Tribe, how much more pain would he know when he himself broke the rules that the humans had fashioned from the gifts of Altos? Kiri only hoped that Sember would not give name to the deeper pain he knew, when he sired a child upon a woman other than the one written in his heart.

As they approached the campfires of the One Tribe, Kiri silently thanked Aussas for the one gift that she had managed to give Sember. Already he knew too much, and understood too little. Kiri had been tempted to answer when he'd demanded to know who had sired her first child before her time and against her will. She had been tempted to hurl the name at him like a javelin: Tawni Arc, the old Godtalker, the holy man of Altos. At the time she had feared that Sember would not believe her; now she was afraid that he might have and that the knowledge would have sent him utterly adrift.

And Kiri knew also the full price of her firemagic. The aurak hunt had been the last time she had been truly a member of the One Tribe. Forever would she be set apart by the touch of Aussas, condemned to carry a burden of secrets and silence. Among the many, she would always be alone.

Then Kiri remembered Ghilanna's child, and the task of training a firewoman to take her place. It was yet another burden, but in thinking of it her heart lifted just a little. Perhaps in time, firewomen might speak aloud of their power and their goddess. Perhaps in time the children of Altos and Aussas might walk together. That time was not now, and it was not hers. But hope gave a new purpose to the lonely woman and lightened her steps as she walked toward the campfires of the tribe.

## About the Editor

Scott Siegel, with his wife, Barbara, is the author of forty-six books, ranging from fantasy to film reference, from Westerns to biographies. In addition, he has created scores of books as a packager, including *The Whispers*, the first installment in the recently launched *The Gates of Time* series by Dan Parkinson. A former senior editor at a New York publishing house who now runs a successful literary agency, Scott has been immersed in the book business for much of his adult life. He lives in New York City with the lovely and talented Barbara, where the two of them lead yet another life as film, theater, and cabaret critics.

## About the Authors

Elaine Cunningham is the bestselling author of ten elf-infested fantasy books, including *Elfshadow* and *Tangled Webs*, and many short stories. Her most recent fantasy adventure, *Thornhold,* involves a young woman's quest for family and offers a glimpse into the rollicking and tragic life of a dwarven clan. Elaine is a once and future teacher, an occasional musician, and an oft-transplanted New Englander who is currently undergoing yet another uprooting. She lives with her husband and two sons amid several computers, thousands of books, and about twenty billion Magic cards.

Christie Golden has written nine novels and fourteen short stories in the fields of science fiction, fantasy, and horror. Though best known for tie-in work, Golden is also the author of two original fantasy novels, *King's Man and Thief* and *Instrument of Fate*, which made the 1996 Nebula preliminary ballot. She launched the TSR *Ravenloft* line with the highly successful *Vampire of the Mists*, which introduced elven vampire Jander Sunstar. Golden followed up *Vampire* with *Dance of the Dead* and *The Enemy Within*. Other projects include three *Star Trek: Voyager* novels, *The Murdered Sun*, *Marooned*, *Seven of Nine*, and the novelization of Steven Spielberg's *Invasion America*.

Ed Greenwood is a librarian and longtime fantasy and science fiction fan who lives in Canada and writes books (just under one hundred, so far). A member of the Gamers' Choice Hall of Fame, Ed is the creator of *Forgotten Realms*, published by TSR, Inc. Ed's books have been published in over twenty languages and regularly appear on national bestseller lists. When time permits, Ed is an avid cave explorer, fencer, and gamer and has been the guest of honor at conventions around the world, often appearing as one of his characters: the wise old rogue wizard, Elminster.

Mary H. Herbert currently resides in Georgia, writing fantasy in those infrequent spare minutes between family activities, children's activities, PTA, Girl Scouts, and gardening. Little wonder she chose fantasy. In the past year, she has visited three different fantasy worlds (not counting our own) and lived to tell about it. She is the author of the *Dark Horse* series, various short stories, and an upcoming *Dragonlance* novel.

Mary Kirchoff has been a longtime contributor to TSR's *Dragonlance* world, including the bestselling novels *The Black Wing*, *Night of the Eye*, *The Medusa Plague*, *The Seventh Sentinel*, *Kenderhome*, *Wanderlust* (with Steve Winter), and *Flint, the King* (with Douglas Niles). After taking five years off to raise two lively boys, plant gardens, and finish remodeling a 1906 Victorian home, she has returned as executive editor of TSR's novel lines. She lives with her family and their old, red dog fifteen miles from the small southeastern Wisconsin town in which she was raised.

Douglas Niles has recently finished the *Watershed* trilogy, an epic fantasy series published by Ace Fantasy, as well as *The Last Thane*, a new *Dragonlance* novel from Wizards of the Coast and TSR, Inc. He has authored more than two dozen novels and is currently at work on a World War II Alternate History novel called *Fox on the Rhine*, in addition to a new fantasy trilogy for Ace. He is a cheesehead from Wisconsin, though he has never worn a wedge of the yellow foam.

Nick O'Donohoe has been a mystery, science fiction, and fantasy writer. His *Crossroads* novels about veterinarians treating fantasy animals include *The Magic and the Healing* (selected by the American Library Association as a Best Book for Teens), *Under the Healing Sign*, and *The Healing of Crossroads*. Nick's first science fiction novel was *Too, Too Solid Flesh*, about an all-android acting company's performance of *Hamlet*. He has written roughly one dozen fantasy stories for the *Dragonlance* anthologies. Nick is currently working on a fantasy novel and sequel set in Rhode Island during World War II.

Dan Parkinson is the author of thirty-five wide-ranging novels, including multiple bestsellers in fantasy, science fiction, historicals, high-seas adventures, and Westerns. His recent works include *The Gates of Time* trilogy and the *Timecop* book series, both from Del Rey. He attributes his wide range of subject and content to "what interests me, which is practically everything—and what I know, which is less than enough of anything." A Kansas native, the former journalist and professional community development coordinator lives with his wife, Wilma-Jean, in Lake Jackson, Texas. "Family Tree" is one of about one dozen short stories he has written.

R. A. Salvatore was born in Massachusetts in 1959. His first published novel was TSR's *The Crystal Shard*. He has since published more than two dozen works, including six *New York Times* bestsellers. At present, Salvatore has more than four million books in print. His most recent fantasy novels are *Passage to Dawn*, *The Demon Awakens*, and *The Demon Spirit*, the latter two from Del Rey. Salvatore lives in Massachusetts with his wife, Diane, and their three children.